kd easley

Where the Dreams End

NukeWorks
Publishing

NukeWorks Publishing
Fulton, Mo 65251 USA

ISBN 978-0-9825294-1-6

Cover design by Duane Stapp and A&J Creative Services
Cover photo by Justin Easley
Edited by Alice Peck

Visit kd easley at www.kdwrites.com

Printed in U.S.A.

For Mom. My biggest fan, my biggest critic, my best friend.

I couldn't have done this without you.

I miss you.

Acknowledgements

This book exists because I am blessed with friends and family that truly believe in me. This is my chance to say a public thank you. First to Broc, without you Brocs Harley would have never existed, wherever you are, thanks. To the ladies at the truck shop, thanks for reading my rough drafts and keeping me churning out the pages. To Lisa Polisar and Stacy Juba, the two best critique partners a writer could ever have. To Alice Peck, Chief of the Echo Police and the best editor in the world. You make me look good. To Duane Stapp for his help making this dream a reality. To Tim Cockey, all I can say is wow, thanks. To my guppie mates, thanks for sharing your knowledge, there's not a better group for young writers anywhere. For A. Hunt. You know who you are, you know what you've done, now you know how much I appreciated it. For my boys. Thanks for putting up with hamburger helper, for reading my rough drafts, and for learning to do the laundry. I couldn't have done it without your help. And finally, thanks to my Mom, my most honest first reader. How am I going to keep doing this without you?

Where the Dreams End

Chapter 1

ain beat a steady tattoo against the faded canvas of the funeral home tent. I stood alone and watched the man seated at the graveside say goodbye to his favorite son.

That man was my father. I was the other son.

Rain soaked my bare head, dripped off my hair and ran down my neck. I wondered idly why young men didn't wear hats anymore—brain confetti, I didn't want to think about why I was standing there in the rain.

My brother's fiancée, Lori, stopped at my side. Pale with grief and dressed in black, she was still beautiful. I held her close and her small frame shuddered. I rested my cheek against her hair while she cried in my arms. We stood that way for a long time. Finally, she took a trembling breath and stepped away from my embrace. Rain mixed with the tears on her cheeks.

"I loved him so much, Brocs," she whispered.

Lori's dad pulled her under his umbrella and they trudged slowly toward his car. I shivered, turned up the collar of my overcoat, and squinted into the darkness under the tent. Lightning flashed and thunder shook the ground. I flinched. The old man sat unmoving.

Melinda Carver, Drew's secretary, stopped by my side. I tore my gaze from the tent and transferred it to her. Her eyes were puffy and red from crying. She started to speak, and then just shook her head. I gave her a hug.

"Thanks for coming, Mel."

"I don't know what I'm going to do without your brother, Brocs."

I wondered that myself as she slowly walked away. My eyes drifted back to the scene at the graveside. The priest, Father Michael, knelt to speak with Halston. They turned briefly toward me. Halston shook his head, stood and moved away. Father Mike started speaking again. I turned to watch the line of cars parading out of the cemetery. Wil Pinkerton, my best friend since college, stopped and shook my hand. In all the years we've known each other I don't think we'd ever shaken hands. It was awkward.

"Want me to stick around?" he asked.

I shook my head. "Thanks for coming, Wil."

"Call me if you need anything."

I said I would, watched him make his way down the hill to his car, and wished I'd asked him to stay.

The soggy squelch of a footstep sounded behind me and I turned toward the tent. Father Mike opened his umbrella as he ducked out from under the canopy. He stopped, squeezed my shoulder and started to speak. Our eyes met and he sighed. He knew whatever comfort he offered wouldn't help.

"I'm sorry, son," he said.

I clenched my teeth and turned away, fighting for control. He gave my shoulder another squeeze and continued toward his car. I stared once more at my father, Halston Harley—in mourning for the son he loved, left with the one he despised.

My name is Brockston Lee Harley. Brockston was my mother's maiden name. Lee was my biological father's name. Mom gave me the name Lee against her husband's wishes. That single act of defiance may have shaped my entire childhood.

The funeral director huddled off to the side, shivering in his overcoat. The men waiting to fill the grave stood behind the flapping canvas, smoking, talking quietly, waiting patiently for us to go. Thunder crashed and lightning split the sky again. I swore softly to myself, and glared at Halston.

As if he felt my gaze, he turned and stared at me in disgust as he stepped away from the grave. I took his arm when he shuffled past. Shrugging me off, he increased his

pace so we weren't walking together. His thinning gray
hair lay in wet tendrils across his head, his hat twisted
forgotten in his hands. His rain-soaked overcoat billowed
behind him as he stretched the distance between us.

I sighed and trailed him to the limo. A shudder rippled
up my spine as the sound of machinery broke the silence.
I slid into the car next to the man who had raised me, as
my brother's casket settled into the earth.

We rode through town in silence. Rain peppered the
windshield, but the streets were filled with lunch hour
traffic. People hurried through the shower talking and
laughing. Even in a place as small as Stantonville,
Missouri, the death of one person caused only a tiny
ripple.

I closed my eyes and slumped against the leather seat
until the limousine stopped outside the monstrosity Drew
and I jokingly called Halston Manor. Cars lined the circle
drive and lights shone from the front windows. I wasn't
going in. I couldn't imagine anything that would take me
through those doors now that Drew was gone. I'd walked
away from that house four years ago and hadn't set foot
inside since.

Halston and I left the limo from opposite sides. He
started toward the front steps. I headed toward my olive
drab F150 pickup. Halfway there I stopped.

"I loved him, too," I said.

Halston paused when I spoke, but didn't turn around.
Then he stalked up the stairs and pushed through the
front door. He wouldn't even share his grief with me. I
slipped behind the wheel of my truck and lay my forehead
against the steering wheel. The tears I'd been choking on
since Drew died trickled out. I clamped down on them,
jabbed the key in the ignition, and spraying gravel across
the immaculate lawn, shot onto the street.

I drove aimlessly, letting the sound of the wipers lull
me into a daze. A blaring horn brought me out of the
ozone and I swerved into my own lane. A picnic area was
ahead, deserted in the storm. I angled off the road and
parked, looking out at the swollen river. Fat drops
splattered on the roof, ran together and blurred the view
from the windshield. I slumped against the seat, closed
my eyes and thought about the last time I saw Drew.

■ ■ ■

We stood at the bar, glasses held high, singing Happy Birthday. Drew grinned with embarrassment and slipped his arm around Lori. We finished our off-key serenade and yelled for a speech. Drew, fortified by alcohol, climbed onto the bar. He started to speak, then stopped and glanced at Lori. She nodded slightly and he went on. "Lori and I are getting married," he said. Yelps of surprise greeted his announcement. I ordered another round of drinks. Drew's buddies took turns pounding him on the back and twirling Lori around the dance floor. When they finished pummeling Drew, I grabbed him in a bear hug.

"Congratulations, bro. It's about time."

He smirked. "I didn't want to get in any hurry."

Lori appeared at his side, blue eyes shining, cheeks flushed with happiness. Her blond hair fell across her face and she flipped it out of the way. I brushed a kiss on her cheek and gave her a hug. Her head barely reached my chin and the flowery scent of her shampoo tickled my nose. Something akin to regret washed through me. I would have traded places with Drew in a heartbeat, but Lori met Drew first and never spared me a glance. She stepped away and curled her arm around my brother. I envied their happiness.

"You mind if we get out of here, Brocs?" Drew asked.

He turned and gave Lori a wink. She smiled and a blush stained her cheeks. Clearly, they had a more personal celebration planned. I gave Drew a gentle shove toward the exit.

"Get out of here, you guys."

"Meet me for lunch tomorrow, Brocs. I got something I need to talk to you about."

"Sure. Where and when?"

"How about Luigi's around one?"

"I'll be there. See you tomorrow."

His expression darkened for a moment. I thought it was a trick of light until he spoke again.

"Don't stand me up, Brocs. This is important."

His tone was serious, at odds with the party swirling around us. "I'll be there. I promise."

I escorted them outside and waved as they strolled down Allen Street hand in hand. When they were out of sight, I wandered back into the bar. Smoke hung in the air and the jukebox was blasting Metallica. The party was still in full swing even after the departure of the guest of honor, but I'd had enough. I finished my beer, shouted goodnight, and escaped the smoke and noise. The music blared, then became muffled when the doors swung closed behind me. The clock on the bank flashed twelve-thirty. It felt later. I started down the street to my apartment. Other than the diffused glow seeping from a covered window above, the block was dark. The shadows hid the cracks in the sidewalk, the peeling paint and crumbling brickwork. Under the soft moonlight, the neighborhood wore a cloak of prosperity that, in the harsh light of day, had been missing for over a decade.

Fatigue seeped through my body. I trudged up the stairs and turned the key in the lock. I draped my jacket over the back of a chair, eased off my boots and padded into my bedroom. As I peeled off my tee shirt, I noticed a dead mouse at the foot of my bed. I tipped the trashcan and toed the gift inside as I made a brief search for my benefactor, Baldwin, my feline roommate. He's a charcoal gray tabby, invisible unless he wants to be noticed. I flushed his dubious gift, finished undressing and sank onto the bed.

Drew was worried about something. I clicked through the TV channels and wondered what it was, probably something to do with the wedding. Maybe Lori was pregnant. I grinned at the thought. The Flying Tigers with John Wayne was on channel thirty-four. I turned up the sound and settled onto my pillows.

A ringing sound jolted me awake. I sat up and Baldwin slid down my chest with his claws out. I swore and pushed him aside as I reached for the phone. Blood dotted the scratches on my chest and I pressed the sheet against them.

"Hello," I mumbled.

"Mr. Brockston Harley?"

Christ, a telemarketer. I checked the time, 4:00 a.m. Maybe not, even those guys sleep sometimes.

"Harley, are you there?"

I tried to place the voice and failed.

"Who the hell is this?" I asked.

"Your brother should have kept his nose out of our business."

"What are you talking about? Who is this?"

"This is a piece of friendly advice. Stay out of things that don't concern you."

The line went dead. I cradled the handset, rubbed my face and thought about calling Drew. Decided it could wait since I was meeting him for lunch later. I got up, drug the bloody sheet off the bed, and washed the scratches with alcohol. It stung like a son of a bitch. I looked around to glare at Baldwin, but he was MIA. He's big on self preservation.

Back in bed, I wrapped the quilt around me and was just on the edge of sleep, when a thundering noise sounded from the front of the apartment. I shot off the bed like I'd been launched from a catapult and stomped down the hall.

"The building better be on fire," I snarled, as I jerked the door open on the safety chain.

A badge appeared through the crack. I quickly ran through my actions over the last twenty-four hours. I couldn't come up with any reason the police would need to see me.

"Mr. Harley?" A voice demanded from the other side.

The chain rattled as I released it from the catch. I was expecting uniforms. Instead, two casually dressed men entered. Plainclothes detectives? Goose bumps rose on my skin. Cops at four-thirty in the morning will do that to you.

"What's this all about?" I snapped.

"Why don't you get some clothes on, Mr. Harley, then we'll talk."

I glared at the older of the two cops. He seemed prepared to wait me out so I went into my bedroom and scooped the clothes I'd been wearing earlier off the floor. I pulled on my shirt, and the smell of stale beer and old ashtray assaulted my senses. In the bathroom, I splashed my face with water—a feeble attempt to wake up. It didn't help much. The detectives were standing in the living room talking quietly when I entered. They stopped and turned as I came into the room.

The older one was tall and somewhere in his mid fifties. His dark brown hair was beginning to go silver and his skin was weathered as if he spent a lot of time outdoors. His wrinkled suit coat appeared slept in. I couldn't tell if that was the result of a long day, or his natural appearance. The necktie dangling from his right jacket pocket led me to believe it was the former. When I entered the room, his face went pale and he took a step back. As I watched, his gaze narrowed and he shook his head. The blank cop stare was gone. Now his gaze held something I couldn't identify. He was vaguely familiar, but I couldn't place him. He seemed to recognize me, though.

His partner had dark curly hair that needed a good combing. He was a few years younger than me, somewhere in his mid-twenties, and there was no compassion in his face or his stance. His arms were like tree trunks, straining against the fabric of his polo shirt. I knew his type, asshole, full of himself and the idea of being a cop. He was probably an asshole before he got the badge. I motioned the detectives to a seat and lowered myself onto the coffee table facing the older one.

"What the hell is going on?" I asked.

"Mr. Harley, I'm Detective Sergeant Dean Stryker. This is my partner, Detective Morris. We tried to reach your father, but apparently he's not home."

"Probably passed out and didn't hear the phone," I said.

Stryker's expression was pained. I don't know if it was because of the comment or the interruption.

"I'm sorry," I said. "Go ahead. What did you need to talk to Halston about?"

"Mr. Harley, there's no easy way to say this. A patrol officer discovered a body around two a.m. We believe it might be your brother Andrew."

I felt like a fist had just sunk into my stomach. I shifted my stare back and forth between them, but didn't speak, so he went on.

"The body was found in Borders Alley off of Allen Street this morning. The ID with the body belongs to an Andrew Harley. I hate to ask it of you, sir, but we'd appreciate it if you would come downtown and make a positive ID."

Drew. Dead. Impossible.

"There's got to be a mistake," I said. "I just saw Drew last night." I glanced down at my watch. "Just a few hours ago."

"I'm sorry, sir, it could be a case of mistaken identity."

He didn't believe that and neither did I. Why would someone else have Drew's ID? I stared at the floor between my feet, unable to face the truth in his eyes. A picture of Drew and Lori hand in hand walking down the street flashed through my mind. I shook my head free of the image and looked up.

"Mr. Harley, would you please come downtown with us?"

I nodded and stood. Stryker and his partner walked to the door of my apartment and I followed. In a daze, I shoved my feet into my boots, snagged my jacket and trailed the detectives to their car. I sat in the rear seat. The door panels were scarred and stained. The seat back in front of me showed the marks of countless footprints. It smelled like vomit and fear and sweat. I glanced at the doors with no handles and remembered other rides in the back of other police cars. At least this time I wasn't wearing cuffs.

The chatter of the police radio was the only thing that broke the silence as we drove through the darkened town. Here and there, a light shone in a window. Early risers brewing their first cup of coffee. We passed the police station and stopped at the rear entrance of the hospital. The coroner's office and morgue were in the basement. I tagged behind the detectives into the building and onto the elevator. The walls were prison gray. The light was muted by a layer of dirt on the inside of the fixture. No happy healing colors here, this elevator was obviously not for public use. The elevator hissed open onto a vast sea of white—walls, floors, ceilings. I squinted against the sudden glare.

We stepped into an entry hall bracketed by swinging doors. Paper coveralls were stacked on shelves to my left with white lab coats hanging below on hooks. Every detail of the scene appeared in sharp-edged relief. Stryker removed a surgical mask from a dispenser on the wall and held it out to me. A laugh welled up inside at the incongruity of preventing infection in a morgue. I stifled the urge with a cough. The hyper-clarity dimmed as I donned the mask.

The curly-headed detective pushed a button almost hidden behind the hanging lab coats. The face of a young woman appeared at the window. She recognized the detectives and stepped into the hallway. She was beautiful. Her green scrubs and auburn hair stood out in stark contrast to the white walls.

"Good morning, detectives," she said. "Working late, or up early?"

"Late I'm afraid, Sara. We need to ID the body that came in this morning."

"Follow me."

She met my stare, sizing me up. It was not a friendly look. Probably wondering if she was going to have to revive me. Rotten bedside manner, probably why she worked with dead patients, I thought uncharitably. She had succeeded in distracting me until she pushed into the lab. The detectives moved through behind her. I stood watching the doors swing back and forth, willing myself to follow, wishing I didn't have to. Detective Stryker came back through.

"Come on, son. It won't get any easier if you wait."

His expression was compassionate and that was almost my undoing. I took a deep breath and pushed into the lab. Sara moved purposefully across the room and stopped in front of a wall of stainless steel drawers, each one slightly larger than a dorm-sized refrigerator. The detectives halted on either side of her. I held my ground, my feet wouldn't move any closer. She shot me another unfriendly glance, lifted the latch and swung the stainless door open. I didn't breathe as the metal table whispered out, and the sheet-covered form came into view. It wasn't Drew. It couldn't be.

"You need to step forward, son."

I forced my feet to move. Sara lifted the sheet and revealed my brother. His face was slack in death, devoid of the laughter usually there. His right eye bulged slightly and a bruise shadowed his cheek and forehead. I groaned low in my throat and took a step back. The older detective placed a hand on my shoulder and squeezed. I shrugged away and cleared my throat.

"That's Drew."

The words were strangled. I cleared my throat and stared at the detective. "That's my brother."

I spun away, snatched the mask from my face and pushed out of the lab and into the waiting area. A tattered mustard yellow couch with chrome arms stood next to the wall in the hallway. I sagged onto it, rested my head on my hands and closed my eyes. I felt the couch give as the older detective sat next to me.

"Detective..." I stopped, but his name wouldn't come.

"Stryker."

"Detective Stryker, how did he die?"

"It appears to be a suicide."

I snapped upright and glared, pain replaced with fury. "My brother wouldn't kill himself. He just got engaged."

"The location is a bit unusual, but it seems fairly straightforward."

"What do you mean the location is unusual?"

Stryker shifted on his seat before he answered.

"Suicide is a very personal decision. It's somewhat unusual for it to be in a public place. In a car or hotel room, but not usually out in the open. Don't get me wrong, it does happen, just not often."

"Was there a note? What makes you think it was suicide? Oh Jesus, what am I going to tell Lori?"

I ran my hands over my face. My throat was tight. My eyes burned. Stryker laid a hand on my shoulder.

"I'll have someone drive you home. I'm sorry you had to do this, son."

I jerked away from him and glared.

"I don't want to go home."

I pushed the words past the lump in my throat and stared at the detective until he turned away.

"Stryker, I want to know why you think my brother killed himself. What did he die of?"

Stryker, still not meeting my gaze, said softly, "A gunshot wound to the head."

I stared at his face. He kept his gaze locked on the wall behind my left shoulder.

"I didn't see a gunshot wound."

"You were on the left side, it was in his right temple. We won't know for sure until the coroner's report is finished, but the injury appears consistent with a self inflicted gunshot wound."

"Drew didn't own a handgun, he hated them."

Something flickered in the detective's eyes, just a flash and then it was gone, the compassionate expression dropped back into place like a mask.

This wasn't really happening.

"Look, son, you've had a terrible shock. It's normal to throw up roadblocks, reasons why they wouldn't have done it. I'm sorry, the evidence of suicide is pretty clear. He left a note."

"Can I see it?"

"I'll see that it gets to you myself."

God. Drew was dead. I felt as if an enormous hole had just opened in my life. We sat in silence, the detective and I, in the harsh white light of the hallway. He just watched while I crawled through my memories for a reason Drew might have killed himself. There wasn't one. He wasn't sick, he wasn't deeply in debt, he wasn't depressed. I would have known.

"You're wrong, detective."

"Go home, son. Get some rest."

Anger coursed through my body. This man didn't know Drew, but he was willing to believe he killed himself and wasn't going to search any further. It was all I could do not to hit him. I stood and paced down the hall, my hands clenched into fists at my sides. A message board was bolted to the wall at eye level. A purple smiley face surrounded by balloons stared at me from a flyer. That was just too much. I slammed my fist into the grinning purple glob. Pushpins pinged on the floor and rolled away. The now-crumpled smiley floated down to my feet. Stryker watched from down the hall, while I massaged my knuckles and fought to get my anger under control.

"It can't be suicide."

"The coroner's report will tell us for certain, but this isn't television, son. Murderers in the real world are more likely to hide a body than to stage a suicide. Do you have a reason to think it's murder, Mr. Harley?

His tone was different. The comfort and compassion were missing. His voice was hard now. My bullshit antenna went on red alert as I tried to reason out the change. When I looked up, his face still held the same soft expression as before. I shook off my uneasiness and put it down to a long shift. He was tired, I was tired. We weren't getting anywhere here. I tried to ease the tension in my neck and shoulders.

"No one would want to hurt Drew."

"That just leaves us with a crime of opportunity, like a mugging. But that wouldn't explain the suicide note with the body, or the fact that his wallet and watch were still there."

"He didn't kill himself." I wasn't sure who I was trying to convince, the detective, or myself.

Stryker paced down the hall away from me.

"What did the note say?" I asked.

He turned when I spoke. "Son, please. Give yourself some time to come to terms with this trag—"

"What did the note say, detective?"

"It said, 'Please forgive me'!"

Why would Drew say that? Forgive him for what? It didn't make any sense.

"The note was in Drew's handwriting?"

"Mr. Harley. I know you're upset over the death of your brother. Rest assured if the coroner doesn't rule his death a suicide, I'll be the first one out there trying to find his killer."

I interrupted again.

"You didn't know Drew. If you did, you'd be out there trying to find the killer now, not making excuses. I want that note, Stryker."

The detective placed a business card into my hand.

"I'll get the note to you, son. You're right. I didn't know your brother. Why don't you come down to the station this afternoon? We'll talk and see if we can come up with any ideas."

I eased the card underneath the cellophane around my cigarette pack and stuck it in my pocket. I had no intention of talking to him about Drew. I knew he was just trying to placate me so I'd get out of his hair and he could go home. As far as he was concerned, the case was closed. I turned to leave and he asked if I needed a ride. I shook my head and punched the button for the elevator. I had to see Lori.

■ ■ ■

Four days since Drew died and I still didn't know why. There was no police investigation. All the evidence said suicide. I dried my face, turned on the wipers, and angled back onto the road. The rain was starting to let up as I passed Drew's office in town. The night he died, Drew had been worried about something. That's why we had planned to meet at Luigi's for lunch the next day. I stopped in the middle of the street as my thoughts darted in another direction. An angry horn blared behind me, the driver flipping me the bird as he swerved around. Maybe Drew did kill himself. Maybe there was something he wanted to talk about and in the end, he just couldn't. I shook my head. No way. Drew wouldn't have considered suicide a solution. I glanced at the Harley Real Estate sign and nodded once to myself. Something was going on that Drew couldn't handle. Maybe it had to do with business. One way to find out was to check into what he'd been working on lately. I was going to toss his office.

I didn't have a key so I walked to the rear entrance. I removed my lock picks from my wallet and checked for nosy neighbors. It was clear, so I finessed the lock, stowed the picks in my pocket and stepped inside. I hadn't picked a lock in years but I guess it's like riding a bicycle. Once learned, never forgotten.

In the belly drawer of Drew's secretary's desk was a set of keys. I pocketed them, pushed into his office and stopped. The picture on the wall behind his desk was of Drew and me, standing together on a riverbank in front of my motorcycle. Pain stabbed my heart and tears threatened. I willed them away and shook my head. I didn't have time for tears now.

I started sorting through the files in Drew's desk. Drew worked in real estate with the old man. From the paperwork, business seemed a little slow, but the books showed steady income. I didn't find anything out of the ordinary. But I didn't really know what I was looking at, either. After one last glance around, I gave it up as a bad idea and started for the door. As I brushed past the desk, I knocked Drew's daytimer onto the floor. I retrieved it and scanned the entries for the previous week—Bfast, Rowan-Morgan, 8am; lunch with Lori; Call Wes 1st Cap re financing; flowers to Mel for b-day. I turned to the current week—b-day party w/guys; update dad Brunner estate. There were more of the same, mostly business meetings. Nothing penciled in for the day he died or about what he wanted to discuss with me. I tossed the date book to the desktop and the blotter scooted uncovering a collection of papers. I sat back down behind the desk, and gathered the collection of sales flyers and email jokes. As I shuffled them into a stack, a scrap of paper fluttered to the floor. I picked it up and squinted at the scribbled words, B Luigi's re Austin-Kline. It had been torn from the note section of his daytimer and was crumpled as if he'd thrown it away, then changed his mind. I opened his organizer to the back and found the page the scrap had been ripped from, but there were no other notes written there. I read the message again.

"B" would be me, but I didn't know anything about Austin-Kline. I dug through the files again, and lifted the one labeled Austin-Kline and tossed it on the desk. I went through his desk once more, searching for anything else with that name on it. In the lower right-hand drawer, I found a blue folder with a rubber band around it. I added it to my stack. Drew's briefcase was on the floor by my feet. I shoved the papers into the case tossed his date book in with them and started out. Halston was coming in as I stopped at the door.

"What the hell are you doing here?" he snapped.

Those were the first words Halston Harley, had spoken to me in four years.

"I could ask the same thing about you. You've got business so pressing you have to work the day of Drew's funeral?"

"Get out of here," he hissed.

I shouldered past him, got into my truck and stared through the rain-speckled windshield. God, this day had been a week long already. I started the engine and fumbled around on the seat for my cigarettes as I drove toward home. The pack I picked up was empty. I crumpled it and felt something hard. I looked to see if there was a cigarette still in the pack. A business card was stuck between the cellophane and the paper. Detective Stryker's card. As I sat at the stoplight, I worked the card from the mangled pack and stared at it. Tapping it against the steering wheel, I made a decision.

Chapter 2

Ten minutes later, I sat on another ugly plastic and chrome couch, a twin to the one in the hospital hallway, and waited for Detective Stryker. After thirty minutes and no sign of him, I rose to go. As I stood, the desk sergeant buzzed the detective into the lobby. I wondered if he'd been watching from behind the door, but that seemed paranoid. He wouldn't have any reason to play that kind of game with me.

"Mr. Harley, how may I help you?" Stryker shook my hand.

His expression, when he stared at me, still held something I couldn't identify, pain maybe, but the compassion was gone. Today they were the hard eyes of a cop. I thought about just leaving, but that wouldn't find Drew's killer.

"You said I should come down and talk to you about my brother."

"Andrew, right? His funeral was today. I'm sorry." I swallowed the lump in my throat, but my voice still came out husky.

"Thank you, sir. Can we...do you have time to talk with me today?"

"As long as you don't mind doing it over lunch. I haven't eaten."

I did mind. I'd had enough already. I wanted to go home, drink away my headache and forget the whole rotten day, but that wasn't going to help find Drew's killer. "That's fine."

"Good, let's go to Luigi's."

I started in surprise and stared at Stryker. "I'd uh, rather go somewhere else if you don't mind."

"Sure, how about the Wagon Wheel?"

"Anywhere but Luigi's is fine."

He turned to the sergeant behind the desk.

"Morris will cover anything that needs to be handled right away. Send everything else to my voicemail. If the captain calls, send him to Terry. She has the information he wants. I'm going to be out for a couple of hours. I'll check in when I'm available."

"Yes, sir."

I trailed Stryker to the parking lot. He stopped at the unmarked Crown Vic in the next parking space.

"Come with me," he said.

I bristled at the implied command, then shook it off, and shoved my keys into my pocket. I sank into the worn springs on the passenger side, and for the first time in my life, I rode in the front seat of a cop car. We drove down Westwood without talking. Traffic was sparse in the rain. The brick shop fronts glistened in the fading afternoon light and the trees dripped onto the sidewalk below.

We whipped onto the interstate bypass that allowed travelers to avoid downtown Stantonville and circled into town from the north. Stryker drove with small precise movements—no wasted motion—I stared out the window. I wondered why this visit with me was such a priority. The only information I could share, was the phone call I'd received the night Drew died. I could have told him about that at the station. If I had been in my truck, I would have just gone home. Probably why he wanted to drive—to make sure I didn't back out.

We exited the bypass, turned onto Ellis, then into the parking lot of the Wagon Wheel. The fake log siding was dank and depressing. We drove around and parked in the rear next to an overgrown empty lot.

"We'll go in this way," Stryker said.

We pushed through Old West style swinging doors into a small private dining room. Track lighting around the ceiling did little to relieve the gloom. Stryker motioned past a handful of tables to a booth next to the window and farthest from the entrance.

"Have a seat," he said. "I'll be right back,"

I sat and stared out at the overgrown lot. The remains of a wind-damaged billboard lay scattered across the ground. The rain had almost stopped, but the sky was leaden. Headlights shone on the wet pavement. Cars threw up rooster tails of water as they passed. I jumped as Detective Stryker eased in across from me.

"We won't be bothered in here," he said. "Renee, the waitress, will be in to take our order in a few minutes."

I shrugged and watched the passing cars as the sky faded to dark. If it hadn't been for the phone call I wouldn't be here at all. Renee came in to get our drink orders and left menus. Detective Stryker studied his and asked me what sounded good. I ignored him. He didn't seem put off by my silence.

Renee returned with drinks—beer for the detective, bourbon for me. Detective Stryker ordered a T-bone, with a baked potato, when she got to me, I shook my head.

"Make that two, Renee," he said.

I took a sip of bourbon and stared out the window. Night had fallen. The only visible light was puddled beneath the streetlamps at the far side of the field. Cars were reduced to a flash of headlights in the darkness.

Renee set salad plates in front of us. The detective speared a tomato and started to eat. I shoved the lettuce around with my fork. When the steaks came, I scooted the salad plate aside to make room. Detective Stryker smiled and sliced into his steak. I picked up my knife and fork, stared at my plate, and put them down. I wasn't hungry. My gaze went back to the rain-swept window. This was a bad idea. I needed to get out of here. Before I could turn thought into motion, Detective Stryker spoke.

"Do you remember me?" he asked.

I turned away from the window and stared directly at him for the first time.

"What do you mean?"

"We've met before. Do you remember?"

"You look familiar," I said.

"Your name rang a bell with me the other night so I did a little research. Your hair's not quite as long as it used to be and the earring's gone, but it was you all right."

I tried to place him and failed.

"You still don't know where we met?" he asked, a half smile curving his lips.

I shook my head.

"I busted you for car theft about ten years ago."

A light blinked on. He was a little older, but I recognized him now. He'd had me in the rear of his cruiser after I got busted joy-riding in a brand new Corvette. I stifled a grin and focused on my plate.

"I see that I've jogged your memory."

"Yeah. Didn't recognize you without the uniform."

"If I remember right," he said around a bite of steak, "you got off on an evidentiary technicality."

"I got off because my old man had a lot of money."

"There's always that," he said. "I also seem to remember that car theft wasn't your only talent."

My mind flashed over the bit of breaking and entering I'd done that afternoon at Drew's office. I quelled the urge to swallow, didn't change my expression, and kept my hands steady as I cut into my steak. He continued to speak.

"I couldn't get into your juvenile records, but I spoke to a couple of officers who remembered you. Seems you were a pretty fair hand at breaking and entering, as well."

"I wasn't very good. I usually got caught."

"They seemed to think maybe that's why you did it."

I looked up in surprise. It had taken me the better part of ten years to understand that.

"Your old man was always there to bail you out," he continued.

I shrugged. "He'd do anything to keep his name out of the papers."

"You must have cost him a bundle before you left home."

"I hope so."

He raised his eyebrows at that and went back to his steak.

"So, what have you been doing since you gave up your life of crime?" he asked.

"Did a hitch in the army, went to college, started a business."

"Why'd you get out of the service?"

"I'm not very good at taking orders."

"They bust you out?"

I smiled and shook my head. "No, I did my hitch and didn't re-up."

He nodded and went after his baked potato. "What'd you major in at the university?"

I paused before I spoke. "Criminal justice."

Detective Stryker choked on a bite of potato, coughed, took a long pull of his beer, and cleared his throat.

"An unusual choice," he said when he could speak again.

"Not really. My dad was a cop, a highway patrolman. He died before I was born."

Stryker went still and stared at me without speaking for a long time.

"I thought your dad was in real estate."

"Halston Harley is not my father. Mom was pregnant when she married him."

"I didn't know that."

"What does this have to do with Drew?"

"Nothing really, sometimes it helps me to understand the family dynamics involved in a case."

"Well, I'll tell you a little about the Harley family dynamics. My mom broke up with Halston and got engaged to Dad. After Dad died, she married Halston, then told him she was pregnant. When he found out, it was like my Dad reached out from the grave and slapped him in the face. Halston has hated me since before I was born. I'm surprised you didn't already know all this. It's common knowledge around here."

"I'm not from around here. I left the Springfield police force and moved to Stantonville just a couple of years before you and I met the first time."

I didn't really care if Detective Stryker had moved here from the police force on Mars. I wanted to tell him about the phone call and get the hell out of there. I swirled the bourbon around in my glass and waited for him to speak. I wasn't buying his bullshit about family dynamics either, so I shut up. Never got into any trouble by keeping my mouth closed.

He finally broke the silence. "The situation between you and your...you and Halston, must have made things difficult between you and Andrew."

"There was never anything difficult between Drew and me. I protected him all my life. I loved him. After Mom died he was my whole family."

I stared out the window. Before my mom died, I hadn't really noticed how much Halston hated me. Without her to run interference, it didn't take long to find out. But instead of tearing Drew and me apart, it made us closer. Mom and Drew were the only two people I'd ever loved and now I'd lost them both. Detective Stryker interrupted my memories.

"So, Mr. Harley, tell me, what kind of business are you in? Not a private cop or our paths would have crossed before now."

I shuffled through the business cards in my wallet until I found one of mine and tossed it across the table. 'H & H Recovery' and a phone number were all that was printed on it.

"What does that mean?" he asked.

"I'm a recovery agent, a repo man."

Detective Stryker erupted into laughter. I finished my steak.

"So, you're still stealing cars."

"Seemed a shame to waste the talent," I said.

Detective Stryker was chuckling when Renee reappeared to clear the dishes. She brought fresh drinks with the check. He signed it, handed it back, and watched as she pushed through the batwing doors before he spoke. "So, what did you want to talk to me about?" he asked.

"My brother."

"He the other H in H & H recovery?"

"Hmm, I guess. He loaned me some money when I was just getting started."

That was part of it. The other reason for the name was that I wanted to make sure no one thought my business was connected to Harley Real Estate. I didn't think the detective needed that bit of information.

He nodded and stared across the table at me.

"You still think it wasn't suicide?" He asked.

"I know it wasn't."

"Convince me."

"My brother was a very happy man. He made good money. He had a wonderful girlfriend. Happy men don't kill themselves." I started to mention the phone call, but Stryker interrupted.

"Maybe he wasn't as happy as you think."

"I would have known. I told you we were close. If he was in trouble, or upset about something, he would have talked to me about it."

"It wouldn't be the first time a seemingly happy individual decided to end it all."

This wasn't getting us anywhere. He wasn't listening. I tried again.

"He wouldn't have done that to Lori. He wouldn't have done that to me," I paused. "Detective?"

"Call me Dean."

"Dean, if my brother was upset enough to take his own life, and I don't think he was, he wouldn't have done it with a gun."

"Why do you say that?"

"He hated guns. He didn't own one. He wouldn't have shot himself."

"You, on the other hand, own several."

I paused and stared at the detective. Why was he digging around in my background?

"We're not talking about me, we're talking about Drew."

My voice cracked on his name. I took a long swallow of my bourbon and stared down at the table.

"Did you find a gun with my brother's body?" I asked.

"A twenty-two. Funny thing...it was registered to you."

The glass slipped from my hand and smashed on the hard floor. Bourbon and glass mingled together on the tiles.

I looked with disbelief into the eyes of Dean Stryker.

"Why didn't you tell me this before?" I whispered.

"Why would your brother have your .22?"

"The last time I saw that gun, it was locked in Halston's gun safe. I left it there when I moved out. I haven't been there in four years."

Renee pushed into the room with a broom and a dustpan, cleaned up the mess, and left. A few minutes later she returned with a fresh drink and disappeared. I relaxed against the seat back and stared at the dark window. We were there in reverse; it was like staring into a black mirror.

"You're investigating my brother's death as a homicide?"

"I am."

"Do you have any suspects?"

Our eyes met in the black window.

"Just one," he said. There was no mystery to the expression on his face now. It was all cop.

"You're barking up the wrong tree, Detective. I got a—" He didn't let me finish.

"You never felt the least bit jealous when Drew got all the attention from your dad?"

"No, sir. Halston wasn't my father."

"I think you did get jealous. I think all these years it's been building up inside and finally you just cracked. All those years of neglect by your father, watching Drew become a success in your father's business, get engaged to a beautiful woman—I think it was finally too much for you. I think after he announced his engagement, you followed him to Lori's place, waited for him to leave, and shot him. Then you went home to your lonely little apartment, crawled into bed and slept the sleep of the innocent, secure that finally you'd have all of your dad's attention."

Anger coursed through my system. I clenched my fists on the table in front of me and leaned toward Stryker.

"You're wrong, detective. I loved my brother and I don't give a rat's ass if Halston Harley ever speaks to me again."

"I think you do."

"This is a waste of time." I stood and glared down at Detective Stryker. "I thought you could help me find out who killed my brother. I came to you hoping you would, but you won't even listen to me. I didn't kill Drew, Detective, but I will find out who did."

I started out of the room and Stryker called me back.

"How did you know your brother was shot with a handgun?"

"What?"

"At the hospital, you mentioned a handgun. I didn't. How did you know, Mr. Harley?"

"You're grasping at straws, Detective."

I pushed out into the hallway and reached for my cell phone. It was in the truck. Figures. At the pay phone hanging next to the restroom. I called a cab and went out into the damp night to wait.

Chapter 3

The rain that had tapered off while we ate started again while I stood outside the Wagon Wheel. An hour and a half-pack of Marlboro's later, the cab finally arrived. By that time, I was soaked. I could have walked to town faster. At the police station parking lot, I tossed the fare onto the front seat and jumped out before the cab rolled to a complete stop. The driver was snarling about the lousy tip as I slammed the door. Stryker's unmarked cruiser was already in its space next to my truck. I resisted the urge to plant one of my size elevens in the middle of the door panel before I climbed behind the wheel.

I drove to my apartment, wet, angry, and with a splitting headache. I dropped Drew's briefcase on a chair and slung my sopping overcoat on top of it. I toed off my soaked shoes, walked across the room and notched a CD into the stereo. An old Dire Straits album played, dark and mellow—suitable for my mood, easy on my aching head.

Baldwin trotted silently behind me as I entered the bedroom. He hopped onto the dresser and inspected my pocket treasures while I unknotted my tie. I draped it across him and he batted it around while I peeled off my shirt and pants. Baldwin escorted me to the bathroom, vaulted onto the counter, and curled up in the sink. I turned on the shower and rubbed him behind the ears as the bathroom filled with steam. When the mirror was fogged, I stepped into the shower and let the hot water

loosen the knots in my shoulders and neck. My headache
started to recede. Toweling my hair, I let Baldwin lead me
out of the bathroom. He hopped onto the bed and the
covers moved. Lori sat up. Her face, flushed from sleep,
turned bright red when she realized I was naked. Her hair
was tousled and her mascara had made dark smudges
under her eyes. She was gorgeous. I covered myself with
the towel and ducked into the bathroom.

"Jesus, Lori. What are you doing here?" It came out
sharper than I intended. I wasn't angry, just surprised. I
cringed at the hurt in her voice.

"I...I'm sorry Brocs. Your dad wouldn't let me come
back to the house after the funeral. I couldn't face going
home yet, so I came over here. I'm sorry I was in your bed.
I've been here for hours. You didn't come home. I didn't
think you'd mind."

Christ, I'd made her cry. I could hear the bedspread
rustle as she got up.

"I'll just go wait in the kitchen," she said.

Baldwin was in stealth mode so I dressed without his
help. I zipped into my jeans and found Lori at my kitchen
table, shoulders slumped, forehead resting on her palm.
She straightened when I came in.

"You want a drink or something, Lori?"

"No. I should get home. Brocs, I didn't mean to barge
in on you. I got tired of sitting in the hall. Then I
remembered I had Drew's—" her voice cracked, then she
continued. "Drew's keys, so I came in."

"Don't worry about it, you're always welcome here. You
know that. You need a ride home?"

"No. I'll be okay. I feel like walking."

I sat down across the table and took Lori's hand in
mine. It was cold.

"Why would he kill himself, Brocs? She whispered. "I
thought we were happy."

"It wasn't suicide, Lori."

"How can you be sure? Something was bothering him.
Maybe he was sick or maybe it was me. Maybe he didn't
really want to get married."

I didn't want to tell her the police knew it was murder,
not while I was the only suspect.

"Lori, Drew loved you and he loved me. He wouldn't do that to us."

Silent tears made tracks down her face as she stared at me.

"Somebody killed him, Lori, and I'm going to find out who did it and why."

"That won't bring him back."

I sighed. "No, it won't bring him back."

I let Lori's fingers slip from mine, walked into the living room, and stared unseeing at the neighborhood below. Lori lifted my overcoat from the chair and started to hang it on the coat rack.

"Is that Drew's briefcase?" she asked.

"Yeah, I guess he left it here the other night."

The lie came without conscious thought. I immediately felt like a bastard, but I didn't want her to know what was going on until I had more information.

"You want me to take it home?" she asked.

"Do you mind...I'd like to keep it for a while?"

Lori stepped to my side and squeezed my arm.

"I'm sorry, Brocs. Of course you can keep it. I'm so wrapped up in myself I forget that you're hurting, too."

Now I really felt like a shit. I wrapped her in my arms. Her shoulders shook and tears ran in warm rivulets down my bare chest. Her body was soft and curled into mine. I felt a sharp tug of desire, my body's way of affirming life in the face of death. I tamped it down. I wasn't going to sleep with Lori, whatever the reason. She eased out of my arms and wiped away her tears. With soft fingertips, she brushed my cheek. I shuddered at the touch and grabbed her hand.

"You have his eyes," she said. "When I look at you, I can almost see Drew staring out."

I let go of her hand and took a step back. The yearning on her face was painful to see.

"I'm not Drew, Lori."

"I know that," she whispered.

I wanted to pull her into my arms and keep her there all night. Our eyes locked and I knew she would stay if I asked her.

"I'd better go," she said.

"Let me give you a ride home, Lori."

She shook her head. "Find out who did this, Brocs."

She closed the door softly behind her. I sank onto the couch, and rubbed my temples. My head was still pounding as I tried to shake off what had just happened between Lori and me.

The Dire Straits CD still played softly on the stereo. Muscles that had been tense all day started to loosen and my lids got heavy. I dragged myself off the couch before I fell asleep there, scooped up Drew's briefcase and let Baldwin lead me down the hallway to the bedroom. If Detective Stryker thought I killed Drew, it would be a bad idea for Drew's briefcase to be found in my house. I scooped his office keys from my dresser, popped the latch on the briefcase and tossed them inside. If I'd been thinking, I would have stopped off at my office and put everything in the safe. I was too wiped out to head over there now. I stowed the briefcase behind a panel at the rear of my closet, covered the hole, and pushed the clothes into place so you couldn't tell they'd been moved. It wouldn't hold up to a balls-out search, but it would do for tonight.

Thinking about Stryker tightened the knots in my neck and shoulders. I stretched out on the bed and tried to relax. Lori's scent wafted from the pillow. I thought about calling Crystal or Bev, just to have a warm body to hold, but decided it wasn't worth the trouble. Sex wasn't what I wanted tonight. Baldwin hopped up beside me and rumbled against my ribs. I closed my eyes, but sleep was a long time coming.

■ ■ ■

"Take care of your little brother, Brocs; he's much smaller than you."

"Mom, he's such a pest."

"Brockston Harley, do not be selfish. He's the only little brother you have."

"Yes, Mama."

I went outside to play, told Drew to stay out of my way and ignored him.

"Brocs, honey, where's your brother?" Mama asked a few minutes later.

I looked around, but Drew was nowhere to be seen.

"He was just here, Mama."

"Brocs, what have you done?"

"I'll find him, Mama, I promise I will." I searched frantically, but Drew was gone.

"Brocs, I am so disappointed in you."

I was crying now. "I'll find him, Mama," I sobbed. "I will. Drew," I called. "Drew, where are you? Drew!"

I jerked awake with Drew's name ringing in my ears. Baldwin was hunkered down at the foot of the bed staring at me and someone was pounding at my door. The clock on my bedside table read 2:30 a.m.

I tried to gather my scattered wits as I pushed off the covers and pulled on my jeans. My nine-millimeter was in the drawer of my bedside table. I grabbed it and stuck it in my waistband. The doorbell joined the pounding. I shrugged into a tee shirt and walked down the hall. Through the peephole I could see Detective Stryker standing in my hallway. I twisted the dead bolt and slipped the safety chain.

"Jesus, don't you ever sleep?"

"Let me in," the detective said.

"Didn't we already do this, Stryker?"

"Open the damn door, Harley."

I swore softly to myself and stepped aside. Detective Stryker brushed past me and sat down at the kitchen table.

"Where's your partner?" I asked.

"I sent him home."

"He's been watching my house?"

"Getting a little antsy, Mr. Harley?"

I narrowed my eyes and didn't answer.

"Could I get a drink of water?" he asked.

I motioned toward the sink. I wasn't feeling very hospitable at the moment. He fumbled through cabinets until he found the glasses, filled one with water, and sat down. I waited for him to start. He let the silence go on long enough for Baldwin to come out and investigate. He sniffed at the detective's pant leg. Stryker reached down to pet him and Baldwin hissed. Detective Stryker jerked his hand away. I swallowed a smile.

"Your cat doesn't seem to like me very much."

"He's a smart cat."

"Hmm. Did you enjoy comforting your brother's fiancée this evening?"

I jumped as my mind went over last night. "What do you mean by that?"

"Oh come now, Mr. Harley. She's a beautiful woman."

"Detective Stryker, I think you should leave now."

"Brothers have been killed for lesser reasons."

"I didn't kill my brother."

"So you say."

"You don't have any evidence or I'd already be downtown."

"Don't get too comfortable, Mr. Harley. I have a murder weapon with your fingerprints on it, and you don't have an alibi."

"I think it's time for you to go."

I stood and waited for the detective to get up from the table. When he rose to leave, Baldwin slunk away hissing and snarling, I felt like hissing and snarling myself. I moved to the entryway and held open the door while Detective Stryker glanced around the apartment.

"You won't get in here again without a warrant," I said as he clomped down the hallway to the stairs.

He just smiled. "Sweet dreams, Mr. Harley."

"Bastard," I muttered.

I closed the door gently and rammed the bolt home. If I'd had a dog, I would have kicked it. Baldwin, not taking any chances, disappeared. I went to bed, but sleep was far away. Between the dream about my mom and Detective Stryker's visit, I was wide-awake. As the sky lightened outside my window, I finally drifted off.

The phone rang and I thrashed around trying to untangle the blankets. The machine kicked in before I could get to it.

"Come on, Harley, I know you're there. Answer the damn phone."

I picked up the receiver.

"What do you want, Nick."

"Got a job I need done. Thought I'd give you first crack at it."

"What is it this time?"

"Got a car out at Lone Ridge I need brought in."

"Christ, Nick. Why do you keep selling to those losers?"

"Those losers are paying for my 'Vette."

"You're a real piece of shit, Nick."

"Yeah and you're a car thief. Now that we've got that settled, get your ass down here. I've got another one you can take care of today while you're at it."

"Give me an hour, I'll meet you at the lot."

"You got it."

I fumbled the phone into the cradle and slid out of bed. I took a quick shower and dressed for work in loose cut Levi's, a long-sleeved tee shirt, windbreaker and hiking boots. I hooked the holster over my belt, snapped the nine into it and shoved my .22 into the pocket of my jeans. Baldwin jumped on the dresser and patted the pocket flotsam until he unearthed my lock picks. I rubbed him under the chin and dropped the picks into my pocket. My slim jim was in the bottom of my underwear drawer. I dug it out and tucked it up the left sleeve of my tee shirt. Baldwin left as I checked my pockets to make sure I had all my tools.

The rain had moved east overnight and the sky was a sparkling blue. I squinted in the glare and groped around the seat for my shades as I drove. Ten minutes later, I parked at "Buy and Fly Automotive", Nick Ascosi's car lot. It's a pretty apt name. A lot of his customers make a couple of payments and fly the coop. It's good for my business.

Buy and Fly is what's known in the business as an Iron Lot. Nick buys junk, spiffs it up and overprices it. The payments are minimal, the interest is astronomical. He collects from his customers weekly and if you miss one, he calls you on the phone. You've got two days from the contact to get caught up. If you don't, he hires me. For this kind of work I get a flat hundred-dollar fee. If I get beaten up, Nick pays the doctor bills and I get an extra fifty. If I get shot at, it goes up to two hundred. If I get hit, it's a grand plus the doctor bills. I've never been shot. Nick hopes if I do it's fatal.

When I arrived at the lot, Nick was at his oily car salesman best, sleazing some poor kid out of his paper route money. Nick is somewhere between forty-five and sixty and looks like a cross between a mafia don and a GQ cover model. He's got a pencil thin mustache and his dark hair is slicked back. A linen jacket over a silk shirt, pleated pants, and Gucci loafers with no socks complete the Nick ensemble. He nodded toward the showroom as I angled out of the truck. I ducked inside and sat down in his office.

The tile on the floor was yellow with ground in dirt. A brick was wedged under the corner of the battered wooden desk, standing in for a missing leg. A hole in the front was patched with duct tape where it looked like someone had aimed a well-placed kick. The hole was new since my last visit.

A Rigid Tool calendar girl aimed a sultry stare at me from behind the desk as she fondled a cordless drill. Over my left shoulder, a vintage Snap-On tool calendar was open to July of '81. A blonde this time, in crotch length cut offs and a bikini top, draped over a '69 Charger. It was a sweet car.

From my vantage point, I could either watch Nick work his magic on the kid, stare at the '68 Mustang sitting on the showroom floor or riffle through the junk covering the top of his desk. I'd seen Nick fleece enough customers, and even from across the room, I could tell the Mustang had more Bondo than metal under the paint. I chose the desk. I pawed through the auction flyers, loan applications, and the Springfield newspaper without finding anything interesting. I lifted a file from his in-box and found a new issue of Playboy tucked underneath.

I was checking out the centerfold when Nick finally slumped into his chair. The poor kid was just driving off the lot in his new treasure. I turned the centerfold toward Nick.

"You think those are real?"

"Give me that."

He snatched the magazine out of my hand and shoved it back into the in-box. I lit a cigarette while Nick fanned through the mess on his desk for the two files he was turning over to me. The first was on Lewis Clancy. I laughed when he handed it to me. Lewis is a regular customer. He gets flush, buys a car, makes his payments for a month or so then goes on a binge, drinks his paycheck, and Nick sends me out to get the car. I've been to Lewis's place a dozen times. The second one was at Lone Ridge, a neighborhood outside the city limits, overlooking the river. The inhabitants keep to themselves and guard their territory with buckshot. It's the kind of place that gives Ozark Mountain People a bad name. Every time I have to do a repo at Lone Ridge I come home swearing to hire a partner.

My target this time was Julius Manchester. He was the soon to be former owner of an eighty-two Chevy pickup. Recently out of prison, he'd been in town about three months. He was a no good piece of shit and it was a pretty safe bet he'd be back inside soon.

"Why don't you just wait till this asshole gets arrested again, Nick?"

"Nah, the truck will be totaled before that. I want it now. What's a matter, you going soft on me?"

"I'll get it for you, but you know the deal."

"Yeah, yeah."

He dismissed me with a wave of his hand. I removed two contracts from my jacket pocket, flattened them out and slid them across the desk.

"I'm insulted, Brocs. I'm one of your best customers."

"Just business, Nick," That and the fact he was about as trustworthy as Julius Manchester.

Nick scribbled his name and tossed the paperwork to me. I folded the contracts, and stowed them in my pocket as I left. The first one would be easy. I'd take care of Lewis then head out to Lone Ridge and see what I was up against there.

Chapter 4

I parked at the curb in front of Lewis's house. The shades were down, but as I stepped onto the stoop I could hear the canned laughter of a TV game show. I reached through the broken screen and knocked. Shuffling sounds came from inside and Lewis swung open the door. The smell of stale beer and unwashed male rolled out over me. I stepped back to get away from the stench. Lewis scratched his belly through his undershirt and grinned. "'Lo, Brocs."

"Morning, Lewis. I need to pick up the car."

"I was expectin' you 'fore long."

"You want to drive it into town? I'll give you a ride home."

"Sure, sure."

The door closed. I watched a tiny lizard skitter up the siding. It disappeared beneath the leaves of a vine clinging to the gutter. I could hear Lewis rustling around inside, then it was quiet. I turned and stared across the dirt yard to the street where a small boy rode his Big Wheel back and forth through the lone mud puddle in front of his house. I gave it a couple of minutes and when Lewis didn't reappear, I opened the broken screen door and knocked again. The TV stopped in mid laugh. There were more shuffling noises from inside. Finally, Lewis opened up. He stared at me in surprise.

"Hey, forgot you was out here."

He belched and started to close the door. I stuck the toe of my boot in to keep it from closing. It banged against my foot and bounced open. Lewis backed up and stared in confusion. After a pause, he wandered down the hall into the kitchen for his keys. I stood there and tried not to breathe until he shuffled back.

He followed me out of the house and got into his car. I tucked in behind him and made sure he stopped at the lot. Nick met us at the office, and Lewis handed over his keys. I gave Nick the paperwork. He slipped me the hundred and glared.

"Easiest money you'll ever earn."

"Yeah, makes up for having to go out to Lone Ridge."

I motioned for Lewis to get in the truck. He closed the door and I almost asked him to ride in the bed. I opened the windows instead. Good thing it was only a couple of blocks. I drove with my head out the window until we stopped in front of his house. He crawled out and ambled up the cracked sidewalk.

"See you in a couple of months, Harley."

I laughed and waved as I backed away. I drove toward Lone Ridge with the windows down, but it didn't do much good. Eau de Lewis was imbedded in my nostrils. I eased onto the shoulder at the bottom of the hill below the ridge and decided to climb the road on foot. Dotting the ridge were ancient mobile homes sporting satellite dishes. The yards were decorated with derelict cars, old bedsprings, and broken-down furniture. Feral cats slunk around the cars, hissing if you got too close.

I found the trailer I was aiming for, but the Chevy wasn't there. I glanced around for neighbors. I didn't see any so I ducked into the woods, found a log to sit on, and waited for Manchester to make an appearance. I didn't have to wait long. Fifteen minutes later, the Chevy ground up the hill and came to a stop in front of the trailer. Manchester went inside carrying a six-pack. Looked like he was in for a while and he didn't lock the truck. I smiled. Maybe this wasn't going to be so bad after all. I eased out of my hiding place and crouched at the rear of the truck. A cat shot between my feet. I grabbed the bumper to keep from falling and swore under my breath. I bobbed up for a peek over the tailgate. Still no one around. Crouching, I made my way to the driver's side and eased behind the wheel. This was going to be a piece of cake. I hummed to myself as I reached under the dash and started to hot-wire the pickup. As I peeled the insulation from the wires, the trailer door flew open and a black and tan hound ran, snarling, toward me. "Shit!" Slamming the truck door shut, I fumbled with the wires while the dog hurled himself at the driver's window. I glanced toward the trailer as a rifle barrel appeared between the edge of the screen and the doorframe.

"Shit!" I ducked as he fired. The bullet starred the windshield and thudded into the seat beside my head. "Dammit!"

Fumbling under the dash, I finally made the connection. The engine groaned to life. I dropped it into reverse without sitting up. A trash can clattered off the bumper and overturned as I swung the Chevy around. I shifted into drive and mashed the throttle. The engine stumbled, coughed, and sputtered.

"Take off you piece of shit!" I yelled.

I pounded the steering wheel in frustration as a gunshot pinged off the tailgate. I heard a third shot and felt a sting above my right ear. Pellets of safety glass showered my head and shoulders.

"Son of a bitch!"

My eyes blurred. I blinked them clear. Another shot and my right arm went numb. I rammed my foot to the floor. The engine coughed, caught, and gravel sprayed behind me as I lurched out of the drive. I risked a glance in the rearview mirror. The rifle lay on the ground at Manchester's feet. He was shielding his eyes from the gravel with one hand and giving me a one-finger salute with the other. I grinned. I love my job.

I drove the Chevy onto Nick's lot. A throbbing ache replaced the numbness in my arm. Blood dripped off my elbow onto the seat. My hair was matted to the side of my head and blood soaked the neck of my shirt and jacket. I probably looked like something from a horror movie as I stumbled from the truck. My knees buckled as my feet hit the ground and I clung to the window frame for support. Nick stepped out onto the sidewalk, took one look, and ran back inside. I hoped he was going for the first aid kit and not barricading himself in his office. I really didn't feel like driving myself to the emergency room.

He reappeared with a bleach-mottled shop towel and ran toward me as I released my hold on the window frame and leaned against the bed. I hoped the rag wasn't soaked in gasoline or brake cleaner. Just in case, I jerked away as Nick moved the folded scrap toward my head, snagged it from his outstretched hand and held it against my arm.

"Jesus, Harley. What the hell happened up there?"

"Julius wanted to keep the truck."

"He shot you?"

"No, Nick. I shot myself."

"Un-fucking-believable. Christ, get inside or something. You're gonna scare away all my customers."

"You're all fucking heart, Nick. Just give me a ride to the ER. I think I need a couple of stitches." I moved the now crimson shop rag and fingered the rip in my sleeve.

"Yeah, sure. Just a sec."

Nick left me. A few minutes later he reappeared from behind the building in his 'Vette. I scrunched into the passenger seat still holding the towel against my arm.

"Don't get any blood on the seats, pal. This is my ride."

I glanced around the car lot and back at Nick. "You couldn't find something else to drive?"

"When Nick drives, Nick drives the 'Vette. The ladies love it."

I swallowed a groan and rested my head against the seat ignoring Nick's warning about bloodstained upholstery. Nick parked outside the ER, opened my door and pulled me none too gently out. I stumbled to the desk and an aide hustled me behind the curtain. Nick moved the car and found me a few minutes later.

The nurse, Celia Alley according to her name tag, soaked a gauze pad in Betadine solution, stuck it on my head and told me to hold it there. She had the body of a goddess and the hard-faced appearance of someone who had fought her way up from the bottom. She might have been pretty once.

While I held the gauze pad in place, she prepped a syringe with a local anesthetic.

"I don't want an injection."

"What's a matter, big guy, are you afraid of needles? I promise it will only hurt a little."

"I'm not afraid of needles, I just don't like lidocaine."

"Sure, tough guy. I gotta go talk to the doc. Be right back."

While I awaited her return, I removed the Betadine soaked pad from my head and probed the crease above my ear. The bleeding seemed to have stopped, but it was beginning to swell. I could feel the skin around my eye and cheek starting to tighten. I scooted off the exam table to check out the damage in the polished metal front of a supply cabinet against the wall. Before I made two steps the doctor entered, followed by Nurse Alley. One glare from her and I sat back down. The doc took a quick look at my injuries and frowned.

"These are gunshot wounds."

"Yes sir."

"I've already called the police," Nurse Alley said.

I waited for Nick to throw in his two cents, but he remained unusually silent.

The doctor probed my arm and I tensed.

"This is pretty deep. It's going to be painful to get it cleaned and sutured. You sure you don't want a local anesthetic?"

"I'm sure."

He made a notation on my file and handed it to the nurse. I thought I heard Nick mumble the word 'masochist' under his breath, but when I glanced up, he was examining his cuticles.

"He wants to do it the hard way, Celia. There doesn't appear to be any muscle damage. Clean him up, stitch him up, and turn him over to the cops."

"Yes, doctor," she answered.

I'm sure I imagined the malevolent gleam in her eye as she rolled the suture tray closer to the exam table.

She told me to remove my jacket, and proceeded to cut the sleeve out of my tee shirt. When I was properly disrobed, she soaked a new pad with antiseptic and told me to press it against my arm. Holding the gauze pad, I forced myself to stay still while she cleaned the crease above my right ear. I was only moderately successful. As I winced away from her fingers, she stopped and looked me in the eye.

"This doesn't have to hurt, Mr. Harley."

"I know."

"But you still don't want the injection."

"Right."

"Then be still."

I laughed. "Yes, ma'am."

Nick muttered something I couldn't hear. Nurse Alley's lips twitched as she held back a grin.

I made damn sure I didn't move a muscle as she stitched my head together. She put the bandage in place and flipped my hair down to cover it.

"Your hair should hide the scar, hon."

"I'm sure he's real worried about the cosmetic damage," Nick said.

I knew his silence was too good to last. I glared at him, but he ignored me. Ms. Alley shot him a look and he flashed her one of his car salesman smiles. She grinned and set to work cleaning my arm.

Over her shoulder, I could see a police officer waiting patiently for her to finish. I decided to take care of business before Nick disappeared. He was admiring Ms. Alley's 'technique' and mumbling to himself about the bloodstains on his Vette. I think the quiet was starting to wear on him.

When she stepped away to prepare a new suture tray, I fished the contract out of my jacket pocket and tossed it to Nick.

"Hey, brother." I said to Nick. "You owe me two thousand bucks, a tee shirt and a new windbreaker."

"What!"

"If a gunshot wound is worth a grand, two of 'em ought to be worth two grand."

"Ah, that's bullshit, Harley. I gotta get the glass replaced. You got blood all over the truck seat. It's gonna cost me a bundle to get that thing ready to sell. And to top it off, you bled all over the Nickmobile. Besides, you should have been out of there before he got off the second shot."

"I would have if that piece of shit truck would run."

"I tell you what, I'll give you a thousand and replace your clothes. That's more than fair. Hell the truck's not worth much more than that."

"Deal."

"You son of a bitch. You played me. All you wanted was the grand."

I grinned, and then winced as Nurse Alley started stitching my arm.

"Hold still, it wouldn't hurt if you'd let me give you a local," she said.

"Sorry."

"You're a rotten piece of shit, Harley."

"You're not so bad yourself, Nick."

"How 'bout I go get your old Ford while this nice lady finishes her handiwork?"

"Better watch it, Nick. It'll get out that you're really a nice guy."

"Don't start with me, Harley."

Nick stood and started out of the cubicle.

"How bout you pay up before you go, Nick?"

He glared and reached for his wallet.

"You're not very trusting."

I smirked while he peeled off eleven one hundred dollar bills and handed them to me.

"You can pick out your own clothes," he said.

I folded the money and shoved it into the front pocket of my Levi's. "My truck's parked at the foot of Lone Ridge Road."

"I'll find it," said Nick.

He edged around the curtain and disappeared from view.

"Hey cowboy, what ya doin' for dinner?" Celia Alley asked with a smile.

"All booked up, darlin. Sorry."

"That's okay," she said. "My old man probably wouldn't take it too well anyway."

The smile was gone, the words sounded defeated. My mom had sounded like that before she died. I had a sudden vision of Celia's old man smacking her around. I glanced up at her face and caught the faint trace of a fading bruise around her left eye.

"Your old man, he hit you?" I asked

Her shoulders stiffened. She ignored my question and bandaged me up. I thanked her and started to shrug into my damaged jacket.

"I'm not finished yet," she said.

"I don't have any more bullet holes."

"Tetanus shot. You just thought you were gonna get out of here without an injection."

I sighed and sat down. She pushed up my sleeve and the slim jim fell out. She picked it up off the floor, stared at it for a minute, then glared at me as she tossed it on the bed. She knew what it was. Her old man probably had one.

"What exactly is it that you do for a living?" she asked.

"I'm a repo man."

"Sure you are, sugar."

She shot me in the arm with more force than necessary, then motioned to the policeman that I was all his.

"Celia, wait," I said.

She stopped and turned around.

I handed her my card. "He hits you again, you call me."

Her eyes widened, then her face went blank. She shook her head and turned to walk away without looking at me again. But she didn't throw away the card. I hoped she would call me. I don't have much use for guys that hit women. The officer took her place at my side and I explained what had happened.

"Mr. Harley," he said, when I'd finished. "You just made my week. We've been dreaming of a reason to put that sack of shit Manchester back behind bars ever since he came to town."

"Glad I could help."

"Just make sure you're around to testify."

He shook my hand before he walked out of the exam room. I followed him out and started toward the entrance when I heard my name. I turned toward the desk. Celia waved a piece of paper at me and motioned me over. She gave me my wound care briefing and I signed the insurance forms. Celia started down the hall. I tossed my pen down on the completed form and caught up with her before she entered the exam room to clean up.

"Celia, I meant what I said. Call me."

She glared at me and I took a step back.

"I think you need to spend a little more time taking care of yourself and a little less time sticking your nose where it doesn't belong."

I tried again.

"Just keep the card, okay. No one should have to be afraid to go home at night. I promise, if you call me, I'll come."

"I've wasted enough time talking to you, Mr. Tough Guy. I have other patients."

She stepped into the exam room, dismissing me. But her hand was in the pocket of her scrubs fingering the business card she'd tucked in there earlier.

I hoped she would call. Actually, I hoped she wouldn't ever need to call, but that wasn't likely. I sighed and turned down the hall to the ER entrance and stepped outside. My truck was parked at the curb, the keys dangling from the ignition. I eased behind the wheel and headed home twelve hundred dollars richer than when I'd left. Not a bad day's work even with the stitches. I'd have to call Drew when I got home and tell him about the recovery. Grief washed over me as I remembered he was gone. For just a little while, I'd forgotten.

Baldwin came in, sniffed the air as I stepped inside, and backed away growling low in his throat. I didn't blame him. In the bathroom, I took the bandage off my head, flipped my hair over the stitches and washed off most of the blood. My right eye was starting to darken and a bruise showed on my cheek. I threw the jacket and tee shirt into the trash and gingerly pulled on a sweatshirt. My arm was going to be sore as hell for a couple of days, and last night's headache was nothing compared to the one I had now. I retrieved the packet of pain pills from my pocket and tossed them into the trash. Not my kind of painkiller.

I stepped into sweat pants and threw my jeans into the washer to soak. In the kitchen, I broke the wax seal on a brand new bottle of Maker's Mark. I poured a double shot, drained it and poured another. History's original anesthetic burned in my empty stomach. I fixed a ham sandwich, and washed it down with the second drink. The throbbing in my head started to subside as the bourbon went to work. I left the glass in the sink and decided on a nap.

Two hours later I awoke in the dark. Baldwin's eyes shone like gems in the glow from the streetlight. I sat up and turned on the bedside lamp. Baldwin blinked in the sudden glare. My head started pounding. I stretched and cringed as the stitches pulled. In the kitchen, I took a couple of Tylenol and washed them down with iced tea. Wide-awake, I dug Drew's briefcase out of the closet, popped it open, and started going through his papers.

It was time to find out if Austin-Kline Investments had anything to do with Drew's death.

Chapter 5

hree hours of wading through Drew's papers, trying to find something that raised a red flag, left me with nothing. My eyeballs felt like they were going to pop out of my head. I shuffled the jumble of files into the briefcase, swallowed a couple more Tylenol, and decided to call it a night. As I went down the hall toward the bedroom, a knock sounded at the door. I wasn't in the mood for cops. I picked up my gun, flung open the door and prepared to give Detective Stryker an ass chewing he'd never forget.

Lori stood wide-eyed, staring at the weapon in my hand.

"Uh, maybe this isn't a good time. I'll leave you alone."

"I'm sorry, Lori. Its okay, come on in."

I tucked the gun in the back of my waistband and followed her to the living room. "You want a drink or something?"

"Sure."

She looked better today, not so bruised. Her hair was fixed, her makeup flawless. Only the eyes gave her away—there was no sparkle there, only sadness. Outside, Lori was back to normal, the inside would take longer to heal. She stopped in front of a picture of Drew and me, ran her fingers lightly over his face and took a deep breath. I watched from across the room. She moved toward me and softly touched the bruise around my eye. Her touch sent tremors through my body. I stepped away. Detective

Stryker's words echoed in my head, "Did you enjoy comforting your brother's fiancée this evening?" Lori's voice snapped me back. "Good God, Brocs. What have you done to your face?"

"I repo'd a truck from a guy who wanted to keep it."

Anger replaced the sadness in her eyes. "One of these days some lowlife is going to kill you. Is that what you want, to get shot over a damn car?"

I stared open-mouthed at her. "Uh...let me get you that drink." I poured bourbon over ice, added soda, and handed her the glass.

"I'm sorry, Brocs. That was out of line."

"It's okay. I didn't know you cared one way or the other."

"Of course I do. You and I were the most important people in Drew's life."

I didn't know how to respond so I fumbled around mixing another drink. I didn't even like bourbon and soda. I took a taste, made a face and put it down on the table. "What can I do for you, Lori?"

"I wasn't thinking straight when I was over here before. I guess I was still in shock over..." She made a 'you know' kind of motion with her hand, then pressed her fingers to her lips. She paused and took a sip of her drink before she continued. "Drew had been acting different lately. Brocs, do you really think he didn't kill himself?"

"What do you mean, he was acting different?"

"It started a couple of weeks ago. I...I think Drew found out something and didn't know what to do about it. He was distracted, upset, grouchy. He was never like that. You know how he was." She paused again and forced back her tears. "I think he found out something he wasn't supposed to and that's why he's dead."

I sat up in my chair. If that were true, the phone call I got the night he died made sense.

"Tell me what was going on the last couple of weeks."

"I don't know really. He was just distracted like I said. I asked him what was wrong. He said he couldn't tell me, but he needed to talk to someone about it."

"Did he?"

"Not that I know of. I think maybe that's what he wanted to talk to you about at Luigi's."

"He didn't mention what it was about?"

"He wouldn't tell me anything, Brocs. I thought he was trying to work his way up to breaking up with me."

"He would never have done that, Lori."

She smiled. "I wish he would have told me what was wrong."

"It might be a good thing he didn't. If someone killed him to keep it quiet, they wouldn't think twice about doing it again."

Lori tensed in her chair. Shit, I'd scared her. I hadn't meant to do that.

"Do you think I might be in danger?" she whispered.

"Maybe. Could you go stay with your dad for a while?"

"If you think I should. I can't sleep at my place anyway. It's too quiet."

"It might be a good idea if you got out of town until we can figure out what's going on."

"God, Brocs. This is just too much."

She covered her face with her hands. I went over and held her in my arms. She relaxed against me for a minute before she leaned away. The tears were under control. She took a deep breath and brushed her fingers over my bruised cheek again.

"I don't want you hurt, Brocs. Maybe you should just let the police handle it."

"That's not really an option, Lori."

She didn't ask why. For that I was thankful. I still didn't want her to know Stryker thought I'd killed Drew.

"What can I do to help?" she asked.

"Can you remember what Drew was working on before he died?"

"A sale for some investment firm, Eldon or Elston something."

"Austin-Kline?"

"Yeah, that was the name. That was all, though. It was a pretty big deal. He'd been working on it for a long time. Brocs, I don't think it was anything to do with business."

"Why don't you think it was work-related?"

"I don't know. Maybe it was. I can't imagine what he'd be involved in at the office that could...that could get him killed. He sold real estate."

Her voice dropped. I gave her hand a squeeze. She took a minute to gather herself. I resisted the urge to fold her into my arms again.

I had a hunch work did have something to do with Drew's death. I didn't have any reason for it, just a gut feeling and a page from his daytimer that I'd found in his office. I was glad Lori didn't know much about Drew's latest deal. If the Austin-Kline account had something to do with why he was killed, the less Lori knew about it the better. Even so, I was glad she was getting out of town.

"Lori, did Drew keep any papers at home?"

"Well, he had an office there. I never went in it. I don't know what he kept there."

"Can you get in?"

"Halston won't let me in the house. There was a picture Drew had on his desk. I asked Halston if I could have it. He slammed the door in my face."

What a bastard. "I'll try to get your picture," I said.

She waved me off like it wasn't important. I'd get it for her, though. If I had to, I could get into Halston's house. I installed the security system. That was one B&E I was sure I could do without getting caught.

I straightened from the stool in front of Lori's chair and moved to the couch. I picked up my glass and stared into the amber liquid, trying to sort out what I needed to do next. I hadn't found anything in Drew's papers so far.

"Drew left some files and stuff at my apartment. Do you want me to bring them over?"

My head snapped up. Yes, I wanted those papers. No, I didn't want Lori to bring them over. Not with Detective Stryker and his watchdog around. They were probably outside right now.

"I want the papers but you probably shouldn't bring them over. I don't know if the men who killed Drew are watching you or not. Why don't you mail them to me when you get to your dad's?"

"Isn't that a little extreme?" she asked.

"Maybe. Just humor me, okay?"

"Alright."

"If you need to get in touch with me, while you're at your dad's, call my cell."

Lori was staring at me now. Wondering what I knew, which was nothing really, not about the killers anyway. I did know that Stryker and his bird dog were watching my place. I didn't think they were tapping my phone, but it seemed silly to take chances.

"Brocs, what's this all about?"

"Just trust me, Lori. I promise I'll explain when I can."

"I trust you, Brocs."

"If you think of anything else about the last few weeks that I need to know, leave a message on my cell phone."

"Brocs, maybe we should talk to the cops."

"NO!"

Lori jumped in surprise. "Couldn't you at least call that friend of yours, Wil? He might be able to help."

Wil was a cop and we'd been friends since college, but I didn't want to put him in the middle—between me and the police department. I'd handle this alone. At least for now.

"Lori, we don't have anything to tell them right now."

"I don't know, Brocs. Whatever you think. I wish you would at least talk to him."

"Maybe later, Lor."

I escorted Lori to her car and watched her drive away. A quick glance around the parking lot didn't reveal Stryker or Morris. Didn't mean they weren't around.

Back inside, Baldwin twined himself around my legs as I picked up the dirty glasses from the living room and dumped them out in the sink. I wondered if I should get in touch with Stryker and tell him about the phone call. He probably wouldn't believe me now. It had been too long.

I sat down at the kitchen table. Baldwin hopped up and blinked at me. I dropped my head in my hands and tried to decide what to do next. Baldwin tiptoed over and rooted under my arm. I rubbed behind his ears and he started to purr. I tried to remember exactly what the voice on the phone had said the night Drew died. It was something about minding his own business. I couldn't think of the exact wording. Too much had happened since then. Shit. I wish I had caller ID. Then I'd at least have a place to start.

I had no doubt that Drew was murdered. Now I just had to discover why. Drew was concerned about something the last couple of weeks. It had to be connected to Austin-Kline Investments, but none of the papers I had seen so far gave me any idea how. I dug them out and read through them again. I just didn't have enough knowledge of the business to see anything wrong. I wished Drew was here to explain it to me. I smiled at the thought. If Drew was here I wouldn't need it explained.

Halston could probably clear it up. I'd have to get someone else to ask him. He wouldn't take my calls and he probably wouldn't let me through the door of his office. I knew he wouldn't let me into the house. I thought about calling my old roommate, Billy Rayburn, and asking him. He was into real estate among other things. I went as far as picking up the phone, but I hung up before I dialed. It was late, I was tired, and I felt like shit. It was time to give in to my pounding head and hit the sack. First thing tomorrow, I'd take a little trip to Riker and see what Billy could tell me about Austin-Kline Investments.

Chapter 6

Riker, Missouri is thirty miles east and several tax brackets north of Stantonville. Billy Rayburn had his office there and I was hoping to pick his brain. I stalked out of the elevator on the eleventh floor of his building at five minutes after nine. The receptionist looked up and gasped in surprise as I pushed into the reception room. I was wearing Levis, black motorcycle boots, and black leather chaps. My leather motorcycle jacket gaped open as I strode in, showing the shoulder rig housing my nine-millimeter. My rainbow eye and bruised cheek only added to the effect.

"I'm here to see Rayburn," I said, scowling to keep a smile off my face as the latest in a long line of well-endowed blonde bimbos scooted back in her chair.

"I'm...uh, sorry sir, he's um....in a meeting," she stammered. "Would you like to make an appointment?"

"I don't need an appointment."

With that, I brushed past her and pushed in Billy's office. Rayburn sat behind a teak desk the size of an aircraft carrier. His suit was custom-tailored, his shoes were Italian, and his cigar was Cuban. The little blonde followed me into the room stammering an apology. Her boss looked up in anger. A smile broke out when he saw who it was.

"Harley, you son of a bitch. Where the hell have you been?"

We shook hands and I lowered myself into the chair in front of his desk.

"It's okay, Tia. He's an old friend. Brocs, this is Tia Mattingly. Tia, Brocs Harley."

I stood, bowed, and kissed her hand.

"Sorry, I didn't mean to scare you. I just like to make an entrance when I come to see Billy."

She gave me a head-to-toe appraisal, the look on her face changed from fear to interest.

"Pleased to meet you, Mr. Harley. Can I get you anything?"

It was definitely an open-ended question. I gave her the head-to-toe look back. She blushed.

"Tia, hold my calls and reschedule anything I have going this afternoon."

"But, sir."

"Just do it, Tia."

She nodded and slipped out of Billy's office.

"She's a looker, Bill."

"Yep, I don't think she has ten functioning brain cells in that pretty little head of hers."

"When you gonna start hiring them for their brains instead of their boobs?"

"You know me, still trying to find one that has both. Hey, man. I was sorry as hell to hear about your brother. I was in Atlanta when Wil called to tell me. I didn't get back into town until yesterday or I'd have been there."

"Thanks, Bill."

"So, what brings you here, Brocs? Just using me for an excuse to get the hog out on the road?"

"I need your help."

Billy Rayburn's business interests were very...diverse. He knew most of the movers and shakers in the local business world, both legitimate and otherwise.

"Tell me about Austin-Kline Investments."

His twinkling blue eyes suddenly shuttered. He tipped back in his chair and put his hands together over his belt buckle.

"I don't believe I've ever heard of them. What exactly are they into?"

He was lying.

"That's what I was hoping to find out from you."

"Guess you're out of luck, Brocs. I've never heard of them."

I knew he was lying. Now I wanted to find out why. "No big deal. It's a nice day for a ride. You still got your bike?"

"Yeah."

"Want to play hooky?"

He lost the shuttered look and a small smile touched the corners of his mouth. "Why the hell not?"

He shrugged into his suit coat and punched the intercom button. "Tia, I'm going to be out of the office the rest of the day. Send messages to my voice mail."

"Can I reach your cell phone?"

"Nope, I'm going to be in a meeting all afternoon."

"Yes, sir."

I winked at Tia on the way out. She blushed and busied herself with the telephone. I got the impression from the blush that she hadn't been serious about her earlier offer.

I straddled my Heritage Softail and waited for Rayburn to retrieve his BMW from the underground parking garage. When he drove out, I tucked in behind him and we wound our way up into the Ozark foothills to his little five thousand square foot hideaway. I parked the Harley in the drive out front and ducked under the garage door as it lowered behind the Beamer. Rayburn bleeped the security system on the car and opened the door into the kitchen. I tossed my jacket on a chair and stepped down into the sunken great room. The west wall was all glass. Cedar Lake was just visible through the trees. While Rayburn changed from businessman to biker, I checked out the view. It was incredible.

I strolled around the living room, stopping to admire the tiny treasures tucked on the shelves between leather-bound first editions. Billy has a thing for tiny works of art; paintings, sculpture, anything in miniature. My wanderings brought me in front of the window again. The room was outstanding, rich but comfortable and everything was keyed to the view. I went to the bar, poured water over ice and sat down. The chair enfolded me like it was custom built for my six-foot-two frame. The whole place was like that. At first glance it took your breath away. Then it just wrapped itself around you and you didn't want to leave. If I had a place like that, I'd never get any work done. I'd never get out of the house.

Rayburn came out of the bedroom dressed to ride, grabbed his leather jacket out of the closet and slung it over his shoulder.

"Let's hit the road, Brocs."

I started my Harley and waited for Billy. We rolled over the winding hill roads around Riker and Stantonville all afternoon. Tiny burgs were scattered along the lightly traveled blacktop—places where if you needed more than gas and a pit stop, you were out of luck. We were maybe five miles from Billy's place at Cedar Lake, close to twenty from my house, but it felt like a different world. It was the perfect place to kill an afternoon on a bike.

We stopped at an overlook. I always meant to bring a camera with me when I came up here. Drew was going to remind me the next time we took off for an afternoon. I turned away from the view and got back on my bike. God I was going to miss him.

A few miles from the overlook, we stopped at a no-name inn outside of Linden—the only town between Riker and Stantonville that still boasted a post office, grocery store, and restaurant. I stood and stretched. I hadn't been in the saddle for that many hours in a long time. My butt and back were complaining and my bullet wounds were starting to throb. Maybe riding today hadn't been such a hot idea. I shrugged out of my jacket, eased out of my shoulder rig and stowed it in one of the saddlebags. We were intimidating enough in our leather; I didn't need to give someone a heart attack with the gun.

"You look like shit. You okay, Brocs?"

"Just a little stiff."

"Yeah, I always get pale and start to sweat when my muscles get stiff."

I shrugged at him as we went inside. We took a booth at the back. I tossed my jacket on the seat and eased in. We ordered a couple of beers and watched the waitress as she removed the bottles from the ice and came across the room trading insults with her regulars. She put our beers down and dropped menus on the table in front of us.

She was close to forty and had probably looked the same since she was twenty. She'd probably still look forty when she was sixty. Her name tag bobbed on an ample bosom and her skirt swished invitingly over nicely rounded hips. She wasn't beautiful, but she was all woman. I glanced at Billy and saw him smile appreciatively.

She told us the specials, then leaned in for a closer look at me and said, "Hon, I've got just the thing to make you feel better."

She left and a moment later reappeared with a brandy snifter. "Drink," she said.

I took a sip.

"All of it."

"Yes, ma'am." I drained the glass and handed it to her.

"That's better. Now, what can I get for ya?"

We ordered, and then watched as she swayed across the room to the kitchen.

"That's the woman that should be answering your phones, Rayburn."

He tore his gaze from her retreating form and shook his head. "Too smart, might take over."

I snickered. Might make him get off his ass and do some work is what he meant. The bandage on my arm peeked out from under the sleeve of my tee shirt as I picked up my beer.

"What happened to your arm?" Rayburn asked.

"I got shot."

"Man, you need to find a different line of work. Why don't you come to work for me?"

"And do what?" I asked.

"I could find something for a man with your talents."

"Sorry, Billy. I'm strictly on the side of angels now."

I dug two Tylenol from my pocket, swallowed them with the beer and willed the headache to subside. We talked about old times while we waited for our food. Billy was one of my roommates in college. He got through on charm and luck while I busted my ass for grades. Now he was living in a mansion on top of a mountain and I had a three-room apartment just outside the low rent district. Some guys are born under a lucky star—Billy Rayburn was one of them. We ate dinner and drank a couple more beers before I brought up Austin-Kline again.

"So," I thunked my half-empty bottle down on the table. "Tell me about Austin-Kline."

"Never heard of them, told you that already."

"Don't lie to me, Rayburn. I've known you too long."

"What's Austin-Kline to you, anyway?"

"Just curious."

"That's not going to cut it, Harley."

I sighed and took a long pull from my beer before I spoke. "Drew didn't kill himself."

Billy stared at me with narrowed eyes. "What's that have to do with Austin-Kline?"

"Before Drew died, he was working on a deal for them."

"I'm not following you, Brocs. What's the connection?"

"Maybe there isn't one. I'm fishing."

"We're not dealing with fish here, Brocs. These are sharks, great whites with big sharp teeth. I'm not going to tell you anything unless you give me something to go on."

I sighed again and finished my beer. Then I told Billy what little I knew.

"Detective Stryker is trying to pin Drew's murder on me." I finished. "Someone went to a hell of a lot of trouble to make it appear I had something to do with his death. I want to know who, and I want to know why. I had to do something so I started with you. You've got a connection to everything and everyone that does business in the area."

Billy slouched against the booth and stared out the window.

"You may not like what you find out, Brocs."

"Dammit, Billy. They are trying to pin my brother's murder on me. I'm not doing this for the fun of it. The police have evidence against me and they're not looking very hard at anyone else. I don't have any choice. Either I find out what the hell's going on, or I go to prison."

Billy sighed and rubbed his hand over his face.

"Austin-Kline is huge. I don't even know who the kingpin is. He's hidden away behind a lot of legal paperwork. They have a finger in every pie—drugs, prostitution, you name it. They've had their hooks in your old man for years. I'd venture a guess that most of the money that goes through Harley Real Estate comes out a hell of a lot cleaner than when it went in."

"You think Halston is laundering money for those guys."

"It's just a guess. He spends a hell of a lot more money than he earns on real estate in that two-bit town of yours."

"Lori said Drew was working a real estate deal for Austin-Kline. Would they have killed him if he found out what was going on?"

"It's possible. If rumor can be believed, it's happened before."

"How could they have gotten my gun? It was at Halston's."

"Hell, they probably thought it belonged to Drew or your old man. You said they tried to make it look like a suicide. Face it man, you're just a casualty of war."

"Yeah, but whose war?"

"That's the ten thousand dollar question isn't it?"

"I've got to find out more about these guys. Can you help me?"

"I can't, Brocs. I'm a small fish compared to them. I'm sorry, man. I've just got too much to lose."

Yeah, so did I. I picked up my jacket from the seat next to me and stood. "Thanks for nothing, Billy."

He started to speak, then shook his head and picked up his beer. I was fuming on the ride home and I had more questions now than when I started.

Chapter 7

By the time I made it into town, it was full dark. I rolled my Harley into the parking space next to the Ford and climbed the stairs to my apartment. My head was pounding and my arm throbbed with every step. I fumbled the key into the lock, left my jacket on the floor in the entry, and shuffled down the hall to the bedroom without turning on the lights. Baldwin uncurled himself from my pillow and came over to say hello while I pulled off my boots.

"I got a two-bourbon headache, Baldwin."

He cocked his head and trotted down the hallway. I sank onto the bed, fully clothed, and closed my eyes. From the kitchen, I heard Baldwin batting his food bowl across the floor. He was hungry. With a sigh, I got up and changed into sweats. Something heavy toppled to the floor and Baldwin yowled.

"Keep your shirt on, beast."

Baldwin was giving me the evil eye when I walked into the kitchen. His food dish was in the middle of the floor, my Maker's Mark rested against the table leg—the thump I'd heard from the bedroom. Luckily it wasn't broken.

"You're getting on my last nerve, cat."

Baldwin put on his innocent angel kitty face, and wound around my ankles as I scooped the dish and the bottle off the floor.

Dodging the cat, I filled his dish. He purred and chattered as he started to eat. I opened the Maker's Mark and poured downed my first dose of pain reliever. As it burned it's way to my stomach, I poured a second and took it with me to the bedroom, leaving Baldwin alone to enjoy his evening snack.

I picked up a legal pad from the bedside table and wrote down everything I could think of that might have some bearing on Drew's death. The list was depressingly short. I had the name Austin-Kline Investments and a gut feeling they were involved, but no proof. I had a rumor that Harley Real Estate was laundering money for Austin-Kline, but no proof. And I had the phone call from I don't know who, the night Drew died. Nothing. Just unrelated tidbits and instinct. I knew that Drew hadn't killed himself and had not one shred of evidence to prove it. I needed to find a connection of some sort before Detective Stryker stopped playing around and hauled me downtown. As I stared at the list waiting for inspiration, the phone rang.

"Mr. Harley?"

My stomach clenched. A woman was trying hard to control the tremor in her voice. "Who is this?"

"C...Celia...Alley...from the hospital."

She took a shuddering breath before she spoke again. "Can you... you said if I ever needed... if..."

Recognition dawned; Celia was the nurse who had sewn up my bullet wounds.

"P...Please, can you help me?"

She was sobbing now and I could hardly understand her. I held the phone with my shoulder and started shrugging into my clothes.

"Celia, you gotta calm down. Has he hurt you again?"

"Oh, God."

I shoved my arms through the sleeves of a flannel shirt and winced as the bandage on my arm snagged on the fabric. "Relax, Celia. Calm down and tell me what's going on. Is he still there?"

I heard her take a couple of hiccupping breaths before she spoke. This time her voice was stronger, the tremble not as noticeable. "Quentin's gone. He probably won't be home for a couple of hours."

Quentin Alley. A picture of a mean-faced little jerk popped into my mind. He was a bully I'd once repo'd a brand new Ford pickup truck from. No surprise that he got his kicks smacking around on women. I snapped my holster in place behind my right hip and shrugged into my jacket. Celia was still sobbing quietly.

"Give me your address, hon."

She stuttered it out and I told her I'd be there in ten minutes. I found my keys and ran out to the truck. Brocs Harley, knight in shining armor.

When I parked in front of Celia's house, all the lights were on. She was huddled in the entry watching for me. I went up the steps two at a time. Celia's face was a mess, her nose looked broken. She had one arm cradled against her chest and she moved bent over, protecting her ribs.

I guided her into the living room and sat on the coffee table in front of her chair.

"Celia, I gotta get you to a hospital."

She nodded once, but wouldn't meet my eyes. I touched her knee. She jumped and grimaced with pain. I moved my hand away.

"Celia. Please look at me."

Her gaze slowly met mine.

"This is not your fault. You do not need to feel guilty about this. Do you understand me?"

She nodded and stared down at her lap.

"You've got to report this to the police."

She jerked her head up, eyes wide with fear, and pushed herself back into the chair.

"I...you don't understand. He'll kill me," she whispered.

"No he won't. That's why I'm here. Report this. Let me call a friend of mine who is a police officer."

"I don't know," she whispered.

"If you don't get out now, next time he might kill you. I'll help you Celia, but you're going to have to help yourself, too. Report this, file charges."

Tears leaked from her eyes, mixed with the blood from her nose and ran over her split and swollen lips. Finally she nodded.

"I won't let him hurt you again, Celia. I promise."

"Thank you."

I helped her into my truck and drove to Regional Medical Center. It was a longer drive, but Celia didn't need to deal with this in front of her coworkers. While the nurse got her settled, I called Wil Pinkerton, my buddy on the force. He wasn't on duty. I could have caught him at home, but I didn't want to get into the mess with Stryker so I talked to his partner, Greg Rawls, instead. As soon as I knew Rawls was on the way, I ducked around the curtain and sat by Celia's bed until the doctor arrived. Celia clung to my hand as silent tears ran down her face. I wanted to kill the son of a bitch who did this to her.

When the doctor finally got there, I motioned him outside. He was tall and clean cut, somewhere in his late fifties. I could tell from his clinical glance at Celia that he'd seen his share of the damage domestic violence could do.

"Doctor, this is a domestic. There's an officer on the way to take her statement. We need photographs, details on her present injuries and any old injuries or bruising that you notice. Can you do that?"

I think he assumed I was a cop. I didn't do anything to change his mind. He said he would help as long as the patient agreed. I thanked him and he followed me back into the exam room. While I spoke to Celia, he waited by the bed.

"Celia, this is Doctor." I paused and glanced at him.

"Stephenson," he said.

"This is Doctor Stephenson. He's going to get you patched up. Officer Rawls is on his way down to take your statement. Doctor Stephenson will treat your injuries, but he needs to take some photographs first. Is that okay?"

She looked from me to the doctor and whispered, "Okay." I squeezed her hand.

"I've gotta go, but I'll be by to see you in the morning. You're safe here, Celia."

She tried to smile. "Be careful, Quentin can be a mean sonovabitch," she whispered.

"So can I."

I left the hospital and drove back to Celia's. The lights were still on and there was no car in the drive. I parked around the corner and strolled through the shadowy streets. I went through the rooms righting tables and turning off lights. It was a small bungalow, two bedrooms, and looked like it was usually neat. The dishes were all done, no piles of laundry waited in the hall by the washer. The bed was made, but the contents from the top of the dresser had been knocked to the floor. I picked up the bottles and brushes and arranged them on the polished surface, shut off the overhead and sat down in the living room in the dark to wait for Quentin Alley.

I was sitting in what was probably his chair, legs stretched out on the coffee table, my gun loose on my lap when he stumbled in. He tripped on the rug in the entry, swore, and flipped on the light-switch in the foyer.

"Celia, where the hell are you?" he shouted. "Why the fuck'd you turn off all the lights?"

He turned from the hallway into the bedroom, snapped the switch and looked around.

"Where you hidin', bitch?"

He came into the living room, flipped on the overhead light, and stopped when he saw me.

"Who the fuck are you?"

"Are you Quentin Alley?"

"What's it to ya? Where the fuck is my wife?"

I stood from the chair and he took a step back. He didn't recognize me, but I knew him, and he hadn't changed a bit. He was well under six feet, and drunk. I had an unfair advantage even without the gun.

"I'm here with a warning, Alley. You lay a hand on your wife again, and I'll kill you."

I held my gun at my side next to my right leg. His glance shifted from my eyes to the gun.

"What's it to you whether or not I smack my 'ole lady, you ain't no cop?"

I took a step forward. He took one back and came up hard against the wall. I moved in close and jammed my gun into his groin. I had his attention now.

"Celia is a friend of mine. I don't intend to see her beaten again. If you lay a finger on her, I will kill you. Do you understand me?"

Quentin swallowed hard and tried one more time for bravado.

"She's my wife, you got no right to come in here and threaten me."

I eased away to get position and kneed him in the nuts. As he fell forward, I caught him with an uppercut. His head snapped against the wall and his eyes glazed as he slid to the floor. I knelt in front of him and waited until his eyes came into focus.

"Did I make myself clear, Alley?"

He had one hand holding his jewels and one holding his chin. I stayed at his level until he managed to answer.

"Clear," he choked out.

"Good, I don't want to have to come over here again."

I hoped I wouldn't have to. If Celia was smart, she'd find another place to stay and get a divorce from this loser, but abused spouses don't always do the smart thing. When I stalked out of Alley's house, he was still on the floor holding himself and trying not to puke. I hoped he'd still be there when the cops got to him.

I started the truck and drove back to the hospital. I could feel something warm on my arm and knew I'd pulled out at least one of my stitches. I'd felt it let go when I hit Alley. When I got to the hospital parking lot, I unbuttoned my shirt to check the damage. The bleeding had already stopped. Nothing to worry about.

I went in to check on Celia. The nurse in the ER said they had moved her to a room and she was sleeping. She had no internal injuries, and no, I couldn't go see her; come back tomorrow.

I thanked the nurse, pondered sneaking up to Celia's floor and decided against it. Now that the confrontation with Alley was over, my headache was back with a vengeance. I needed to get some rest. Tomorrow I had to decide what I was going to do about Austin-Kline.

Chapter 8

Baldwin was waiting for me when I got to the apartment. He twined himself between my legs and hopped onto the kitchen table when I sat down. My head ached, my arm throbbed and my knuckles were bruised and swollen from Alley's chin. I got up to make an icepack for my hand.

As bad as I felt, I wasn't tired. Too much adrenalin coursed through my system. I pondered making a drink. Decided it was too much trouble. When the ice started dripping through the dish towel, I tossed it into the sink and went to my bedroom. I shrugged off my clothes and washed the blood from my arm. After replacing the bandage, I settled against the pillows. The legal pad was still on my night table. I picked it up and read through my list hoping for enlightenment. The information there still didn't add up to anything.

Baldwin curled up beside me and started to purr. I tapped my pencil on the pad and tried to decide what to do next. I needed to find out if Harley Real Estate really was in bed with Austin-Kline. To do that, I needed to see Halston's financial records.

Harley Real Estate wasn't a publicly held company. Their financial records weren't public and I certainly didn't have access to them without Drew, unless I could convince their secretary, Melinda, to help. I got the impression from thing's Drew had said a few times that there wasn't a lot of love lost between Mel and Halston. If I could catch her away from the office, I bet she'd help. I grabbed the phone book and thumbed through until I found her number, but thought better of it before I dialed. A request like mine would take a while to explain. Better to do it face-to-face. I tossed the phone book back in the drawer and tried to figure out how to engineer a meeting with Mel without Halston finding out. I was almost asleep when the answer came to me. Back when I was working-out regularly, I used to run into her a lot at my gym. Maybe it was time for me to put in an appearance there and see if we could hook up. I flexed the muscles in my right arm. They still throbbed, but if I was careful, I might be able to manage a light workout without popping any more stitches. If I was lucky, Melinda would be there in the morning. I set my alarm and switched off the light. When I closed my eyes, I saw Celia Alley's poor battered face. Anger washed over me. I forced myself to relax. Baldwin moved to my pillow and his gentle purring finally put me to sleep.

■ ■ ■

Shouting brought me awake and made me cringe. I sat up in bed and stared through the darkness at Drew. He was huddled in the center of his blankets hugging his teddy bear and rocking back and forth. I motioned him over and he crawled in next to me. I wrapped the blanket around him and held him close. He cried, leaving wet blobs on the teddy bear's head. I pulled him closer and tried to calm him. The voices coming from down the hall grew louder, but the words were indistinct. Drew flinched as something crashed to the floor.

"Don't you threaten me!" Mom yelled.

A door slammed and footsteps came down the hallway.

"Marilee, get your ass in here. This isn't finished yet."

"Oh yes it is. It's been finished for a long time."

The sound of a slap came through our closed bedroom door. Drew flinched again and a small groan escaped from

*his lips. I stiffened and wished I could kill Halston for
hurting her.*

"It's okay, little bro," I whispered.

*Drew turned toward me and mashed his face into my
pajama top. I patted his back, whispered nonsense until he
relaxed into sleep, and tried not to listen to their shouting.*

*"You leave if you want to and take that bastard with
you, but Drew stays with me."*

*Instinctively I held Drew closer. He squirmed and I
loosened my grip. I knew Halston was talking about me.
Tomorrow I would ask Mom what a bastard was.*

. . .

The alarm jolted me out of the dream. The sheet was
wound around my legs and the pillow was crumpled in my
arms. I hit the snooze button and rolled onto my back.
The dream was still playing in my head. I knew it wasn't a
nightmare. It was a memory, one that I'd buried a long
time ago. I guess seeing Celia last night had brought it all
back.

I untangled myself from the bedclothes, shuffled into
my sweats, and headed out. I felt the twinge of the stitches
in my head, but no headache. Progress. Maybe tomorrow
I'd take them out. I crawled into the truck, stopped at the
grocery store for flowers, and drove to the hospital. Celia
was bruised and sore but a thousand times better today.
She smiled when I handed her the flowers and blushed
when I kissed her cheek.

"You look better today." I said.

"I look terrible," she said. Her fingers traced the
outline of the bruise around her eye. "They're going to let
me out of here this afternoon."

"Hey, that's great. You have someplace to stay?"

"I'm going to crash at my sister's for a while."

"Call me when you're settled in. And let me know if
Quentin comes around again."

"I don't think he'll come around. My sister, Julie, hates
him, always has."

"I hope he doesn't, Celia, but promise me you'll call if he does."

She stared at my flowers, still clasped in her lap.

"Celia, please."

She raised her head, her eyes shiny with unshed tears. "My life wasn't supposed to turn out like this."

I wrapped her in a hug. "Hey, forget what's happened in the past. This is your chance to start over and get it right."

She leaned away, smoothing the now crumpled bouquet, and sniffed. "I ruined your flowers."

Her voice trembled, but a tentative smile shone through her tears.

"I'll get you some more."

She sniffled as I kissed her on the forehead.

"Thank you, Brocs," she whispered.

I left the hospital and prepared for some self-induced torture. I'd gotten lazy about working out the last couple of months and, with or without stitches, this was going to hurt.

The only folks there when I arrived were professional gym rats—guys with trapezius muscles so enlarged they looked like they were carrying a butt roast on each shoulder. I chose a stationary bike and watched the news while I warmed up. When I'd worked up a good sweat and my lungs had started to burn, I crawled off the bike and started the real abuse. I took it easy on the upper body stuff, but felt the tug when I popped another stitch. The rate I was going, I'd have them all out in a couple of days.

I lifted my tee shirt sleeve and checked the damage. Everything was holding together so I stopped pushing my luck and finished up with legs and abs. Melinda came in while I was doing leg presses. Her hair was in a perky ponytail, but she wasn't wearing makeup or snazzy spandex, just gray sweats and an oversized tee shirt. She was still a knockout. Even the gym rats managed to take their eyes off their pecs long enough to admire her image in the mirror. I finished my reps and got on the exercise bike next to hers for a cool down.

"Hey, Mel."

"I'm still in shock about Drew. You doing okay?"

"Yeah, I'm alright."

"I just can't believe it. I feel so sorry for Lori."

"It's been rough for all of us."

I turned quickly away and wiped my face with my towel. Melinda stopped pedaling her bike and laid a hand on my arm.

"Brocs, I know this has to have been hard on you, what with the way things are between you and Halston. Let me know if you ever need a shoulder to cry on or someone to talk to. Lord knows I know what Halston can be like."

"I don't understand why you keep working for him, Mel."

She smiled. "Because working for your brother was a joy. I'm not sure how long I'll be able to stick it out now that he's gone."

She wiped her eyes and started pedaling again. "I meant it Brocs, if you need a friendly ear…"

"Thanks, Melinda. I really appreciate that. Maybe we could grab dinner sometime?"

I felt like an ass as soon as the words were out of my mouth, using her sympathy for an ulterior motive, but I was staring at twenty years to life. I squelched the feelings of guilt and gave her a lopsided grin.

"I'd like that."

When she smiled, the gloom around my heart eased just a little.

"How about tonight, around seven?" I said.

"That'd be fine."

"Can I pick you up?"

"Why don't I just meet you? Mondays can be a real bitch at the office and sometimes I get stuck late. Be nice to have an excuse to get away from Halston."

"I know that feeling. Where do you want to meet?"

"The Silverleaf Café okay with you?"

"Sounds great. I'll see you in the bar around seven."

I said goodbye and headed for the shower, grinning inside because my plan had worked and feeling like an asshole for trying the plan in the first place.

I arrived at the Silverleaf at a quarter till seven and perched on a barstool. The bartender, dressed in a tux with tails, poured my drink and set a bowl of mixed nuts out on the bar. No cheap-ass peanuts for this place. The

Silverleaf wasn't really my kind of hangout. I felt underdressed in slacks and sport coat. Sound was muffled by ankle-deep carpet and thick tapestry hangings on the walls. Candles flickered and gleamed on the silverware. The lighting was low and each table had an intimate feeling—it made me want to speak in whispers. I resisted the urge to pull at my necktie and turned to lean my elbows back on the bar to wait for Melinda.

When she came in, I almost didn't recognize her. She was wearing "a classic little black dress" and it looked like it was painted on. Long shapely legs started at about her neck and went on forever. I smiled in appreciation as she swayed toward me. Wives glared as their husbands turned sheepishly to their dinners. Melinda was going to be responsible for a boom in the flower business as those guys tried to make amends tomorrow.

She stepped in front of me and I kissed her cheek.

"You look terrific," I said.

"Thanks."

"Can I get you a drink?"

"I'll have white wine."

I ordered the wine and followed her through the dining room, enjoying the view. There is definitely something to be said for the little black dress.

We sat at a table overlooking the garden. Our waiter left menus and I tried to concentrate on what to order for dinner. Melinda chose Asian chicken salad; I opted for the prime rib. We talked about work, the weather and the chances for the SMS basketball team. I tried in vain to keep my eyes on her face while we chatted. My gaze drifted south and she caught me when I glanced up.

"I'm sorry, Melinda. That is one outstanding dress."

"I guess it's worth what I paid for it then."

"I don't know what you paid for it, but it was definitely a sound investment."

She laughed as the waiter brought our entrees. Conversation dwindled while we concentrated on the food. When the waiter picked up our plates and asked about dessert, we settled for coffee. I leaned forward, elbows on the table, and wondered how to get the conversation around to the subject of Drew. Melinda beat me to it.

"Brocs, do you really think Drew committed suicide?"

I glanced up at her in surprise.

"No, I don't."

"Are the police checking into it? Do they have any suspects?"

"Just one."

"Really, do you know who it is?"

"Me."

Her eyes widened in surprise. She stared down at the table and stirred her coffee for a long time before she looked up. I tensed as I waited for her reaction.

"That's ridiculous."

I blew out my breath in relief. "They don't seem to think so."

"What can you do?"

"Somehow, I've got to find out who really killed him."

"Is there anything I can do to help?"

"Actually, there is."

"Is that why you asked me out tonight?"

"Um...that's part of it."

"Well, what do you need?"

"Just like that? You're not mad?"

She cocked her head. "The night's not over yet."

"Yeah," I laughed. "Never underestimate the power of that little black dress, right?"

"Something like that."

She smiled and sipped her coffee. I tried to remember what it was I wanted her to help me with. I finally gathered my scattered wits. "I need to see the books for Harley Real Estate. The real ones, not the ones he's cooked up for the tax man."

"You think Halston had something to do with Drew's murder?"

"No, but I think maybe someone he's doing business with might have."

Melinda stared into her coffee cup like it held the answer to my question. I was almost ready to tell her to just forget it when she raised her head.

"I can probably get you copies of the accounting files I have. If Halston's gone tomorrow, I'll take a look on his computer and print his files as well."

"Are you sure about this? I don't want you to do anything if you think you might get caught, Melinda. I don't want anyone else to get hurt."

"I'll be careful. It might take me a couple of days though."

"That's fine."

She pushed away from the table and shot me a saucy look. "Good, glad that's settled. Now, I think you need to take me out dancing."

"You have anywhere special in mind?"

"Nope, I chose the restaurant, you pick."

"I know the perfect place."

I took her arm, tucked her into her car, and drove slowly through town so that she could follow me to my apartment. She got out and walked toward me looking up at my building.

"I don't think I've ever been dancing here before."

"It's great—good music, good whiskey, and the dance floor's never crowded."

She tucked her arm into mine. "Sounds perfect."

I unlocked the apartment and stood aside for Melinda. Baldwin blinked down at us from the top of the refrigerator. I toed off my boots and Melinda left her shoes next to mine. While I put the music on, she wandered around the apartment, finally stopping in front of a framed drawing hanging over the bookcase.

I stepped up behind her and slipped my arms around her waist. She leaned back against me and I could smell the flowery scent of her shampoo.

"Who's that?" she asked.

"My mom, I did that in high school from a portrait she had taken a few months before she died."

"It's amazing. Do you still draw?"

"Not really, no time."

She turned in my arms and we swayed to the music. When she raised her head from my shoulder, I kissed her. Shortly after that, we moved our dance from the living room to the bedroom. There I found out just what made that little black dress so spectacular.

Later, we lay against the pillows. Melinda ran her fingers lightly over the gauze and tape on my arm and I told her about my adventure on Lone Ridge. She lightly kissed the bandage, raised up to kiss my temple and asked if I was feeling any better.

"Hmm. Feeling pretty good right now."

"That's good. I wouldn't want you to pop a stitch or anything."

I leaned against the headboard and tried to look needy. "Well, maybe I'd better let you do the hard part this time."

She draped herself across my chest and pressed a kiss on my lips. "I was kind of counting on you for that part, cowboy."

I pulled her close, captured her lips with mine, and we didn't laugh anymore for a while. I slept without nightmares until Baldwin pounced on my pillow the next morning. I woke with a smile on my face, stretched and sat up. Baldwin batted a piece of paper around the bed. I took it away before it was riddled with tooth marks and spread it out to read:

Brocs, best dance hall in town. We'll have to try it again some time.

I grinned and tossed the note onto the quilt. Baldwin picked it up and continued filling it with holes. I checked the stitches in my head in the bathroom mirror and decided they had been there long enough. Baldwin joined me and sat on the counter watching closely, as I snipped them out and dropped them in the trash. I peeled the bandage away from my arm and checked the progress. Those stitches weren't quite ready to come out yet. I took a bath and covered them with a new bandage. The pounding pain of yesterday was gone and I'd have the rest of Celia's handiwork undone by the weekend. I patted Baldwin on the head and got dressed.

Chapter 9

I started out the door wearing a smile. It slipped a notch when I barreled into Detective Stryker at the foot of the stairs.

"Mr. Harley."

"Detective."

"I wonder if I might take a moment of your time."

"You already have."

He smirked. "How about another one, just for old time's sake?"

"I'm on my way out. If you can say your piece between here and my truck, go right ahead."

I marched toward the parking lot with Detective Stryker locked in step beside me.

"I wanted to ask you again," he said, "About the night Andrew died."

"I've told you everything I know."

"Did you have an argument with your brother that day?"

"No."

"What'd you fight about? Was it Lori?"

"I didn't have an argument with Drew."

"Maybe it was about the business. Was that it? He wanted out and you couldn't afford to stay in business by yourself."

I stopped next to my truck and turned to face the detective. "Stryker, you might find this difficult to believe, but I didn't have a fight with Drew the night he died. I'm not in love with his fiancée, and if he wanted out of the business all he had to do was say the word. I do manage to make a pretty good living all by myself."

"So, you killed him to get back at your father."

I unlocked the truck and jerked open the door. Stryker had to duck away to avoid losing his nose to the window frame. I ignored his grunt of protest and tossed the papers I was holding onto the seat. The paperclip popped loose and pinged off the dash, the papers fanned across the slippery vinyl. I hopped behind the wheel before Stryker could get a look at them and shoved the key into the ignition. Stryker was still talking. I glared him into silence, then I spoke. "Detective, I am not ignorant of the way the criminal justice system works. If you could pin the murder on me, I'd already be behind bars. Instead of harassing me, why don't you take whatever evidence you have that's kept me out of jail until now and use it to find my brother's killer."

I slammed the door of my truck, started the engine and backed out of my space. Detective Stryker jumped aside to avoid the front bumper and glared after me. I could feel his cold stare on the back of my neck as I drove. He wasn't following me, but it felt like it.

I was headed for the office, but before I got there, my cell phone chirped. It was Lori.

"Hey, hon. How ya doing?"

"Better. I was wondering if, uh...you could meet me at the apartment. I wanted to go through some of Drew's things, but I don't think I can do it alone."

On a scale of one to ten of things I wanted to do right now, this was probably a zero, but I couldn't say no to Lori.

"Yeah, I'll head that way right now."

"Thanks, Brocs."

I snapped my phone closed and drove down Allen street and turned into the cul-de-sac where Lori waited for me. Her hair was clipped into a barrette at the back of her neck, and she was dressed in a worn pair of jeans and a faded SMS sweatshirt. She looked like a college kid. I parked and gave her a hug. She shuddered, but her eyes were dry when she pulled away.

"Let's get this done," she said.

I followed her to the upstairs apartment. She slipped the key into the lock, but didn't turn it.

"I hate it here since Drew died," she said.

"We don't have to do this today, girl. Let's go in and if you just can't face it, we'll do it some other time."

She took a deep breath and unlocked the door. I followed her in, and waited as she paused in the foyer.

Silent tears ran down her cheeks as she walked around the room. I stayed near the door. She sniffed and wiped her eyes on the sleeve of her sweatshirt.

"You okay?" I asked.

She nodded and we walked down the hall to the bedroom. It only took a couple of hours, but it felt like days. I wondered if Halston had gone through this when mom died. I couldn't imagine him in tears as he packed away her personal items. Maybe I wasn't giving him a fair shake. He had to have loved her. Lori headed back to her dad's, and I continued my interrupted trip to the office. It wasn't even noon yet, and I was already drained.

I parked in a small lot near the corner of two red brick buildings just off the main drag downtown and scuffed across the broken asphalt to the rear entrance of the smaller of the two. A telemarketing firm used the offices on the ground floor. I could hear the murmur of voices and the clack of computer keys as I made my way upstairs. A sculptor had recently vacated the other room on my floor for a ground level space that required less lifting and now I had the whole level to myself. I slipped my key into the old-fashioned lock and pushed inside. I glanced around and shoved the heavy pebbled glass door closed. Dust motes danced in the sunlight, stirred by my entry. The room felt abandoned, even though it had been less than a week since I'd been there. It looked abandoned as well. Faded yellow paint covered the walls, some previous tenant's attempt to brighten things up. The couch sagged in the middle and dust coated the plastic leaves on the fichus tree in the corner. I'd taken over the office and the furnishings and had never gotten around to adding or changing anything. I tossed the papers I'd hidden from Stryker onto the desktop and sank into the chair behind my battle-scarred wooden desk. The light on my answering machine was blinking. That meant work.

I dug out a pen and punched a button on the machine to get my messages. Someone wanted to sell me aluminum siding. "No thanks." The Police Chief's Association wanted to sell tickets to their ball. "Nah." Rudy Macklin had a skip for me. That was a keeper. I wrote down the number and worked my way through the rest of the messages. I made callbacks to four car lots, got the information on their repos, and wrote it all down on my desk blotter. Macklin I saved for last. He only called me with the really good stuff.

"Rudy, Brocs Harley."

"Hey, heard you got shot out at Lone Ridge. Thought I was going to have to find a new man."

"Just a flesh wound. I'm still in business."

"Good, got a real sweet one for you."

He gave me the details. Rudy was trying to recover a brand new Lincoln. Unfortunately the owner, Lester Crawford, got wind of the repo and skipped. No phone, no forwarding address. My job was to track him down.

"Anything I need to know about this guy, Rudy?"

"Like what?"

"I don't know, he carry a gun, deal drugs, steal candy from little kids?"

Laughter came over the phone line. "Far as I know, none of the above."

"Right, Rudy. Fine upstanding citizen just decided to do a bunk with a forty thousand dollar car."

"What can I say, Harley. I don't do background checks on my customers. I just sell them cars."

"This is gonna cost you."

"I can afford to spend a bit to bring this one home."

"That's good. You're paying daily, plus expenses."

"Just find the car, Harley."

"I'll send you a contract."

I hung up the phone, made out contracts on the five new jobs, addressed them and set them on the desk to mail. Finished with the paperwork, I booted up my computer and did a quick search for Lester. I didn't find anything and wasn't in the mood to spend a couple of hours in front of the monitor. I logged off, propped my feet on the desk and tipped my chair into thinking position. Detective Stryker was beginning to piss me off. If he kept after me long enough, he'd find some reason to put me behind bars and I'd be in no position to help myself.

The web of cracks in the ceiling plaster didn't hold any answers so I sat forward and fanned the papers from Drew's office across the desktop. After an hour of slogging through them, I still couldn't find anything that set off any warning bells. They were a dead end until I had more information. I shoved them into a manila envelope, took them into the bathroom and locked them in the wall safe hidden behind the toilet tank.

My pager went off as I spun the lock on the safe. It was Drew's office. I went to the phone and dialed.

"Harley Real Estate."

"Melinda."

"Yes."

"Ready to go dancing again?"

"I'm sorry, sir, he's been out all morning."

"Ah, the old man showed up after you paged me?"

"He's here in the office now, sir. Sorry for any inconvenience."

"So, I need to use my intuitive powers to find out what you wanted?"

"That should be fine, sir."

"Okay. You've found something?"

"I'm sure we have something you would find interesting, sir."

"Good, you want to meet me somewhere."

"I think we could probably schedule you in."

I grinned. "How about eight o'clock at your place. I'll bring dinner. You provide dessert. Dancing shoes optional."

I could hear the laughter in her voice when she answered. "That should be fine, sir. I'll just wait to hear from you."

I smiled and hung up the phone. Thinking about Melinda and dinner got me out of the mood to work, so I left. I drove around for a while and finally stopped at a pull-off overlooking the river. The water level was starting to recede. Muddy grass and tree trunks poked through the chocolate brown water. I turned off the ignition, and opened the window. The sound of the river rushing in the background covered the highway noise and gave me solitude for my thoughts. I let them drift and tried to come up with a reason for Drew's murder.

I didn't have enough information. I didn't even know what direction to go next. I really needed to find out what the police had that was keeping me on the streets. I decided to call in a favor. I flipped open my cell phone and dialed the police department.

"Stantonville PD."

"This is Sherwin Williams. I need to speak to Officer Pinkerton."

"One moment please."

I listened to McGruff the Crime Dog tell me how to take a bite out of crime while I waited for Pinkerton. Wil Pinkerton roomed with Rayburn and me at the University. He was a sociology major, but he drifted into the criminal justice department and ended up with a double major. With a name like Pinkerton, a career in law enforcement was almost preordained. I hated to call him, but he was my best contact on the police force.

"Pinkerton here. How can I help you Mr. Williams?"

"It's Harley."

A long silence came over the phone before he spoke.

"Right. Rawls took care of Alley. He's in the county lockup. What did you do to that guy? He was almost happy to see us."

"I never met the guy."

"Right, Harley. That it, you just want to check up on your good deed?"

"I actually need a favor, am I persona non grata at the PD?"

"Oh, you bet. Stryker's got a real hard-on for you. What'd you do, make a pass at his daughter?"

"Give me a break, man. I didn't even know he had a daughter."

"I don't think he does."

"Would you get serious for a minute? I need your help. Can you meet me for lunch?"

The laughter was gone from his voice when he answered.

"Not officially, Stryker would have my ass."

I was testing Wil's loyalties. Putting him in between my mess and his job, but I didn't have anywhere else to turn.

"Harley, you there?"

"Yeah, sorry. How 'bout if I just happened to sit down next to you at Doc's about one-thirty."

There was a long pause before he answered. I was sure he was going to say no.

"I'll be there."

"Thanks, Wil," I said, but the phone had already gone dead.

I checked my watch and drove into town. It was already a quarter after. I stopped to fill up with gas, bought a pack of cigarettes, and drove into the parking lot of Doc's at one thirty-five. Wil was sitting at the counter, his blond hair gleaming in the sunlight from the windows. I sauntered through the door, acted surprised to see him, and perched on the next stool.

"Hey, Doc." I said. "Give me a cheeseburger and fries."

Doc set a Coke down on the counter in front of me and turned back to the grill.

I swiveled on my stool to face Wil. "Long time no see, man. How you been?"

"Good, Brocs."

"Keeping the streets crime free these days?"

"I'm doing my fair share. How 'bout you? I heard you got shot."

"Yeah, Julius Manchester took offense when I tried to repo his ride."

"One of these days one of those deadbeats is gonna put a slug in your head. Pretty lame reason to die, man."

"Wil, I didn't think you cared."

"I just don't want to deal with all the paperwork. Homicides generate a truck load of paper."

Doc set a plate down in front of Pinkerton.

"See you around, man." Wil said as he picked it up and headed for a booth in the rear. The women in Doc's turned to watch him amble across the room. I don't know if it was the blond hair or the tailored uniform, but he had an appreciative audience. If he was a motorcycle cop they'd probably swoon.

Doc's gray head was hunched over the grill working on my burger, his small frame almost hidden behind the counter. He was wearing chef's whites and he looked like a diminutive doctor huddled over a patient.

I fiddled with sugar packets and waited for him to finish my lunch. When it was ready he presented it to me with a flourish. Doc's talents were wasted in a Stantonville diner. I picked up my plate and scooted into the booth across from Pinkerton.

"What the hell," he said, as I sat down. "Can't a cop eat in peace?"

I ignored him and dug into my burger.

"What was with the Sherwin Williams bullshit?" he asked.

"I didn't think they would forward my call if I told them who it was. I didn't really want to talk to Stryker again. Saw him once today already."

"I think he's still mad 'cause you got out of that car theft thing."

"Cops don't hold grudges over car thieves. He's pissed about something else."

"What?"

"I have no fucking idea."

"It'll probably come to you."

"I need some info, Wil," I said around a mouthful of burger.

"Like why Stryker is so pissed at you?"

"No, more like what's Stryker got that's keeping him from locking me up and throwing away the key?"

"Thought you might be interested in that."

"A little. Can you help me?"

"Yeah."

Wil finished his burger, dropped a tip on the table, and stood up.

"I need to take a leak," he said. "Last stall," he whispered as he turned away.

I watched Wil head for the john and finished my burger. He gave a slight nod as he strolled out. I added my tip to the one on the table and headed for the toilet. Wedged behind the tank in the last stall was Stryker's murder book. I sucked in my breath. This was above and beyond the call of duty. The file was about an inch thick already. I took off my coat, tucked the file in the waistband of my jeans at the small of my back, and checked to make sure my jacket covered it, before I went out. I paid Doc and walked outside. Wil was already gone.

I slid behind the wheel and wondered how to get the file copied without getting arrested. The Quick Copy shop was out of the question. Old man Kramer would skulk at my elbow as I made the copies and call the police department before I was halfway through. I thought about going to the library but it would be faster to get it transcribed by monks than to use their ancient machine. As I pulled out of Doc's lot, I flipped open my phone and called Melinda.

"Harley Real Estate."

"Melinda, is Halston there?"

"No, he's gone for the day."

"Can you make some copies for me?"

"Sure, park in the alley. I'll meet you there."

"Thanks, Mel. Just take the copies and the original home with you. I'll get them tonight. Oh, by the way, look out the window, I'm here."

She waved and hung up the phone. I handed her the file when she came out, winked, and drove out of the lot.

I stopped at the grocery store on the way home. I needed to get food for Baldwin or he was going to stop leaving mice at the foot of my bed and start putting them on my pillow. After I stocked up on dry cat food and a few cans of something stinky that he really liked, I replenished my liquor supply and drove to the apartment. When I stepped inside, Baldwin made a lap around the apartment without ever touching the floor. He does that every time I bring home cat food.

I filled his dish, emptied and refilled his water, and set the bowl down next to him. Baldwin growled low in his throat when my hand brushed too close to the food dish.

"Relax, Baldwin. I'm not going to take your dinner."

He glared at me until I stepped away. The rumble continued until he was sure his dish was safe. I broke the seal on a fresh bottle of Maker's, and sampled it to make sure it was good. It was, so I topped off my glass, turned on the stereo, and sank into my recliner.

I jerked awake when Baldwin landed on my chest. It was dark in the apartment. I brushed the cat off my lap and stared at my watch, trying to focus. After seven thirty already.

"Shit!"

I took a quick shower and changed into clean clothes. Baldwin smirked from across the room as I stepped into my boots and ran out the door. The Dragon's Claw restaurant was on the way to Melinda's so I called and ordered dinner for two as I turned out of the drive. A quick stop at the liquor store around the corner for a bottle of wine and I was off again. It was already after eight. I was so in trouble. At the Dragon's Claw, I threw a twenty and five singles on the counter, snatched the sack out of the waiter's hands, and ran to the truck. I stopped in the lot outside Melinda's apartment at eight-thirty.

She opened the door before I could ring the bell wearing faded Levi's, a form fitting white scoop-neck sweater and a frown. She looked hot in more ways than one. I stepped inside, kissed her cheek and followed her into the kitchen. It was bright, clean and unused-looking. I don't think Melinda cooks much more than I do. She put the food out on plates while I opened the wine.

"You're late," she said.

"Sorry, I fell asleep. Thank Baldwin for waking me up. If it wasn't for him, I'd still be out."

"Remind me to bring him a treat next time I'm over."

"He likes shrimp."

"I'll try and remember that," she said, as she took the wine glass from my hand and sat down. I sat across from her and took a bite of sesame chicken.

"Mel, can I use your phone?"

"Sure, I guess."

I dialed Wil Pinkerton's home number. He picked up on the first ring.

"Wil, I got something that belongs to you. What do you want me to do with it?"

"It's not at your place is it?" he asked.

"Huh, uh."

"Is it somewhere you can leave it?"

"Yeah."

"Give me the address and I'll pick it up on the way in to work in the morning."

"Let me make sure that's okay."

I asked Melinda if it was alright for Pinkerton to stop by for the files around seven. She agreed and I gave him directions. I hung up the phone and sat down at the table.

"Did you remember dessert?" I asked.

"Hmm, you were late. I'm not sure you deserve it."

"Maybe I can do something to make it up to you."

"I don't know, gonna be pretty tough to make up for being half an hour late."

"I think I might be...up to the task."

She smiled and took a bite of fried rice. "We'll see."

We finished dinner, emptied the bottle of wine and retired to the bedroom. Like the rest of the apartment, her room was full of deep rich colors and light wood furniture, a perfect compliment to Melinda's personality. The room faded into the background when she stood undressed before me. My clothes quickly joined hers on the floor.

Later, relaxed against the pillows and with Melinda tucked in beside me, I opened the real estate file and flipped through the paperwork. The murder book I left for later when I was alone. I had copies from both sets of accounting files so I could compare them. The numbers were substantially different.

"Halston has a pretty neat deal of some sort going, Mel. Have any idea what it is?"

"No, I was surprised at the difference."

"Do you think Drew knew?"

"I don't know, Brocs. He was pretty distracted before I left on vacation. I asked him if everything was all right. He said it was, so I just assumed he and Lori weren't getting along. I wish I'd followed up. He might still be alive."

Melinda's eyes filled. I took her in my arms.

"Don't cry, babe. Even if you knew what was going on, there's no saying you could have stopped what happened."

"I guess you're right."

Her head was tucked under my chin. She shifted and put her head on my shoulder.

"Has Detective Stryker been to see you?" I asked.

"No."

"If he sees us together he will."

"Why?"

"He still thinks I murdered my brother."

"Brocs, that's ridiculous!"

"That's why I need to find out what really happened."

"Let me know if I can help."

"You already have."

She tipped her head away. I brushed the tears off her cheeks and kissed her. A soft friendly kiss that deepened and led to other things. It was after two before I got home.

I took a quick look around the parking lot, trying to spot my watchdog. He was sitting in an unmarked Crown Vic parked under a streetlight. I entered the front door of my building making sure he had a good view, then scuttled through the hallway to the service entrance and stepped out into the alley. Stryker was still parked under the light and now I was behind him. I snuck up to his car, edged next to the driver's side and tapped on the window. Stryker jumped in surprise and glared as he rolled down his window.

"I'm in for the night, Stryker. You can go home now."

"Don't underestimate me, Harley."

"Oh, I don't, but I think you might be underestimating me. I'm not seventeen anymore."

Before he could say anything else I strode across the parking lot, into my building and up the stairs to my apartment.

Chapter 10

Because I was half expecting my early morning visitors, it wasn't a shock when I heard the pounding on my door, but I still wasn't at my best after less than four hours sleep. I dragged on my sweats, slipped the safety chain off, and swung open the door. Detective Stryker handed me a folded paper. I stepped out of the entry to let him by, and unfolded the warrant. Three uniforms followed him in. I ignored them all and went into the kitchen. I tossed the warrant in the direction of the table, and reached into the cabinet for coffee. Stryker came in behind me, scooped the warrant from the floor and placed it carefully in the center of my kitchen table.

"What are you doing?" Stryker asked.

I turned to glare at him, but it was a wasted effort, he was impervious to my annoyance. "I was planning to make coffee."

"Go ahead."

"Why thank you."

He missed the sarcasm, or ignored it. He stood watch while I filled the coffee pot and turned it on. Baldwin glared from the top of the fridge and hissed as Stryker moved past. I didn't even try to stifle a snort of laughter.

"I'm not sure you understand the gravity of this situation, Mr. Harley."

"Tell me what you're trying to find, and maybe I can tell you where it is."

Stryker ignored me, snapped on latex gloves and started going through my kitchen drawers. I lounged against the counter to wait for Mr. Coffee to finish dribbling into the pot.

"Get the cat off the fridge," Stryker said.

I shooed Baldwin away. He shot me an injured look as he slunk out of the room. Stryker opened the freezer and removed everything. He even opened the paper wrapped packages of meat and checked the contents. Satisfied I hadn't hidden any evidence in the pork steak, he moved to the refrigerator. He again removed everything, opened containers, peeled the paper from the butter sticks and dumped lettuce from the bowl into the sink. I stayed propped against the kitchen counter watching him work. He was very thorough. If I'd hidden anything in the apartment, I had no doubt he would have found it. When everything from the refrigerator and freezer was out on the counter, he moved to the cabinets and continued the search.

The pot finished gurgling and I poured a cup of coffee. I could hear the other officers going through the house, opening cabinets and drawers, digging through my life. I heard them remove the panel from the rear of my closet. I stayed relaxed, lids lowered, coffee cup in hand, watching as the detective took my kitchen apart.

"You're very calm about this." he said, glancing up.

"I don't have anything to hide."

"Or you just think it's hidden well enough we won't find it."

"I don't know what you're searching for, Detective, but I haven't broken any laws since the last time you busted me."

"I find that hard to believe."

"I don't really care."

He closed the pantry and stared at me. "You have a real attitude problem, Harley."

"You need to quit rousting me and start looking for the killer. If I remember right, most murders that aren't solved within the first forty-eight hours don't get solved."

"Sounds like you paid attention in class at least one day."

"Nah, heard it on TV."

He smiled in spite of himself. I poured another cup of coffee.

"Okay if I go sit in the living room?"

"Sit anywhere you like, just don't leave the premises."

I took my coffee cup and stretched out on the couch. Immediately my lids grew heavy. I definitely could have used another couple hour's sleep. I parked my half-full cup on the coffee table before I dropped off and dumped it on my chest, and let Morpheus take over. Detective Stryker's voice brought me awake.

"Mr. Harley."

I opened my eyes.

"We've found a couple of things we'd like to take with us. I need you to verify what we've gathered and sign a receipt."

Curious about what they had found, I got up and let him lead me into the kitchen. Drew's briefcase sat open on the table. His keys, minus the one to the office, were on the table next to it. The office key was now on my ring. My toothbrush rounded out their finds.

"Is that your brother's briefcase?" Stryker asked.

"Yes."

"Are those your brother's keys?"

"Yes."

"Why do you have them?"

"I picked them up from his office after the funeral."

"Why?"

"I wanted to find out what he was working on before he died."

"Why?"

"Just curious. Why are you taking my toothbrush?"

"Oh come now, Mr. Harley. Surely you didn't sleep through your forensics class." He tossed the plastic evidence bags holding the keys and toothbrush into the briefcase and snapped it shut.

"DNA?" I asked.

"Very good."

"Help yourself. Where do I sign?"

Stryker handed me a receipt. I signed and pushed it across the table to him. I could tell he was disappointed in what they'd found.

I motioned around the kitchen. "You gonna put all this stuff away?" Yeah, right.

"We'll leave that to you."

"Thanks, Stryker. Cops like you make innocent citizens think about committing crimes."

"Good thing you're not an innocent citizen then, isn't it?"

With that parting remark, he motioned his merry band of home wreckers out. I stared at my ransacked apartment. It was going to take the rest of the day to put it together again. I went to the kitchen, stuffed the food into the fridge and the freezer, and decided the rest could wait until I caught up on my sleep. After my nap, the mess hadn't improved any, so I decided to let it wait until I got home from the gym. To put it off a little longer I went to the office after my workout. My files should be safe here for the time being, Drew was the owner listed on the building and the office space I occupied wasn't in my name. Stryker wouldn't have any reason to search here. I removed the files from behind the toilet and sat down at my desk.

I tossed the murder file onto the desk, lined it up even with the blotter, brushed some imaginary specs of dust off the surface and waited for the courage to open it. When I started to feel silly staring at the blank manila surface, I opened it and sucked in my breath. A crime scene photo was on top. I turned away from the picture and stared unseeing out the window. It took an act of will to turn back to my desk.

The photo was still there, still horrible, but at least not a surprise this time. I flipped through the other photos from the crime scene, passed up the autopsy pics and started reading the coroner's report. Nothing new there. Death was caused by a single gunshot to the head, small caliber bullet, probably a .22. I noticed it didn't read self inflicted in the report. Stryker probably knew Drew was murdered the morning I went down to ID the body. Bastard.

I slowly deciphered the scrawled handwriting as I made my way through the ream of papers. Finally, at the bottom of the stack, I found out why I was still among the free—there were smudges on the gun on top of my prints.

Unfortunately for me, no other prints were found. Forensics thought the smudges were made by someone wearing latex gloves. I rolled my eyes. Apparently Stryker thought I was smart enough to wear gloves to commit the murder, but too stupid to wipe my prints off the gun first. Maybe I was giving him too much credit. I felt a little better about my chances as a free man.

I stacked the papers into a neat pile, locked them up, and decided to try and find a few cars. I drove downtown and parked outside my first target's house. She was sitting in her driveway in the car. I smiled—this was perfect. Before she backed all the way out of the drive, she paused, reversed direction and jerked to a stop. She popped out of the car and ran into the house. I ducked down in my seat and pondered doing the snatch right there, but before I could move she came out carrying a piece of paper. Guess she forgot her grocery list. She backed out again. I tailed her across town and smiled when she pulled into Tony's Market. I parked two rows over and waited until she went inside. As soon as she disappeared, I ducked between the rows to her car, jimmied the lock and drove out of the lot. A gurgle came from the rear of the car as I turned onto the street. I glanced in the rearview mirror. A baby smiled from a car seat and waved a stuffed dog at me.

"Shit!"

I slammed on the brakes, pulled a U turn and squealed back into the parking lot. The woman was standing in the empty parking space holding a box of tampons and screaming into a cell phone.

Jesus Christ. Not just a panicked mother, I had to try and repo a car from a panicked mother with PMS. I hoped she didn't have a gun.

I stopped the car outside the parking space, got out and stepped away. The woman ran toward me still yelling into her phone. I glanced around and took another step back. I could hear sirens coming closer and a few seconds later two police cars whipped into the parking lot. Not a minute too soon as far as I was concerned. This woman was scary. They braked to a stop and the first officer jumped out with his gun drawn. I raised my hands and took another step back. At the rate I was moving, I'd be home soon. As the officer approached, the panicked woman leaned into the car to check on the baby.

The cop jerked his gun in my direction. "Don't move, slimebag."

I looked over his shoulder as the officer climbed out from behind the wheel of the second car. It was Wil Pinkerton.

"Uh, Wil. You mind calling off the dogs here," I said.

He grinned and started to speak.

The officer holding the gun on me yelled, "Shut up, asshole."

Pinkerton snickered. The crazy woman backed out of the car and turned on him. "There's nothing funny about this. I want this man arrested. He kidnapped my baby."

Wil swallowed a smile, told one of the officers to take her aside and made his way over to me. "Put your gun away, Mike," he said as he passed the first officer.

"But."

"Put it away. You got paperwork on this ride, Harley?"

"Yeah."

I reached into my inside pocket for the papers and Officer Gung Ho whipped his gun back out of the holster. I hit the deck. Wil turned around, peeled the gun out of his hand and told him to check on the baby. I got up from the ground, brushed myself off and handed Wil the paperwork.

"Just stay here a minute," he said. "I'll talk to her."

He showed the recovery paperwork to the PMS queen.

"This is bullshit and you know it!" She shouted, slapping the papers out of Wil's hands.

He spoke softly to her. She flounced away a couple of steps and gave him a stop sign motion with her hand. "Oh, I get it. He's a man so you take his side. I want your badge number."

She had wandered out of the parking space and into the traffic lane. Wil took her arm and tired to guide her out of harms way.

"Let go of me," she screamed. "That's harassment. I'm calling the newspaper."

This time, when Wil spoke, his voice was loud enough that the whole parking lot could hear.

"Ma'am, you need to settle down."

"I'm not going to settle down. That man stole my car and kidnapped my baby, and you're going to let him get away with it."

"He's a recovery agent. He repossesses cars. You're behind on your payments. You're going to have to let him take the car."

With no warning, she swung her purse by the shoulder strap and round-housed Wil on the side of the head. He spun, grabbed her arm, jerked it behind her back and snapped on the cuffs. She tried to head butt him, but he ducked out of the way. The whole maneuver was so smoothly done, it looked choreographed. He led her, still screaming, to the police car, shoved her in the rear seat and told one of the officers to put the baby in the other car.

"What you going to charge her with?" I asked as he walked over.

"Child endangerment, resisting arrest, creating a disturbance. I'll think of something."

"Think it'll do any good?"

"I doubt it."

"Thanks, man. I thought she was going to kill me."

"Yeah, do me a favor. Check the back seat for kids from now on."

I told him I would, got in her car and drove it to the lot. One of the squad cars trailed me. My guess was Officer Gung Ho, making sure I didn't decide to drive off into the sunset with the crazy woman's Subaru. I collected my fee, bummed a ride to my truck, and decided I'd rather clean house than deal with a woman with PMS. Maybe I did need to get into another line of work.

My cell phone chirped as I drove into my lot. It was Celia.

"Celia, how ya doing?"

"I'm a lot better. Still pretty sore, but it's going away a little every day."

"That's good. So how are you really?"

"I'm Fine."

I stayed silent. After a minute she continued.

"I hired a lawyer. He filed a restraining order and he's working on the divorce papers."

"How do you feel about that?"

"I...I don't know," she said, her voice sinking to a whisper. "I'm seeing a therapist."

"Celia, remember you're not the one in the wrong here. You don't need to feel guilty because you want to get out of a bad situation."

"That's what my sister and my therapist keep telling me."

"They're right, give yourself a break."

"I'm trying."

"Do you need anything? Do you have a place to stay?"

"I'm staying at my sister's. That's where I'm calling from. I don't need anything right now. I just...I just wanted to thank you, Brocs."

"I'm glad I could help. Take care of yourself and call me if you need anything."

"I'm fine now, but thanks."

She wasn't fine yet, but she was at least heading in the right direction. I grinned as I saved her number in my phone and tucked it in my pocket. Every once in a while the guys in the white hats win one.

Chapter 11

At my office the next morning, I fired up the computer and started digging for something on Lester Crawford, Rudy's skip. Two hours later I had his last known address and addresses for all his relatives. I also had his driver's license number, social security number and his most recent employer. Not bad for a couple hours work. Now for a little sweet-talk. I dialed the Stantonville PD number and waited through eight rings. Busy day at the cop shop, I guess.

"Police Department," a frazzled voice answered.

"Officer Pinkerton, please."

The phone clicked, McGruff came on, then Pinkerton answered.

"Pinkerton."

"Safe to talk?"

"You already owe me, Harley."

"This is about something else."

A sigh came across the wire. "What do you need?"

"I'm tracking a skip."

"And?"

"I need you to run a DL, and social for me, see what comes back."

"Okay, but this is it."

"Sure, I know."

The phone went quiet. I could hear computer keys clacking in the background and breathing over the phone, so I was pretty sure Wil was still there.

"Wil?"

"Yeah."

"How come you're still in uniform?"

"What?"

"Why haven't you made detective?"

"Sometime when you've got a lot of liquor, a lot of time, and aren't wanted for murder I'll tell you about it."

"That bad, huh?"

"You don't know the half of it."

I spun my chair around and stared out the office window while the computer keys continued to clack across the phone lines. "You could always quit and come to work for me," I said.

"That's assuming Stryker doesn't put you away for the next twenty years."

"Well, yeah."

"Hang on," he said.

The phone clunked on the desktop. I cocked my chair and propped my feet on an open drawer while I listened to bits and pieces of conversation. A loud burst of laughter, then Wil's voice came back on the line.

"I got something on your skip, he's a frequent flyer with us. Lester's been a bad boy for a very long time."

"Let me have it."

"I don't have that much time. How 'bout I print it out. Your boy Lester is quite familiar with the judicial system."

"So, how we going to do this? In the old days I'd just meet you for lunch somewhere."

"That's what we're going to do. I'm over on hours this week and we're double-covered today. Besides, I've had the brass on my six all day."

"Ooh, I love it when you throw out all the military jargon."

"Stuff it, Harley. I'm taking the rest of the day off. I've reached my limit on ass chewing. They don't like it, I'll turn in my piece."

"Meet me at Doc's in an hour. Wait for me if I'm late, I've got an errand to run on the way.

"Will do."

I hung up and felt the stitches pull in my arm. Time to undo the rest of Celia's handiwork. I snipped out the stitches, flexed my arm, and ran my fingers over the new scar, still tender but not bad. I grabbed my jacket from the back of the chair and fired up the truck. I stopped by Harley Real Estate first, but Mel said Halston was at home, so I pointed the truck toward "Halston Manor." I almost turned around, but I'd promised Lori I'd get her picture from Drew's office, so I kept going. I knocked on the door, but there was no answer, so I rang the bell. Footsteps sounded in the hallway and the door banged open.

"What the hell do you want?" Halston asked.

I had wanted to ask him about mom—about what he went through after she died. Helping Lori with Drew's things must have unhinged me if I thought he'd talk to me about anything.

"There is a photograph on Drew's desk. It belongs to Lori and she'd like to have it back. I told her I'd stop by and get it."

"You can tell that bitch to kiss my ass."

I slapped the doorframe next to Halston's head. He jumped away.

"Halston, quit being a dick and go get the fucking picture. It's not going to kill you to do something nice for someone else."

"She wants that picture, she can come get it herself. I ain't giving you shit."

I fought the urge to draw my gun and shoot the smug look off his face.

"You're really something special, Halston—a real tribute to mankind."

He didn't answer, just slammed the door in my face, and slid the bolt home.

I jumped into my truck and spun out of the driveway. I know better than to set myself up for failure where Halston was concerned. It was a mistake I wasn't ever going to make again.

I pointed the truck back toward town, thinking vile thoughts about Halston Harley. If Stryker could read my mind right now, I would never convince him I hadn't committed murder. The wind gusted and the truck skittered toward the shoulder. I glanced at the sky toward the west where clouds were starting to build. We might be in for a storm, but right now, it was warmer than it had been in a couple of weeks. I parked at Docs and walked inside. Wil wasn't there yet, so I snagged a stool at the counter.

"Whaddya drinkin?" Doc asked.

"Just water."

Doc thunked the water glass on the counter. He wasn't his normal sunny self, must have had the health department in today. I ordered two burgers with the works and moved to a booth to stay out of the line of fire. Wil strolled in out of uniform a few minutes later. He eased into the seat across from me just as Doc sat down the burgers. Wil ordered a Coke and Doc headed back to the grill.

"God, I need a drink," Wil said.

"Bad day, huh?"

"You could say that."

"What's up?"

"Stryker just discovered we were roommates in college."

"Oh."

"Yeah."

We ate our burgers and crunched our fries without talking.

"Got any plans for your afternoon off?" I asked.

"Not yet."

"I could use your help."

"I gotta run to the bank. I'll meet you at your office."

I dropped a five on the table, picked up my jacket and left.

I was sitting, feet propped up on the desk when Wil came in. He handed me a file. I shoved Drew's papers and the office accounts across the desk. Wil picked them up and flipped through the pages.

"What am I trying to find?" he asked.

"Good question."

I opened the bottom drawer of my desk, retrieved a half-full bottle of Maker's Mark and two glasses. Wil's face lit up as I splashed some in the glasses. He picked one up and headed for the couch. While he ran through Drew's papers, I checked out Lester. I started through the printout with a grin that slowly disappeared. The guy was forty-two years old and had a rap sheet as long as my arm. He'd been busted for everything from jaywalking to murder and had spent exactly six months behind bars.

"This guy got some powerful friends, Wil?"

"Either that or he was born under a lucky star."

"Any way to find out who posted his bond last time?"

"Hmm. Maybe. Might be worth checking out."

I continued through the sheet, but it was just more of the same. Busted, out on bail, charges either dropped or case dismissed for one reason or the other.

"I'd really like to find this asshole."

"Better watch out, Harley. You're starting to sound like a cop."

I ignored his comment.

"You come up with anything?" I asked.

"Halston's up to his neck in something."

"I got that, anything else."

"Not really. You know who he's in bed with?"

"Yeah."

Wil dropped the file on the seat next to him and stared at me from across the room. I sipped my bourbon and tried to ignore him.

"You mind sharing?" he asked.

"Are you asking as a cop or a friend?"

"I'm always a cop, Brocs. I can't turn it on and off."

I sighed. "I know."

"Well?"

I put my glass on the blotter and watched the moisture soak a ring into the paper before I answered. "Rumor has it he does a little business with Austin-Kline Investments."

"They're pretty heavy hitters."

"That's what I hear. Why do you know that?"

He didn't answer my question, just asked one of his own. "Who told you Halston was fronting for Austin-Kline?"

I raised my eyebrows and grinned.

"Rayburn," he said. "I might have known."

"Would it make you feel any better if I said Billy's not involved with them?"

Wil shook his head. "Just marginally."

I refilled my glass. Wil held up his empty so I dragged myself out of the chair and filled his too. The sky had darkened and the wind whipped dust and gravel against the office window. I stared out over the parking lot as the trees snapped back and forth. We were in for a gully washer.

"How long are you off work?" I asked.

"Three days, then I go on nights for a month."

Wil glanced out the window.

"I could do with a few days at the lake."

"Yeah, this is great weather for the lake."

"That's what I was thinking."

Wil picked up the phone. "Let me call in and tell 'em to put me on pager."

He stood with the phone to his ear waiting for an answer. "I need to go out and see Anne before we take off. How bout I leave my truck there and you pick me up."

"How's Annie doing?"

"Same as always, still in love with you."

"No she's not, she's in love with who she thinks I am."

"Whatever. She'd love to see you."

"Man, I don't mess with married women."

"Dammit!"

I looked at Wil in surprise. He hung up the phone and redialed.

"We got a new phone system. Half the time instead of forwarding the call, it hangs up."

He waited through the greeting, pressed a number and waited for the call to transfer.

"So what's up with Anne. Why the check-up visit?"

"I just like to keep tabs. I don't trust that dickhead she married. I'd like to kick his ass."

Visions of Celia danced through my mind. At the thought of Annie in that position, my heart clenched. I would be guilty of murder if anything like that happened to her. That is if I beat Wil to the punch.

"He's not hitting her or anything, is he?"

Wil spoke into the phone and then dropped it on the desk. "All set. No, he's not beating her up, at least I haven't seen any signs of it. He's just a worthless piece of white trash. Annie deserves better."

I handed the file on Lester to Wil. He shuffled it in with the others and shrugged into his jacket.

"I'll pick you up in an hour or so," I said.

He waved and I listened to his footsteps clump down the hall. I shut down the computer, turned on the answering machine, and closed and locked up the office. Thunder rumbled as I crunched across the lot and eased into my truck. I drove to my apartment and grabbed clothes for a couple of days. I called my next-door neighbor, Mrs. Chancellor, and asked her to keep an eye on Baldwin while I was gone, and headed out. Baldwin glared at my back as I left. I think he knew I wasn't going to be home for a while.

Hopefully, Stryker and his watchdog were harassing someone else right now and they wouldn't see me leave. I drove out of my parking lot and wandered through town for a while, giving Wil a chance to catch up with Anne. I also wanted to make sure I wasn't being followed. I didn't spot a tail so I turned around and drove to Anne's house. Rain was starting to fall in big fat drops when I parked in front of the split foyer. Wil ran down the front steps and crawled in the passenger side. Anne waved from the doorway as a little carbon-copy peeked around her leg. My gaze lingered for a minute, taking in her still slim figure and short blonde hair. I shook my head, waved and backed out of the drive hoping Wil hadn't notice my hesitation. I'd doomed any chance Annie and I ever had back in college. I hoped Wil was joking earlier, I'd treated her like dirt back then. She deserved better.

We wallowed along in the late afternoon traffic on Route 18 and stopped at a liquor store outside of Riker. Wil filled the cooler with ice and beer while I tucked the whiskey behind the seat. Then we loaded up and made our way to the cabin at Langdon Reservoir. The fat raindrops were falling faster. The road was greasy and I drove with care as the light faded from the sky. As we stopped outside the cabin, the heavens opened. We wrestled the cooler out of the truck and onto the porch and got thoroughly soaked as I fiddled with the temperamental lock. As soon as we were in, Wil hurled himself back out into the storm to get the rest of our stuff. I turned on lights, lowered the windows from the top to get rid of the musty smell and started laying a fire in the big stone fireplace.

The cabin at Langdon belonged to Billy Rayburn. The reservoir was small and not very popular because it was a joyous pain in the ass to get to, so it hadn't ever built up like Cedar Lake. There were only ten or twelve cabins around the whole thing, and you seldom ran into anyone on the water, especially during the week. It was an excellent place to go if you were looking for peace and quiet. Billy bought his cabin four or five years ago and gave us each a key. We'd get together up here two or three times a year to fish, hunt, or drink. Drew and I came up last summer for a few days. I quickly brushed that memory away.

There was an old leather couch and a beat up coffee table in front of the fireplace. Braided rugs were scattered across most of the main room and big floor pillows were piled up in the corners. Have to check them out. They didn't get put away last time they were used, and were probably full of mouse nests now. The beds in the downstairs bedrooms were made up. I turned on the tap in the kitchen. It sputtered a little, then came on, I left it to run and did the same in the tiny bathroom. The fridge was cold and there was ice in the freezer. I dug the coffee pot out of the cabinet for in the morning.

I turned from the kitchen sink as Wil dropped our bags and paused to drip onto the mat. I snagged a towel from the bathroom and tossed it to him. The temperature had dropped and the cabin was cold. I lit the fireplace and sank into the broken-down easy chair in front of it to warm up. Wil shivered as he hustled through the cabin with our bags. He clomped into the living room a few minutes later, still toweling off his hair.

"So, now that we've made our escape, mind telling me why we're here?"

"Just needed to get away for a couple of days."

"Right."

Wil cracked open a beer and took a long pull. "It won't take Stryker long to find you up here."

"I'm not hiding from Stryker, just changing my base of operations for a while. Did you bring the files?"

"Yeah, they're in my bag."

"Let's have another look."

Wil brought out the paperwork and I spread it across the coffee table. The rain pounded on the tin roof and ran down the windows as Wil and I went through them all again.

"You know the definition of insanity," Wil asked.

I laughed. "Doing the same thing over and over again —"

"And expecting a different result." Wil finished.

"It's not that bad."

A twelve pack later, I wasn't so sure. We still couldn't find anything to sink our teeth into. I stifled a yawn and poked Wil awake.

"Let's call it a night and start over in the morning."

He stood, stretched, tossed his empty into the trash, and said good night. I stared into the flames, lost in thought.

"I need your help, Drew," I whispered. "I'm missing something."

The fire died down to embers and I shivered in the chill. Drew was with me, but he wasn't talking. Time for bed, I was too tired to think anymore.

Chapter 12

I slid between the icy sheets, huddled beneath the old quilt and waited for warmth to seep in. The moon shone through a break in the clouds and painted a shaft of light across the floor. Then I slept.

The chirp of my cell phone jerked me from a dream I couldn't remember. I fumbled it open and the voice on the other end sent my heart racing.

"Brocs," she whispered. "He's on his way here."

"Celia?"

"They let him out of jail and now he's coming here. He said he was going to kill me. Brocs, help me."

I was already up and stumbling in the dark to find my clothes.

"Where's your sister, Celia?"

"She went out. I don't have the car..."

"Go to a neighbor's house right now, I'm on my way."

I yelled down the hall to Pinkerton. He staggered into my room rubbing sleep from his eyes, caught the urgency in my movements and spun away without a word. He strode into the kitchen fully dressed, two steps behind me. I scooped my gun from the counter and he followed me to the truck. I filled Wil in on what was happening as we flew down the winding lake road. The truck slithered on the curves. I kept the throttle mashed.

Wil used my phone to call the police. Then he made another call to find out how Quentin Alley got out of jail. He slammed the phone onto the seat.

"The fucking judge let him post bail. Christ the system sucks sometimes, Brocs."

I squealed onto Route 18 and floored it. We were running almost ninety when we hit the outskirts of Wardsville. I slowed to make the turnoff, and wound through the unfamiliar streets, looking for the address. Less than thirty minutes after Celia's frantic phone call, we stopped outside the small brick ranch house where she was staying.

The house was dark. I hoped that was a good sign, that she had gotten out. Wil flipped open his badge, unholstered his gun, and pushed me behind him. He moved quickly toward the front entrance. I ducked away from him and headed for the rear. Wil swore under his breath as I edged away, but he didn't try to stop me. In the distance, I could hear the wail of sirens. I hoped they were coming here and I hoped we weren't too late.

I eased around the corner of the house, my hand dragging over the rough brick as I felt my way through the shadows. Light from the streetlamps barely filtered into the backyard. There wasn't any movement on this side of the house, and the only noise, my heart hammering in my ears. I started up the back stairs, stumbled over a flowerpot and cringed as it crashed onto the sidewalk below. I paused, but still there was no sound, no movement. I tried the knob. It turned easily in my hand. I pushed it open and tried to see into the black hole that led to the kitchen. The house felt empty. I prayed Celia had gotten away.

"Celia," I called.

There was a rustle from the front of the house. I flattened against the wall and swung my gun toward the noise.

"Hey, brother. Don't shoot, it's me."

My breath escaped in a whoosh, and I dropped the gun to my side. Wil flipped on the light, and I blinked in the sudden glare.

"Front's clear," he said.

"Check downstairs, I'll go up."

He nodded and opened the basement door. He paused to listen before stepping down into the cellar. I ducked out of the kitchen and took the stairs two at a time. I wasn't even trying to be quiet anymore. There wasn't anyone in the house, at least no one alive.

I flipped on the hall light, and stuck my head into the first bedroom I came to. It was clean and neat. Celia's room I'd bet. I went in, checked under the bed and in the closet. "Celia," I called. No answer. I eased out of that room and moved to the next. It was messy in a comfortable lived in way. Books on the nightstand, bedspread just a little off. No one under the bed or in the closet there either. I stepped out and moved across the hall to the bathroom. I flipped on the light and there was Celia. Blood, still warm and liquid, soaked her clothes and ran from the corner of her mouth. A bloody knife lay on the floor next to her foot. She was huddled against the tub, eyes staring at nothing. My stomach twisted and my mouth went dry. I was too late. I picked up the knife and fell to my knees beside her.

"Oh, Celia." My voice cracked.

I threw the knife into the tub and felt for a pulse. There was nothing. I sank to the floor, and cried as I cradled her head to my chest. I'd promised to protect her from the bastard she was married to and I'd failed. I hadn't protected her, I'd killed her.

"I'm sorry," I whispered. "God, Celia. I'm so sorry."

Wil came in and squatted next to me.

"It's not your fault, Brocs. You did everything you could."

I hadn't. I should have checked that he was still locked up. I glanced up to see two uniforms standing in hallway staring in. I hadn't even heard them come up.

"Sir," one of them said. "Detective Michaels is downstairs. He would like to speak with you before you leave."

"Come on, Brocs," Wil said. "We need to get out of the way and let these guys do their job."

I let Wil guide me from the room and down to the first floor.

"He wouldn't have killed her if I'd stayed out of it, Wil. He might have smacked her around but she wouldn't be dead."

"You don't know that, man."

I did. I was certain of it.

We gave statements to the detective. I told him how I'd originally gotten involved and about the phone call I'd received earlier tonight. He eyed my bloodstained clothing and asked Wil to wait in the other room. Then he went over my story once more. I told him the same thing as before, including the fact that I'd picked up the knife.

When I finished he said, "Were you romantically involved with the deceased?"

"What?"

"Answer the question, Mr. Harley."

"Are you going to arrest me?"

"Not yet."

I stood staring at the detective, as comprehension dawned.

"You think I killed her?"

"I have to look at the evidence. Right now, you're what I've got."

"This is bullshit. I'm out of here."

I spun away from the detective and stalked away. Wil jerked me to a stop.

"What's up?"

I shrugged out of his grasp and didn't answer. Wil turned to the officer following me.

"What's going on here?" Wil asked.

"I need to get your statement, Mr. Pinkerton."

Pinkerton badged him. "It's Officer Pinkerton, Stantonville Police Department."

The detective wasn't impressed.

I watched as Pinkerton went through the whole story again. They were across the room and I couldn't hear what was going on but I could tell Wil was pissed. I guess I was too, but mostly I was numb.

The detective finally flipped his notebook closed, and Wil headed my way. Michaels told us he would be in touch as we stepped outside. I stopped on the porch and turned to speak. "Michaels, where were you guys when Quentin Alley was beating the crap out of his wife, out rousting some other good citizens?"

"Mr. Harley, I could take you in tonight."

"Kiss my ass."

Wil nudged me down the steps and across the drive to the truck before I wound up in cuffs. "Get in the truck, Brocs. They'll find her old man."

"It doesn't matter, Celia will still be dead."

He didn't have an answer for that. He dropped the truck in gear and drove back to the lake while I stared out the window at the darkness.

"They've got nothing to tie you to her murder, Brocs," he said.

I don't know who he was trying to convince, me or himself. We stopped in front of the darkened cabin. The tick of the truck engine as it cooled joined the chorus of night noises around us. I reached for the handle to get out.

"It wasn't your fault, Brocs."

I waved him off and didn't answer. Inside I grabbed the whiskey bottle and took it with me to the bathroom. While I tried to scrub the blood off my hands with soap I let the whiskey clean the stain in my soul. Neither worked very well. I stayed in there until the hot water was long gone. My teeth were chattering with the cold when I walked into my bedroom and slipped into my sweats. False dawn was beginning to show in the east. I stared down at the bed and shook my head. I hadn't had enough whiskey yet to sleep. I sat in front of the fireplace and drank my way through the bottle.

Wil offered to fix something to eat. I shook my head and took another sip. The next time I noticed, he was gone. The fire flickered and the logs popped and finally my eyes started to droop. I dropped the bottle to the floor by my feet and made my way unsteadily to the bedroom.

The room swam when I sank onto the bed and closed my eyes. I stuck one foot on the floor and it stopped. Celia's face wavered before me. Her empty stare the last thing I saw before I slept.

. . .

The house was full of people, drinking, talking, eating. Drew and I sat together in a big chair next to the fireplace. Every once in a while some motherly looking woman would walk over and pat our heads like we were puppies and mumble something like, 'you poor poor darlings.'

Drew hunched closer to me after each visit. I put my arm around him and he went to sleep with his head on my shoulder. I watched the people surge in and out of the house. The motherly women squeezed Dad's hands and blinked away tears. The young beautiful ones gave him hugs and whispered things in his ear, then shot quick looks at Drew and me in our chair. Dad's sister Leda walked over.

"Poor baby, he's worn out. I'll take him upstairs and put him to bed before I go home."

I tightened my arm around Drew. "Let him stay, Aunt Leda."

She smiled and kissed my forehead. "Your mama loved you very much. You're a good boy, Brocs. Don't let anyone tell you any different."

She brushed the hair off my forehead. Blinking back tears she turned and walked away. I closed my eyes and fought the urge to cry. I was not going to let these people see me cry.

I watched my dad across the room. All Mama's friends were gone now along with the sweet motherly women. The only people left were dark men in dark suits with sunglasses peeking out of their breast pockets. They were gathered around my father at the far end of the room. The firelight glittered on whiskey glasses as they talked. One of them said something and slapped my dad on the shoulder. They all laughed. Rage filled me. I held Drew close and stared across the room at the men who were laughing when my mother was dead. One of the men, big with tanned, weathered-looking skin, glanced across the room. His eyes widened when he saw us sitting there. He said something to Dad and headed toward us.

"Time this little one was in bed," he said, leaning toward us.

I shrank back into the chair, pulling Drew with me. The man shot me an ugly look and I released my hold. He jerked Drew from the chair. Drew, woke up and whimpered.

"Hush, kiddo. What the hell are you waiting for, boy?" he asked me. "Come on, get upstairs."

"I want mama." Drew mumbled.

"I told you to hush." He gave Drew a little shake.

I got up from the chair and looked over my shoulder at Dad and the three strangers on the far side of the room.

"Who are those men with my dad?" I asked.

The man cupped the back of my head and shoved me forward. "That ain't none of your business, boy."

"But why are they here?"

"You're as nosy as your mother, close your trap and get up the stairs."

That was too much. I launched myself at the big stranger and pummeled him with my fists. "Don't you talk bad about my mom," I yelled, as tears rolled down my face.

He swatted me aside and I crumpled to the landing. Before I could scramble up, he grabbed my arm and jerked me up the final stairs. I stared down at my dad and willed him to come to my rescue. He never looked our way.

"Which one is your bedroom?"

I pointed and he pushed through, lay Drew on the bed and tugged the covers over him. I sat on my bed waiting for him to leave. He glared at me and strode out of the room. After he left I helped Drew into his pajamas, tucked him back in and hung up our suits so Dad wouldn't yell. Then I eased out into the hallway. I could hear the men talking downstairs. I crept down to the landing, hid behind a potted plant and listened, but I couldn't hear their words.

The men started walking from the room. I hunkered down.

"We should be able to continue business as usual, Harley."

I peeked around the flowerpot to see who spoke. It was the big man that took us upstairs. He eyed my hiding place. A shudder ran through my body and I sucked in my breath hoping he couldn't see me. My dad smiled, shook his hand and they continued away. I let out my breath in relief when the big man disappeared down the hallway.

Drew cried out. I scrambled back to our bedroom and hushed him. He settled into sleep. I crawled into bed. The *cruel face of the dark man swirled around inside my head until I sank into an exhausted sleep. Drew's piercing scream shot me out of bed. I held him and tried to comfort him, but he continued to sob.*

"Hush, Drew. It's okay. Please, Drew. Hush or he's going to come in here."

The bedroom door crashed open and I jumped.

■ ■ ■

I blinked and stared around the room trying to get my bearings. My heart was hammering in my chest and it took a while to remember where I was. I dressed quietly and stumbled to the kitchen. Wil was still sleeping in the other room. I started the coffee pot, poked the fire to life and huddled in front of it. Celia's face still haunted me. I rubbed my temples and swallowed the lump in my throat. I would never again make a promise I couldn't keep.

"I'm sorry, Celia," I whispered.

The whiskey bottle was where I left it last night. I picked it up. There was still an inch or so in the bottom. Christ, I should have hell's own hangover this morning. I didn't. I got up and poured the end of the bottle down the drain and got a cup of coffee. Images from my dream faded in on top of Celia's face. I concentrated on them. I couldn't deal with her right now. I'd grieve for her always, but right now I needed to figure out who killed Drew.

The big dark man from the dream was clear in my mind. I tried to remember if I'd ever heard his name, ever seen him at the house any other time. It was no use. My childhood memories were locked away behind a door for which I no longer had a key. I shook my head, and got up to fill my coffee cup. I picked up a pencil, turned over one of the file papers and sketched the man from my dream, dark hair, air of menace, smile that didn't reach his eyes. I tossed the paper back on the table and stared into the fire while my coffee got cold.

Chapter 13

As I sat transfixed by the dying fire, Wil tapped my shoulder and I jumped in surprise.

"You okay, man?"

"I didn't sleep very well."

He poked the coals until the fire flickered to life, then went to the kitchen and poured a cup of coffee. He sat down in front of the fireplace and cradled the cup to warm his hands. My sketch was on top of the papers on the coffee table. He picked it up and glanced at me.

"What's this?"

"Picture of a guy I dreamed about."

"You had a dream about Marcus Carmichael?"

"Who's Marcus Carmichael?"

"Big businessman over in Rayburn's neck of the woods. Owns a couple of car lots, a motel chain, I don't know what else. We've got a file on him. We think he's dirty but we've never been able to pin anything on him. You being in the repo business, I'm surprised you've never worked for him."

"He was at the house after Mom's funeral."

"You had a dream about your mom's funeral?"

"I've been having a lot of weird dreams since Drew died. Shit I thought I'd forgotten years ago."

"It's just stress, man. Drew died, now the cops are on your ass, then last night with Celia. It's enough to make anybody freak out a little."

"I guess that's it."

Wil sipped his coffee. I got up, dumped mine in the sink, and leaned against the bar in the kitchen.

"How long does the police department keep their accident files, Wil?"

"The old stuff's on microfilm. The newer stuff's all in the computer. Why?"

"Are those records open to the public?"

"You have to pay for the copy, but yeah, you can get 'em."

"I'd like to get a copy of Mom's accident report."

"What the hell for?"

"I'd just like to see it. I was only a kid when she died. Nobody ever really told me all of what happened. They said she fell asleep on the way home from a night class at the University and drove off the Ingersoll Bridge."

"Why do you want to dig that up now? Don't you have enough going on, Brocs?"

"Probably. I'd still like to have it. Can you get it for me?"

"I'll see what I can do."

Wil picked up the files on Drew's deal with Austin-Kline and read through them again.

"Why do you think this Austin-Kline report is important, Brocs?" he asked.

"I was supposed to meet Drew at Luigi's for lunch the day after his birthday party. I found a page from Drew's daytimer that said, "B Luigi's re Austin-Kline.""

"There's nothing in these papers or his daytimer. He must have had something else."

"Lori had some stuff he was keeping at her house. She was supposed to mail it to me when she got to her dad's."

Wil brought his empty cup to the kitchen and rinsed it out.

"Why don't I go into town?" he said. "I'll check your apartment, see if you have a package, try to run down that accident file, then I'll come back up here. While I'm doing that, you might try to get some sleep."

He was right, I did need some rest and I didn't want to go into town and run into Stryker. Not right now. I needed some more information before he backed me into a corner.

"Can you get into the department files if you're not working?"

He grinned. "I'm off duty, not fired. They still let me inside."

I tried to smile, but it was a weak effort.

Wil squeezed my shoulder. "Stop beating yourself up over what happened last night, Brocs. It wasn't your fault."

I wish I were as certain of that as everyone else.

After Wil left, I stretched out on the couch and tried to sleep. I'd just dropped off when my cell phone rang. I picked it up and mumbled hello.

"Mr. Brocs Harley?"

The man spoke with an accent I couldn't identify.

"This is Harley."

"This is Manny from Luigi's."

That got my attention. I sat up and shook the sleep from my head. "Yes."

"I just heard that your brother has passed away. I am very sorry to hear this."

"Thank you, Manny."

"He left some papers here. He asked if I would get them to you as he might be called out of town before he met with you. I thought maybe you would like to have them."

I sucked in my breath and swallowed.

"Yes. Yes I would."

"I will mail them to you."

"No. I'll send someone to pick them up. His name is Wil Pinkerton. He's a police officer."

"Very well, have him ask for Manny. I will give him the papers."

"Thank you, Manny. Thank you very much."

"I liked your brother. He was a very nice man. I'm going to miss him."

"So am I."

I hung up, dialed Wil and prayed he had his phone with him.

"Talk," he answered.

"Wil, it's Brocs."

"I thought you were sleeping."

"I need you to do something while you're in town. Stop by Luigi's, talk to Manny. He has something there for me."

"Shit, I'm almost to the lake."

"Sorry, it might be important."

"Ok, I'll head back."

An hour later my cell phone rang again. It was Wil and something was wrong. I could hear it in his voice.

"You have any idea what Manny had for you?" he asked.

"Some papers that Drew left there. Why?"

"The place is surrounded by cops. I weaseled my way in to find out what was going on. Somebody shot up the place. Manny's dead."

"Fuck!"

"I'm going to get out of here before I get roped in to this thing. I called Rayburn before I went to Luigi's. I'll go liberate him from the office and we'll head your way. This whole case is starting to smell."

I hung up my phone, tossed it onto the coffee table and cradled my head on my arms. My mind was reeling from stress overload. I was a suspect in two murders. Manny was dead. It was probably my fault and I didn't have a clue yet what I was involved in.

"What the hell is going on, Drew?" I whispered.

Chapter 14

Sleep was a lost cause. I started pacing the cabin. Everything I had touched this week had turned to shit. How had somebody found out about the papers at Luigi's? Did they already know the papers were there? Surely they couldn't have set up a hit in the time between when I talked to Manny and when I called Wil. "You're losing it, Brocs," I muttered to myself. They'd have to be monitoring our cell phones to do that. God I was getting paranoid. Shit. Why didn't Manny call yesterday? Why couldn't one damn thing go right?

My phone rang and I snatched it off the table. It was Detective Michaels.

"How the hell did you get this number?" I snapped.

"Mr. Harley, I've been to your apartment several times this morning and you seem to be somewhere else. We need to talk."

"I already told you everything I know."

"Mr. Harley, don't make us come after you. Meet me at the Stantonville Police Department tomorrow morning at nine."

"And if I don't?"

"I'll issue a warrant for your arrest."

"You've been talking to Stryker."

"Tomorrow at nine, Harley. This is the only free pass you get."

I bounced the phone off the wall after he hung up. Phone parts scattered across the floor. I kicked them out

of the way and continued my pacing. I was still at it when
Rayburn and Pinkerton showed up shortly after noon. Wil
tossed an envelope at the coffee table. I detoured my route
and snatched it up. Billy carried Chinese take-out into the
kitchen and unloaded it on the counter.

"That fucking detective wants me to meet him at the
station tomorrow. He's been talking to Stryker. They're
going to pin one of these murders on me, Wil."

"Come on, Brocs. They've got no evidence." Wil didn't
sound terribly confident and that ratcheted my worry
meter up a notch.

"This is unbelievable."

I slumped onto the couch and opened the envelope. It
was the file Lori had mailed. Billy eased down next to me
and handed me a box of fried rice. He rifled through the
mess of papers on the table and came up with the sketch.

"Marcus Carmichael?" he asked.

I glanced up from the file. "You know him?"

"He and I run in the same circles. What you doin' with
his picture?"

"I had a dream about him."

"It must have been in the past. Marcus is gray-headed
now."

"I saw him after Mom's funeral."

"You had a dream about that?"

"Yeah."

Billy stopped talking to eat. I continued reading the
file.

"Brocs, do you know how Carmichael knew your
folks?"

"Not really. I think maybe Halston did some business
with him. Not sure. I was just a little kid."

"I don't know what kind of business your old man
would have with Carmichael. Halston's small time
compared to him."

"Hmm. Like I said. I was a little kid. I might be
remembering it wrong."

It was silent while Billy finished eating and I finished
reading. My food was still sitting on the coffee table
untouched. I dropped the file onto the table next to it. It
was a copy of Halston's accounting files. The same papers
I'd gotten from Melinda. Without Drew here to tell me what

was going on, they still didn't mean a damn thing. I picked up my food, took a bite and put it down. My stomach rolled and I went into the bathroom to spit it out. I came back, sat next to Billy, and stared into the fire.

"Wil told me about that nurse, Celia," Billy said. "I'm sorry, man, but you did the right thing."

I sighed and rubbed my temples. I was setting a world record for headaches in a single week. Maybe Billy was right, maybe I had done the right thing with Celia. Someday I'd see it that way too, if they didn't send me to the gas chamber over it.

Rayburn went out to the truck for his duffel bag. Wil took his place on the couch. He laid the pieces of my cell phone out on the table and started to reassemble them. "You need to go talk to them tomorrow."

"How'd you know I wasn't going?"

He snapped the battery in place and I heard a grunt of satisfaction when he turned it on and it worked. He tossed the resurrected phone onto my lap and leaned against the cushions. "I know you. Now is not the time to show your ass. Go talk to them."

"Jesus, Wil. You were there. She was dead before we even got to the house."

"Relax, if they had anything concrete, they wouldn't be asking you to come in and talk, they'd just pick you up and stick you in a cell."

"Is that supposed to make me feel better?"

"Sorry, that's all I got."

I turned my eyes to the papers in my hand. I was having a hard time concentrating. My mind kept going back to Celia. Wil nursed his drink and stared at the crackling logs.

After a long silence he said, "Brocs, I don't believe in coincidences. If I didn't already believe Drew was murdered, this thing with Manny would have convinced me. What I can't figure out is how they knew Manny had anything we wanted."

"I don't know, it doesn't make any sense, the two of us were the only one's that knew."

"And Billy."

"Okay, three of us. Same thing."

"Phone tap, maybe?" Wil said.

"I'm not buying that, how would they know to tap the phone at Luigi's? I wonder if they had someone watching Drew and just decided to clear a loose end by picking up the file before I did?"

"That still doesn't explain how they knew we were on the way to get it?"

"What's that?" asked Billy as he dropped his duffel inside the door?"

"Just trying to figure out how anyone knew I was on my way to Luigi's to pick up a folder full of papers."

"What makes you think what happened at Luigi's had anything to do with Drew? You guys are getting a little bit paranoid."

Wil laughed. "Your right, man. I think we're reading too much into a random crime."

"Damn right," Billy said. "You guys just need a little decompression time. You've had a rough couple of days."

"You're probably right." I said, but I didn't believe it.

Billy went to stow his duffel bag in the bedroom, then came out and opened a beer before he joined us.

"We can bounce ideas off each other tonight and maybe we'll come up with something," said Wil.

"This would be a lot easier if Stryker and that other fucking detective weren't trying to hang me for the murder."

Wil pushed the papers to one side of the coffee table and propped his feet up. "Maybe we can bring Stryker over to our side, Brocs."

"Not likely."

"It might be worth a try."

"Forget it, Wil. He doesn't want to hear anything I have to say unless I'm going to admit I killed Drew.

Wil huffed in frustration. I didn't know if he was frustrated with me or Detective Stryker. It didn't matter. He was stuck in the middle either way.

"Did you get a copy of the accident report?" I asked.

"I got it."

He reached over the back of the couch for his bag and dug out the report. He handed me a microfilm printout and I started scanning it. Wil said something. I held up my hand to stop him and continued reading. When I finished, I stared at him.

"Did you read this?"

"Haven't had time."

I passed him the report, grabbed a beer out of the fridge and stumbled out to the porch. My hand was shaking as I popped the top on the beer can. Rayburn came out after me and lit a cigarette. He flipped the pack and lighter to me. I lit up and slumped against the cabin wall. Wil joined us a few minutes later and sat on the steps, the report still in his hand.

"This doesn't make sense, Brocs."

"What doesn't?" asked Billy.

Wil gave him the report. I lit another cigarette, sat down on the bench and stared toward the lake while Billy took in the contents of the accident report. He joined me on the bench when he finished.

"Jesus," he whispered. "According to the report, a woman saw someone in a black truck run your Mom off the bridge. It sounds like your Mom was murdered."

"Why would the cops cover that up?" Wil asked. "It doesn't make sense. And what happened to the eye witness?"

"She's dead," I said. "It was old Mrs. Helstrom. She died during a burglary at her house a few days after Mom's funeral."

"How do you remember that, it was twenty years ago?"

I tossed my cigarette over the porch rail onto the driveway. "Mrs. Helstrom was Drew's babysitter. She didn't show up for work one day not long after Mom's funeral. Halston was in a snit because he was planning to go back to work that day and he couldn't because she didn't show. I remember because it pissed Halston off and he took it out on me."

That was the first inkling I had about what life without Mom was going to be like. Mom had been light and happiness, love and warmth. She smelled like flowers and always had a smile for me. She had told me about my father shortly before she died—that he'd been a highway patrolman—that he was hit by a car when he stopped to change a tire for an elderly man on highway 10. She told me she found out she was pregnant a month after my dad died and that she'd turned to Halston because she was terrified to be pregnant and alone. She told Halston she was pregnant with Lee's child a month after they got married. Looking back now, I think she was scared and trying to prepare me in case anything happened to her. I didn't understand all of what she told me. I was too young. I figured it out pretty quickly after she was gone. It was a tough life lesson for an eight-year-old.

Wil's voice snapped me away from my memories.

"Do you think the burglary was just cover for another murder?"

"I don't know what to think, Wil."

"We need to see the police report on that too. There's no way we can get access to all these files unless I go back to work. Brocs, maybe if I let Stryker know about all this he'll get off your ass and start digging in another direction."

"Keep Stryker out of it for now. We don't have anything to give him. Just a bunch of unrelated deaths."

"Brocs, we could really use his help."

"The only help he's going to give me is a ride to the county lockup. Leave him out of it, Wil."

Wil wasn't happy about it, but he knew I was right, especially now with Michaels gunning for me too. We didn't have anything. Just a bunch of unrelated reports, and we didn't know what half of them meant. Rayburn snagged the cigarettes off the bench, lit one and moved over to lean against the side of the cabin. Wil went inside to pack his bag. I tipped my head against the wall and closed my eyes. I had the feeling we were shooting off on a tangent, getting further away from Drew's killer, not closer.

We squeezed into the truck and drove to Stantonville. We dropped Wil off at Annie's house and drove on to my office. I picked up my mail, shuffled through it and left it on the desk. It was all junk. Rayburn drove to the apartment so I could check on Baldwin. I grabbed fresh clothes, then drove Billy home so he could get his car. I started back to the cabin, thinking about what we needed to do the next day. As I turned onto Route 18, a black Lincoln passed me. I glanced at the plates and realized it was my skip.

It was the first good thing that had happened all day.

Chapter 15

I swung in behind the Lincoln, let two or three cars get between us, and tailed Lester Crawford. We wound through the hill roads until good old Lester turned in at a locked entry gate. I drove on past, edged onto the shoulder and parked. There weren't any close neighbors and traffic was light. I eased out of the truck, ducked into the woods and made my way toward the drive where the Lincoln sat. Lester was hanging out of the driver's window yelling into a speaker. I crouched in the brush to watch. Lester snapped something at the disembodied voice, then disappeared back inside the car. A few seconds later the gates swung open and the Lincoln cruised through. I dug a scrap of paper out of my wallet and wrote down the address.

Lester's police record and background made the Lincoln an odd choice of car. The locked entry gate was another piece that didn't fit with my picture of Lester the career criminal. It appeared Lester had moved into the big time. I cut through the weeds and crawled out of the ditch beside my truck. A car swished by and I turned my head away so they wouldn't see my face, but they didn't slow down. I cranked up the truck and continued down the road.

A couple of miles later I passed the entrance to Billy's place. I'd made a complete circle around Cedar Lake. The gated house was directly across the lake from Rayburn's. I jumped on the brakes, reversed and turned into his drive.

My binoculars were in the glove box. I dug them out and ran up the steps to Billy's front door. He opened it before I could knock.

"What's up?" he asked.

"I need to come in for a minute."

Billy stepped aside and I walked down into the living room. In front of the windows I raised the glasses and stared across the glittering lake. The locked gates were visible and the house, made from native stone, was sprawled among the trees. I could see cars parked in the circle drive in front, but no people. I'd guess the house was at least ten-thousand square feet. It made Rayburn's look like a cottage.

"Who lives over there?" I asked.

"Where?"

I handed Billy the glasses and told him where to point them. He studied the house for a minute then handed me the binocs.

"No idea. Is it important?"

"Might be, I just saw one of my skips go through the security gates of that house. Wondered who it belonged to."

He seemed to relax when I said that. "I could probably find out for you."

"That'd be great, let me know what you find out when you get to the cabin."

"Sure. You want a drink or something before you take off?"

"No, I'll see you later."

Billy followed me out and waved as I drove away. The cabin was dark when I parked out front. I poked up the fire, poured a drink and sat on the couch to wait for Rayburn. I finished the first drink and poured a second. I dialed Melinda's number, then flipped the phone closed before I pushed 'send'. I worked my way through my first glass of bourbon and dialed again. I stared at the phone for a long time before I pressed the send button and waited while it rang. After the second ring, I started to flip the phone closed. Before I could do it, she answered.

"Uh, hey, Mel."

"Hey yourself."

Just the sound or her voice eased some of the tension in my muscles.

"Where'd you disappear to?" she asked. "Thought you fell off the end of the earth."

"I'm working out of town for a few days. It sure is good to talk to you."

Melinda heard something in that statement that I hadn't intended.

"Brocs, what's wrong. Are you okay?"

A lump grew in my throat. I swallowed it and intended to tell her I was fine, but that's not what came out. Instead I told her about Celia, what I'd done to try to help, and how it had turned out.

"Brocs, it's not your fault she's dead."

I didn't answer.

"Brocs, listen to me. You did the right thing. It's not your fault."

"Thanks, Mel."

We were both silent for a while. When Melinda spoke again, the subject had been changed.

"So, you gonna be out of town long?" she asked.

I smiled and wished she was there with me. Maybe I'd bring her up here once everything was back to normal again.

"I shouldn't be gone much longer. Did you hear about what happened at Luigi's today?"

"It's been all over the news."

"I think it's my fault Manny's dead."

"What?"

"Drew left an envelope there for me. Manny called and asked if I wanted him to mail it. I said no, I'd have Wil pick it up while he was in town. Before Wil could get there, all hell broke loose."

"How could they have found out Wil was going to stop at Luigi's? Brocs, I think you're reaching."

I sighed. "Maybe. I guess you're right. No one knew Wil was stopping there besides Billy and me. The envelope's probably still at the restaurant."

"I could stop by and check for you?"

I shuddered at the thought. Still not convinced the shooting wasn't connected to me somehow. "That might not be safe. I'll just check when I get back to town. Don't worry about it."

"For Pete's sake, Brocs. Do you think someone's listening in on your cell phone calls or something?"

"I...No, I..." I sighed again. "It's probably not important anyway. I'll just pick it up in a couple of days."

Mel was quiet for a minute and just as I got ready to speak, she mentioned that Detective Stryker had stopped by for a friendly little visit.

"I'm sorry, Mel. I'm sorry you're mixed up in this. What'd you tell him?"

"I told him we went out for dinner and dessert a couple of times, but I hadn't spoken to you for a few days."

I smiled, dessert sounded pretty good. "Dinner and dessert, huh?"

Melinda laughed. "Yeah. I'm supposed to call him if you get in touch with me."

"You probably ought to do that."

"Think so?"

"Yeah, I could be dangerous."

"I think I'll take my chances."

We were going through prolonged goodbyes when Melinda thought of something else.

"Oh, by the way, Halston's in a real snit. He's missing some papers on that big Austin-Kline deal Drew was working on. You wouldn't happen to know anything about them would you?"

"Blue file folder with a rubber band around it?"

"Yeah, that's the one."

"Nah, I wouldn't know anything about that."

She laughed. "Didn't think so. You take care of yourself, Brocs. Something strange is going on around here."

"I will. Melinda, be careful. I can't tell the good guys from the bad ones yet."

"I'll walk on egg shells."

We started the whole round of goodbyes again and I was grinning like an idiot when I punched off the call. God, I was as infatuated as a teenager. I couldn't remember the last time I'd been so hung up over a woman. Maybe never. I got up to pour another drink and snagged the leftover fried rice from the fridge. I ate it cold out of the carton, washed it down with Maker's, topped off my drink and flopped down in front of the fire. I was there, sound asleep, the glass precariously balanced on my chest, when the slap of the screen door startled me awake.

I jumped, and dove for the teetering glass. Whiskey splashed the coffee table and puddled on the rug. I scooted the papers out of the way and retrieved the glass. Billy grabbed a towel from the kitchen.

"Sorry about that, man," he said as I sopped up the mess.

It wasn't the first alcohol related accident that poor rug had suffered.

Billy dropped his briefcase on top of the file folders and papers. He snagged my glass and poured one for both of us before he came in and sat down. I nursed my drink and watched as he removed his laptop and hooked up the phone cord.

"Thought this might come in handy," he said.

He dug my sketch out of the mess on the table and stared at it for a minute.

"I found out who owns that house." He flipped the sketch at me and smirked. "Your old buddy, Marcus Carmichael."

"You're kidding me."

"Nope. That's his place."

"Another coincidence?" I asked.

"Getting to be an awful lot of them."

I stared at the sketch and nursed my drink.

"Tell me about your dream," Billy said.

I glanced at him over my glass.

"It was nothing, just another time when Halston showed what an asshole he could be."

"If that's all it was, Drew's death wouldn't have triggered it. Think. What was it about?"

"Nothing, Carmichael was at the funeral, he put me and Drew to bed. After that, I snuck down to the landing while Halston was talking to Marcus and some other guys, but I couldn't hear what they were saying. That's pretty much all there was to it."

"Come on, Brocs. After all these years, why did you ask Wil to dig up the accident file on your Mom? Something made you do that."

"I don't know, Billy." I put down my drink and pressed my fingers into my temples. "I don't know where the dreams end and the memories begin anymore."

I pushed off of the couch and paced around the small room. "Maybe it was something one of them said and I just don't remember anymore. Mom and Halston were fighting all the time in those days." I paused and thought about the dream of the fight. "Mom wanted to leave. Halston told her she couldn't take Drew. Shit, Billy. This stuff is ancient history. It's not going to help find who killed my brother. And Mom died twenty years ago. That's not connected with Drew."

When Billy relaxed in his chair with a smile, I realized how tense he'd been when he came in.

"You okay, man?" I asked.

"Yeah, why?"

"You just seem a little wound up."

His eyes slid away from mine and he fiddled with the computer. "Just a lot going on right now. Let's get back to what's happening with you. You've been having dreams since Drew died. Maybe you know something. Something you found out as a kid. Something you buried away."

"I don't remember anything."

"You just don't want to remember anything."

"Well it wasn't exactly a party."

"Look, man. I know your old man treated you like shit. I know you've buried the memory of those hurts away, but there's got to be a reason they're coming back to you now. You've got to stop pushing them away."

"Back off, Rayburn. I don't need a shrink."

"I'm not a shrink, I'm your friend."

"Then back off."

Billy raised his hands in surrender. "Okay. Forget I mentioned it."

"Fine."

"Okay."

I perched on the edge of the couch, still scowling at Rayburn. "Let me see your computer, man." Billy handed me the laptop. I started digging further into Lester's past. There were news stories on his arrests, but seldom any follow-up. That went with what I knew about his records. Nothing else of interest came up. I couldn't find any links to Marcus Carmichael. I switched tracks and started searching for Carmichael. I came up with a total blank. That got my attention, so I dug a little deeper. Still nothing.

"I can't find anything about Marcus Carmichael, Billy. It's like he doesn't exist."

"So?"

"So, it's almost impossible not to leave a trace. He's got to have a social security number, bank accounts, something. I'm coming up with a big zero here. I'm tapped into sites that can tell me what size boxers the president wears and what he had for breakfast this morning, yet there's nothing here on Carmichael."

"What's that mean?"

"Marcus has something to hide and he's done a damn fine job of it."

Billy shook his head, but I knew I was right.

"Brocs, Carmichael's been in business for a long time. I don't see how that's possible."

"Are the businesses in his name?"

"I don't know. Let me see that."

I handed him the computer. He checked for business information and came up with a name, Glen Austin. The name Austin rang a bell, but I wasn't making any connections.

"Who's Glen Austin?" I asked.

"I don't know, but if you dig around under Carmichael's business names, it all goes back to Glen Austin."

I took over the computer and fiddled around digging for more information. Billy shuffled the files and papers into a neat stack and started reading them again. I glanced up to see he was admiring Halston's creative bookkeeping.

"I was almost sure Halston had something going on the side," he said.

I went back to the computer. I tried every way I knew of to find information on Austin and Carmichael. The result after two hours—nothing.

"Billy, these guys don't exist. No birth certificates, no social, no driver's license. Nada. It's not possible to live and not leave a trace." I gave up and rubbed my eyes. "Nothing but brick walls."

"Take a break," Rayburn said. "Try to get a good night's sleep. Maybe something will come to you in the morning."

I emptied my glass and got ready for bed. The click of computer keys was the only sound from the other room as I lay down. I stretched out, relaxed my muscles one by one, and waited for the bourbon to do its work. A few minutes later, I was out. After what seemed like seconds, Rayburn rousted me out of my first good sleep in days. "Brocs...Brocs...Dammit, Harley, wake up!"

I sat up and rubbed my eyes. "What!"

"I found something."

"It couldn't wait 'til morning?"

"It is morning," Billy said, laughing.

I nudged the shade away from the window. The eastern sky was fading from purple to orange. It couldn't be much after five-thirty. "Just barely."

"Come on, get up. I've got the coffee pot going."

"I'm coming. Chill out."

Billy left my bedroom and I crawled out from under the quilt. My jeans were on the floor where I had tossed them the night before. I shrugged into them and stuck my head and arms into my last clean sweatshirt. The clothes were so cold they felt wet. I shivered as I stumbled into the kitchen. Billy was waiting with a cup of coffee. I sat on a stool at the counter, wrapped my hands around the mug, and blew across the steaming surface.

"What is so astounding you had to wake me up at the crack of dawn?" I asked.

I took a careful sip of the scalding coffee and willed the caffeine to do its work.

"I found Glen Austin and Marcus Carmichael."

"And?"

"They're the same guy."

I sat my coffee cup down so hard it sloshed over my fingers and dripped onto the counter. I shook my burning fingers and stared at Billy.

"No way."

Billy grinned. "For real, they're the same guy."

I grabbed some paper towels and cleaned up my mess. "How'd you come up with that?" I asked.

"Look."

He handed me a sheaf of papers.

"Where'd these come from?"

"I printed them out after you were asleep."

I started reading and laughed.

"The guy's real name is Bailey Kline?"

"Yup."

"Austin-Kline!"

"You got it."

"Marcus Carmichael is behind Austin-Kline."

"Behind it, in front of it, hell, he is it!"

"I wonder who screwed up with the IDs?"

"I don't know, but I wouldn't want to be in his shoes when Kline finds out."

"Great detective work. Mind telling me how you found it?"

He paused for minute. "Let's just say I have access to some stuff that you don't."

I eyed him over the rim of my cup.

"I thought I was the one with the all access pass."

Billy shrugged. "I called in a couple of favors."

"Thanks, Billy."

"Hey, that's what friends are for. It's kind of fun to run one past you every now and then."

"I wonder what it means, if it really helps? We might be following the yellow brick road to nowhere."

"I found it. I'll let you and Wil decide what to do with it. I've got to go into the office this morning. I'll leave the computer here and come out later tonight."

"Thanks, Billy, I'll see you later."

He waved and the door closed behind him. I read through the printed sheets Billy left behind. I couldn't see how they tied in to Drew's murder, but the Austin-Kline angle was all I had. I checked my watch. It wasn't quite seven. Wil wouldn't be at the cop shop until nine. I put the papers in my overnight bag, changed into sweat pants and tennis shoes and went for a run. Maybe exercise would clear my mind.

Chapter 16

Three miles later, I dragged myself gasping up the stairs to the cabin. Gone were the days I could do six miles and barely break a sweat. I was going to have to start running every day. My laziness was catching up with me. I peeled off my wet clothes and was on my way to the shower when my cell phone rang. I snagged it off the table and answered without looking at the caller ID.

"Mr. Harley."

"Shit." It was Stryker.

"No good morning?" he asked.

"What do you want, Stryker, and how the hell is everyone getting this number?"

"I'm afraid that's a trade secret."

"I'll just have to get a new phone. What do you want?"

"Just wanted to remind you of your appointment this morning."

"Like I would forget."

"Forget, no. Avoid, maybe. I strongly suggest you don't do the latter."

"Is there anything else? I'd like to get in the shower."

"I spoke with your girlfriend. She seemed surprised to find you were out of town."

"First off, I don't have a girlfriend, I date women. I do have some women friends with whom I share dinner from time to time. I'm not in the habit of calling to let them know I'm going to be out of town. Second, what the hell difference does it make to you?"

"You're a suspect in a murder investigation, two of them actually. Everything you do interests me."

"You're barking up the wrong tree, Stryker."

"It's Detective Stryker, Mr. Harley. Show some respect for the badge."

"You haven't earned it."

"I'm going to enjoy taking you down, Harley."

"You're letting your feelings override your common sense, Stryker. You know you don't have enough to nail me."

"I will."

"Then you'll have to manufacture it. I didn't do it."

"The prisons are full of innocent men, Harley. Most of them are guilty as hell."

"Kiss my ass." I hung up before he could respond. In the shower, I let the hot water pound my shoulders till it started to cool, dried off, and pulled on my well-worn Levis. Wil should have gotten to the station by that time so I dialed the PD and asked for him.

"Pinkerton."

"Wil, you talk to Rayburn this morning?"

"No. You coming in to talk to the detectives?"

"On my way." There was a pause. When he spoke again, it was a whisper.

"Stryker doesn't like you for Celia's murder. He's just using it to try and bust you for Drew. He thinks if he gets you rattled enough he'll be able to nail you."

"I appreciate the info, but why are you going behind Stryker's back. You could get fired."

"The motherfucker has had me in here since five this morning grilling me about you, Celia, Drew, and anything else he could come up with. Then, he booted me off regular patrol for a temporary IAD assignment. I don't owe him shit."

"You're in Internal Affairs?"

"Yeah, they do that when they want to keep an eye on you, but they don't have enough to warrant an investigation."

"He's trying to get at me through you."

"Well he can kiss my ass. Shit, here he comes, I gotta go."

I snapped off the phone and shoved it in my pocket. Stryker was playing games and I was tired of it. I checked the time as I walked outside. It was ten after nine. I'd be at the police station by ten. That should have them climbing the walls by the time I arrived.

Sunlight was shining through spotty clouds as I parked behind the station. I strode into the public safety building and told the duty officer my name. He paged Stryker and this time the detective came into the lobby before I could sit down.

"You're late," he said.

"Sorry, some asshole called on the phone as I was getting in the shower."

He propelled me roughly down the hall toward an interview room and told me to sit. I tipped back my chair, lit a cigarette and blew smoke toward the ceiling. I waved and smiled at the tiny camera mounted behind the clock. I thought about flipping it off but I didn't want to push Stryker too far. my gaze wandered around the room taking in the yellow and white tile on the walls, the gray concrete floor, the tile on the ceiling discolored from years of cigarette smoke. Except for the ceiling, the room was bright, almost antiseptic. They hadn't used rubber hoses here in a long time. Psychology was the torture tool of choice these days. I lit another cigarette and watched the clock. Stryker and Michaels strolled in forty-five minutes after they'd put me in the room.

Michaels took up a position against the wall, Stryker sat down across from me. I stubbed out my cigarette and scooted my chair forward so I could rest my elbows on the table.

"Mr. Harley," said Michaels. "You have the right to remain silent. Anything you say can and will be used against you in a court of law."

Shit, Stryker was playing hardball today. I kept my face composed and stared at him as Michaels finished reading my rights.

"Do you understand your rights?" Michaels asked.

I stared up at the detective. "Yes."

He turned on a tape recorder, gave the date, time, and names of everyone present, stated that we were there to discuss the murders of Celia Alley and Andrew Harley, then he looked at me. "Do you wish to call an attorney at this time, Mr. Harley?"

"I do not."

"Fine, let's get started. First go over the events you described to me after the death of Celia Alley."

"I've made my statement, I have nothing to add."

Michaels asked a few more questions. I ignored him and lit another cigarette. He nodded at Stryker. Stryker stared at me. I met his gaze without a flinch. He shook his head and stood.

"I believe Mr. Harley needs a little more time to think about his future."

He leaned out into the hallway and called a uniformed officer into the room.

"Take him down to lockup."

"Am I being charged?" I asked.

"Not at this time."

"Then why are you holding me?"

He smiled. "Because I can."

I was furious, but I didn't want them to see it. I mashed my cigarette in the ashtray and stood as they marched out of the room. Michaels went out first, Stryker stopped in the doorway and glanced back while the unformed officer cuffed my hands behind my back.

"This is wrong, Stryker. You know I didn't kill anyone."

"That's right, Harley. Only innocent men ever get arrested."

The officer led me through the station toward the lower level. Wil looked up from his desk as I passed. "This is bullshit, Wil."

The officer jerked me away and told me to shut up. He unsnapped the cuffs outside the property room. I emptied my pockets and signed the inventory sheet. After they buzzed us into the cell block, he roughly pushed me into the cell. The door clanged shut and I sagged onto the hard cot. I was pretty sure they were just sweating me. They could hold me for twenty hours or so before they had to either press charges or send me home. I didn't think they had enough evidence to make it official.

I lay on the cot and stared at the underside of the one above. I didn't have a book, a radio, a newspaper or my cigarettes. I was stuck in limbo until they decided to cut me loose. I decided to use the time to catch up on my sleep. They hadn't really left me anything else to do. When I woke, it was dark. The wire caged bulb in my cell was off, the only light in the room filtered in through the window of the cell door. A foot scuffed and I sat up. Stryker was leaning against the far wall of the cell. He tossed over my cigarettes and lighter.

I lit one and pressed my back against the cold concrete wall. He waited until I'd taken a long drag before he spoke.

"Why don't you make this easy on yourself, Charlie?"

"What?"

"I said, why don't you make this easy on yourself?"

"You called me, Charlie."

Stryker's face went blank, when he spoke again his voice was hard. "You misheard."

I stared at him through the shadows and wondered what the hell was going on.

"Mr. Harley, I asked you a question."

"Stryker, I've told you before. I didn't kill my brother and I didn't kill Celia Alley."

"They picked up Mrs. Alley's husband in Little Rock two hours ago. He confessed and they're transporting him here now."

"What about Drew's killer. Have you found him?"

"I'm pretty sure I have, but unfortunately I don't have enough evidence to hold you."

"Jesus, Stryker. What do I have to do to get through to you? I didn't kill Drew."

"I don't have enough evidence to hold you, but mark my words, Harley. If I don't get you for this, you will go down for something. I'm going to be right behind you for the rest of your life."

He banged on the door for the guard.

"Stryker, are you even looking at anybody else?"

"I know who killed Andrew Harley. I don't need to search any further."

"This is such bullshit."

The guard opened the door and Stryker strode out. "You're free to go, Harley," he said. "For now. Don't get too comfortable."

He strode down the hallway as the officer escorted me out to pick up my personal property. Wil was waiting for me when I stepped outside.

"You sure you should be lurking around with a suspected felon?" I asked.

"I can lurk with anyone I want. I'm on a two day suspension."

"I'm sorry, Wil."

"Not your fault. I shot off my mouth. Lucky they didn't fire me. You going home?"

"I need to get the files from the cabin. Might as well just stay there."

"I'll meet you out there."

I drove through town and back up the lake road watching my tail and observing all the traffic laws. Stryker probably had the entire force keeping an eye on me tonight. I didn't want to give him any reason to lock me up again. I had to find Drew's killer. No one else was going to bother.

Lights were on at the cabin when I swung into the drive. Rayburn's car was parked by the porch. I got out of the truck and waited as Wil pulled to a stop next to the truck, then followed him inside. Wil went to check on dinner. Rayburn was cooking and the smell of spaghetti sauce filled the cabin. It was the only thing Rayburn could cook besides take-out.

I shrugged out of my jacket and tossed it in the direction of the couch. It missed and slid to the floor. I left it where it fell and sat in front of the fireplace. Stryker was going to manufacture evidence if that's what he had to do to get me behind bars. We were running out of time and still didn't have any leads. I glanced up as Wil came into the living room.

"Beer?" he asked.

I shook my head. Rayburn came in with plates and put them on the coffee table. He and Wil ate. I just pushed mine around and stared into the fire.

"Why's Stryker got such a hard-on for me, Wil?"

"I don't know. I can't figure it out."

"We're not going to have much more time. He's gonna have me behind bars again in a couple of days."

"We'll just have to decipher this mess before that happens."

Rayburn and Wil went quiet. I rearranged my food. "Wil, who's Charlie?"

Wil paused with his fork halfway to his mouth and stared at me. "What?"

"Stryker called me Charlie tonight. I just wondered who Charlie might be. Is he another suspect? Is Stryker just playing with me while he builds a case against this other guy or does he think I'm in on it with someone else?"

"Man, I have no idea. I haven't heard a word about any other suspects. The way Stryker's honed in on you, I'd be surprised if he gave you up if someone walked in and handed him a signed confession."

"Rayburn, you up for some more research?"

"You want me to figure out if there's a Charlie in the woodpile somewhere?"

"Hell it's something, we don't have many other leads."

"I'll see what I can find out. You have anything else to go on? Last name, hometown, anything?"

"All he said was "Charlie." Hell it might be his dog's name, it's just a shot in the dark."

"Thanks, buddy," Rayburn said. "There's probably only about twenty million Google hits for Charlie."

"It's probably safe to say this Charlie lives in Missouri. That should knock the numbers down to a million or so."

"Oh, yeah, that'll be a big help, thanks."

They finished eating and I gave up playing with my food. Rayburn gathered up the plates and went out to the kitchen. When he came back in, he picked up his computer and started searching for the mysterious Charlie. Wil and I split the stack of papers into two piles and went through them again. We still couldn't unlock the puzzle. I wondered if the key had been in the papers Drew left with Manny. If so, it was gone and we needed to find another one.

While Wil and I juggled the papers, Rayburn muttered to himself and punched computer keys. I refrained from asking how the Charlie search was going and turned to Wil.

"You think Drew knew someone was onto him?"

"He must have, otherwise why would he have given the papers to Manny?"

"Why didn't he just give them to you?" Billy asked.

I didn't answer for a minute, just stared into the fire. When I spoke again it was so soft they had to lean forward to hear.

"He was trying to protect me. He knew they were after him and he didn't want to lead them to me. He probably told Manny not to give me the papers until after he left the restaurant."

Tears filled my eyes for the first since the funeral. I buried my face in my hands while Wil and Billy quietly left the room and busied themselves with the dishes. I couldn't believe Drew had died trying to protect me. It was my job to take care of him. It always had been and the one time it really counted, I wasn't there to do it.

Wil and Rayburn were in the kitchen talking quietly. I got up and went to bed without another word. I could hear their voices coming from the living room as I stared up into the darkness and tried to go to sleep.

Chapter 17

I drove to Stantonville the next morning, watching for black and whites. It felt like I was under glass. I hated to admit how spooked Stryker had me. Wil was calling in a few favors to find out more about Bailey Kline. Rayburn was searching for Charlie, and I was going to track down a repo. At my apartment, I flipped through the mail and checked on Baldwin. He was in stealth mode so I topped off his food dish, tossed the mail on the counter and went out to bring back a Firebird. I dug out the paperwork for the recovery and headed for Triple A Printing. Unless I had another runner, the one I was looking for should be there. As I drove across town, I tried to get my head straightened out for work. All I needed for this to be a perfect week was for some deadbeat to knock me on my ass.

I parked on the street in front of the strip mall and skirted around back for a little recon. There it was, a brand new Firebird, shiny as the day it left the lot. I almost felt bad taking a car that was being so well looked after.

I checked out the alley behind the print shop. There were no windows on the rear of the building and no one from the restaurant next door was outside sneaking a smoke. I decided to go ahead and make the recovery.

I sidled up next to the car and looked in the window for any security device. No telltale blinking red lights flashed in the interior. I slipped my picks from my pocket and started working on the lock. Just as the lock popped, a greasy-headed kid pushed through the back door of the restaurant. Shit.

"Hey mister, what are you doing to that car?"

"Just checking it out. It sure is a beauty."

"You'd better get away from that car or I'll call the cops."

I turned around "You don't have to do that. I was just lookin' at it."

The breeze lifted the tail of my jacket, showing the gun on my hip. The kid's eyes widened and he backed toward the door. "I'm calling the cops," he squeaked.

"No, wait."

I reached in my pocket for the repo papers. The kid squealed, dove through the door of the restaurant and slammed it behind him.

"God dammit!"

I slapped the top of the car in frustration and jumped behind the wheel. I reached under the dash and started fumbling with the wires.

An old man wearing an ink-stained apron ran out the back door waving a baseball bat. I slammed the door and tried to get the car started. The old man wound up and took a swing that Stan Musial would have been proud of. The bat smashed into the driver's window. The glass starred and the whole car shook. I swallowed and said a quick prayer of thanks that the bat hadn't connected with my head.

A teenager ran from the print shop and grabbed the old man's arm.

"Grandpa, stop. Don't hit my car."

"Leave that boy's car alone, you hear me?" the old man yelled.

I lifted the door latch and pushed the door open with my foot. I stepped out and stood with my hands up in front of me.

"Sir, my name is Brockston Harley. I'm with H & H Recovery. Your grandson is behind on his car payments. I'm supposed to take the car back to the dealership."

He turned and cocked the bat at the teenager. "You haven't been making your car payments!"

The kid ducked away from the Louisville Slugger and ran inside. Sirens sounded up the street and the punk from the restaurant peeked out to see what was going on. I glared at him.

"You stay right here young man," the old guy said to me.

He turned and strode purposefully into the rear of the shop. I leaned against the car and waited for him to return. A cop car screeched to a stop behind the Firebird as the old man came through the door. I rolled my eyes skyward and sighed. I hadn't made a clean recovery in weeks. The old man walked over and dropped a set of car keys into my hand as the cops exploded from their car.

"I'm sorry I tried to hit you with the bat," he said.

"Don't worry about it. You still got an awesome swing."

The old man grinned and winked as the cops strode up. The first one to recognize me was my old buddy, Officer Gung Ho.

"We get another call out because of you," he snarled. "I'm gonna find a reason to haul you in."

"You'd better make sure the city has a good lawyer."

"Is that a threat?"

"Nope."

He gave me his version of the hard-eyed cop stare. The phone in my pocket vibrated. I reached for the button on my pocket flap and Stantonville PD's "Officer Of The Year" reached for his gun. He jerked it clear of the holster and dropped it. I laughed as it skittered across the parking lot and came to a stop underneath the squad car.

Gung Ho's partner smirked and got back into the car. I got into the Firebird and drove out of the alley. My last sight of Gung Ho was his ass in the air as he fished under the car for his gun. I drove into the car lot and explained what had happened to the window. They cut me a check for the recovery and I bummed a ride to the print shop. In the safety of my truck, I finally got the phone out of my pocket. The missed call number was Harley Real Estate. I dialed and waited for Melinda to answer.

"Hey beautiful," I said when she picked up.

"Um...I checked on that property you were interested in. It's no longer on the market," she said when she recognized my voice.

I didn't say anything while I tried to figure out what she was telling me. Finally the light bulb clicked on. "You went to Luigi's."

"Yes, sir."

"Dammit, Mel."

"It needed to be taken care of right now and you know it." She said, forgetting to code her conversation.

"Shit. Please, please promise me you won't do anything else like this unless we know it's safe."

"I don't think that's possible, sir."

The line clicked in my ear. Great, now she was pissed. I groaned in frustration as I buttoned the phone back into my pocket. I turned into a new subdivision and located my two deadbeats. Neither one had a garage so I decided to try for a nighttime recovery. Maybe I could avoid the cops in the dark. As I drove out of my parking place, a shiny black Lincoln rolled past. I checked the plates and tucked in behind it. Lester parked the Lincoln in the Gas-N-Go lot and went inside. I parked across the street and pondered making a quick run at the car, but decided old Lester might be handy if I let him stay out on the street a while longer. Of course, he might be inside stocking up for a cross-country run for the border, too.

I hunched down and waited for him to come out. He tossed a bottle onto the seat and got in. The way my luck was running, he'd get drunk and run the Lincoln into a tree or something.

Lester eased away from the Gas-N-Go and turned toward Route 18. It looked like he was going out to Carmichael's place. I tailed him out of town until traffic got thin enough that I was afraid I'd be spotted, then peeled off toward the cabin. Something was niggling at me about Lester and Carmichael/Kline, but I couldn't get a handle on it.

My phone chirped again. I checked the readout. It was the Police Department main line. I groaned. I was sick of trying to convince Stryker of my innocence. I punched it on and snapped out a hello. Wil was on the other end. "Hey, man. Glad I caught you."

"What are you doing at work? I thought you were suspended."

I could hear the smile in Wil's voice when he spoke again.

"They had sudden epidemic of the flu around here. I got called in to cover."

"A real epidemic?" I asked.

"Nah, just a little support among officers. I got a lot of friends around here and so do you. Listen, I found out who bonded out your old buddy Lester. Place called Wilder Properties. Apparently he works for them as a handyman."

"That doesn't really help."

"Sorry. It was worth a shot."

"Thanks anyway, man."

I turned onto the lake road. I told Wil to hang on and bounced the rest of the way to the cabin. I parked and picked up the phone again.

"Okay, I'm back. What else you got?"

"I found the report on the burglary at your old babysitter, Mrs. Helstrom's, place. I made a copy of it."

"Have you had a chance to read it?"

"Yeah, they never arrested anybody on that one. Her family all live out east. They put some pressure on the department, but the case was never solved. I just skimmed through it. I'll bring it out tonight."

"Have you heard anything from Rayburn today?"

"Not a word, he's probably still slogging around the internet searching for Charlie."

"I'll give him a shout."

I told Wil I'd see him in a bit, punched off the call and dialed Rayburn.

"How's the search going, buddy?" I asked.

"There are seven hundred and twenty-six thousand hits on Charlie in Missouri, five hundred and twenty-two thousand in Greene County, five hundred and sixty-three thousand in Stantonville. The mayor's brother-in-law is named Charlie as well as the president of the City council and Dean Stryker's kid. According to the white pages, there are two hundred and twenty three Charlie's, Chucks, and Charles' in the Stantonville area. Stryker's kid is the only one even remotely related to this thing and I think it's a pretty safe bet he's not involved.

I sighed. "Okay, let me know if you turn up something."

"I'm going to kick your ass when this little project is over, Harley."

"You'll probably have to get in line. I gotta go, man. Talk to you later."

I punched off before he could answer and stared at the forest around the cabin. Mrs. Helstrom's case was never solved. Another dead end. Everything we turned up raised more questions than answers. We were running in circles and Stryker was closing in. I couldn't see him, but I could feel the net growing tighter. I climbed out of the truck and turned my thoughts away from Stryker. Worrying about him wasn't going to keep me out of jail.

Chapter 18

You know anything about Wilder Properties, Billy?" I asked.

We were sitting on the porch. The laptop was shoved under my chair to make room for a plate of chicken. Billy can almost always be counted on to show up with food. He washed his last bite down with beer before he answered.

"They own a bunch of rental properties in Riker and Stantonville, maybe other places. Why?"

He seemed happy to be talking about something besides the mysterious Charlie.

"I'm looking for a skip who works for them."

"Doesn't have anything to do with Carmichael?"

"No. This is about a repo."

Billy wadded up his paper plate and shot it toward the bed of my truck. It hit the side of the bed and bounced across the driveway. "You hear they called Pinkerton in to work?" he asked.

"Yeah, he called me. Told me about Wilder. Why'd you ask if Wilder had anything to do with Carmichael?"

"Just wondered."

"Try again, Rayburn."

He grinned at me over his shoulder. "I've heard rumors that Carmichael was connected to Wilder's business somehow. Just wondered where you were going with it."

"Connected how?"

"I don't know."

"Can you find out?"

"Probably not without Carmichael finding out who was asking."

"So you're not going to."

Billy turned on the step so we were looking at each other. "Brocs, I can't. It's all I can do to stay in business and not step on any toes as it is. If I go rooting around in Carmichael's business, I'm going to end up broke or dead or both. These guys play for keeps."

I sighed. "Don't worry about it just keep chasing Charlie. I'll find out some other way."

At the mention of the Charlie search, Billy hunched over and stared toward the lake. I dropped my empty plate on the porch and tipped my chair against the cabin wall. If I stayed quiet, Billy would either change his mind about checking up on Wilder or he'd change the subject.

"Get any new information today?"

"Whatever papers Manny had for me are gone. Guess the shooters got 'em."

"Shit."

"I wasn't holding out a lot of hope. You spending the night?"

"No. I just wanted to come out and check on things, see if there's anything you need me to do."

Besides look for Charlie, he meant.

"No, I'm good. Thanks for dinner."

He paused on the steps and turned toward me. "I wish I could do more, Brocs. I..."

I shrugged off his reply. "Don't worry about it. Just find our mystery man."

"You got it. Call me if you need anything else."

Billy left. I finished my beer, and watched the dust settle back onto the gravel road. I lifted the beer can, and found it empty. I crumpled the soft aluminum, and launched it at the truck. It hit the inside of the tailgate and bounced out onto the gravel.

"That's par for the week," I mumbled.

I snagged another beer from the fridge and strolled through the woods to the dock. It was peaceful. Crickets chirped in the tall grass. A slight breeze sent ripples across the lake. A fish broke the surface with a splash. I sat with my back against one of the deck pilings and stared out over the water as the sun sank behind the hills.

Drew and I were up here last summer. Every night we'd come down to the dock and watch the sunset, talk, and drink beer. We'd stay until the beer ran out or the mosquitoes ran us in. The pain of his loss shot through me like a stab wound. I gritted my teeth against it. If one of us had to die young, it should have been me. I must have mumbled that last thought out loud because it got an answer.

"Why would that have been better?"

I snapped my head toward the voice. It was Wil. He was sitting on the dock behind and to my right. He'd come down the path, onto the wooden dock, sat down, opened a beer, and I never knew he was there.

"Jesus, Wil. You scared the hell out of me."

"Better be glad it was me and not a bad guy. You'd be dead."

He was right; my gun was still on my hip. If he'd been out to kill me, I'd be gone.

"You want another beer?" he asked.

"Nah, I need to work tonight. Want to come along?"

"What ya got?"

"Couple of repos. The guys are brothers, live right next to each other. The way I see it, I've got to do them both at the same time or one of the cars will disappear."

"They got garages?"

"Carports."

"Any reason to think this one's going to go like the rest of them have this week?"

"Just Murphy's law."

"That's comforting."

"Up to you. I can disable one, leave with the other and then go back."

"That's just asking for trouble. I'll go with you."

I stood up and stretched. Wil started up the trail to the cabin with me behind him.

As we clomped up the stairs, I said. "I'm gonna crash for a while. We'll head into town about midnight."

Wil nodded and dropped onto the porch steps. I went inside, draped my clothes over the chair next to the bed and pulled the quilt up to my chin. The sky was full dark and stars were just starting to show. I closed my eyes and prayed I wouldn't have another dream.

I woke at eleven-thirty. The cabin was painted with moving shadows from the flicker of the fireplace. I stuck my head in Wil's room and woke him, then went to get dressed. I pulled on a black turtleneck and tucked it into black Levis. I laced up my black running shoes and rummaged in my bag. Inside I found a black stocking hat and shoved it on my head. I loaded the clip on my 9mm, racked a round into the chamber, and snapped it into the holster inside my waistband behind my right hip. I picked up my slim jim, eased it down the right leg of my jeans against my thigh and went out to the kitchen. I fixed a pot of coffee, poured a cup, and was leaning on the counter drinking it when Wil ambled down the hall. He was in black jeans and a black long sleeve tee shirt. He looked at me and grinned.

"That what the well-dressed cat burglar wears these days?" he asked.

"The well-dressed repo man."

He shook his head and buckled into his shoulder rig. He checked the clip in his automatic before he rammed it home.

I rummaged in a drawer in the kitchen until I found a tube of black face paint. I smeared it over my face and hands and tossed it to Wil. He did the same and we both shrugged into our leather jackets.

"We get stopped on the way into town we're both gonna get hauled in," he said with a smile.

"I guess we'd better not get stopped then."

"I'd say with the way your luck's running this week, we don't have a chance."

We got into the cab of my truck and wound out of the hills into Stantonville. Clouds had rolled in again and covered the moon. The cool damp air might settle into fog. That and the lack of moonlight would be good for our plans. I parked the truck two blocks away from our target and we snuck through backyards to get there.

Dark silent houses squatted around us. Our breath made little puffs in the air as the temperature fell. So far, the fog was staying above the trees. No help from Mother Nature tonight. A dog barked when we crept past a fenced-in backyard. We hit the ground and hid in the shadows. The porch light came on. An elderly man in a flowered lady's bathrobe looked around the yard, called the dog inside, and closed the door. The night went quiet. We waited in the shadows until our night vision returned. Wil squatted silent beside me. When I could see, I nudged him and we moved through the yard.

We paused behind a hedge next to a carport. I pointed at the twin cars. They were parked side-by-side in adjoining driveways. Both of them were dark brown Ford Crown Victoria's, maybe a year old, identical in every detail.

"These guys twins?" Wil whispered.

I flashed him a grin in the dark, removed the slim jim and handed it to him. He edged toward the car on the right.

"These guys gonna be armed?" he asked softly.

"Won't matter unless we get caught."

"That makes me feel better."

I stooped at the rear of the car and felt under the bumper. In a little magnetic box I found a key. "Wil," I hissed.

He duck walked a few steps in my direction. I held up the key box and pointed to the rear bumper. He nodded, felt under the bumper and lifted out the hidden key. He pushed open the lid, and dropped the box. It clattered across the concrete driveway. We hunched in the dark behind the two cars and waited, no one came running out with a shotgun. I let out my breath in relief. Wil felt around on the ground until he came up with the key. I motioned him over.

"Put the car in neutral and let it roll out of the drive before you start it. A car on the road won't be noticed as quickly as one starting up in front of the house."

Wil nodded, opened the driver's door and pulled it closed until the latch clicked. The dome light stayed on. I saw him reach up and turn it off. I eased into the other car and did the same. Wil rolled silently out of the drive. No lights flipped on in the sleeping houses. So far so good. I trailed him out of the neighborhood and breathed a sigh of relief as we turned onto the main drag. We were halfway to the car lot when two police cruisers raced up behind us with lights and sirens blaring. I saw Wil glance over his shoulder. He pulled to the side of the road. I parked behind him. Guns drawn, the cops raced up to the cars.

I already had my hands on top of the steering wheel when the officer got to my open window. The guy was in his late forties, paunchy but not soft. He looked like he'd love to have a reason to shoot me.

"Get out real slow and keep your hands where I can see 'em."

I reached through the open window to open the door from the outside. I didn't want this guy to shoot me when I reached for the door handle. I released the latch, pushed the door open with my knee and stepped out.

He spun me against the car. From the corner of my eye, I could see Wil getting the same treatment.

I stood spread-eagled against the ugly brown Taurus while the cop frisked me. I heard him chuckle when he lifted my gun from the holster.

He leaned in close to my ear. "What do we have here, asshole?"

"I'm a licensed recovery agent doing a registered recovery for a client."

"Sure you are, sport."

"Hey, Nicholson," the one frisking Wil yelled. "This one says he's a cop."

"Yeah and I'm the Easter Bunny, Miller. Give me your arm, sleazebag," he growled at me.

He twisted my right arm behind me, snapped on the cuff, pulled the other arm around and repeated the maneuver. I sighed. I hate handcuffs. The cop called Miller had disarmed Wil, cuffed him, then removed something out of the inside pocket of Wil's jacket.

"Uh, Nicholson. You might want to take a look at this."

The kid with Wil was young and now he sounded nervous as he called to his partner.

Nicholson looked over his shoulder at me as he moved toward the kid. "Don't move, jerkoff."

I stayed still and waited while he stomped over to Wil, snatched the wallet out of Miller's hand and flipped it open. Wil's badge glinted in the streetlights. Nicholson stepped closer to Wil and shook his head.

"Pinkerton?"

"Nice to see you too, Nicholson. What the hell were they thinking give you a rookie partner?"

Nicholson ignored Wil's question, closed the badge wallet with a snap and handed it to his partner without a word. Some of the aggression went out of his stance as he returned to my side. He still looked like he'd enjoy an excuse to shoot me.

"What'd you say your name was?"

"I didn't. You never asked."

"Listen smartass, I asked you a question. What's your fucking name?"

"Harley, Brockston Harley. I own H & H Recovery. We repossess things."

"What's he doing with you?" he pointed at Wil with his chin.

"Moonlighting."

Nicholson stalked back to Wil. "You working for him?"

"Yeah."

"Sonovabitch," he muttered. "Unlock him, Miller. You got paperwork say's you can repo these cars?"

"Yeah."

He unlocked the cuffs and hung them on his belt.

"Let me see it."

I reached into the inside pocket of my jacket and pulled out the contracts. He read through both papers and jabbed them back at me.

"Guess you guys can get outta here."

"My gun," I said.

"What?"

"You've still got my gun."

"You got a permit to carry?"

I sighed, removed my wallet and showed him the permit. He grudgingly removed my gun from the overloaded waistband of his uniform pants and handed it over.

"Why'd you stop us?" I asked. "We didn't break any traffic laws."

"Got a call from a lady saw you two skulking around some houses. Then she called again and said you stole two cars."

I nodded and eased behind the wheel of the Taurus.

"We'll just follow you guys till you stop at the lot."

"Of course."

We finished the short drive to the lot with a police escort. They stayed with us until we parked, then peeled off into town.

I got out of the car, lifted my cell phone from my pocket and called Anton Richards. He's the owner of the lot.

"This better be good if you woke me at three in the fucking morning," he answered.

"Got a couple of cars down here I think belong to you."

"Harley, God dammit. Why don't you ever make my recoveries in the daytime?"

"Then I wouldn't get to have these late-night chats with you, Anton."

"I guess you want me to come down there right now and pay you."

"Well, I didn't do it for free."

"Shit. I'm on my way."

"Give us a ride to my truck and I'll buy ya breakfast."

"You're all heart, Harley."

He slammed the receiver in my ear. I returned my phone to my jacket and sat down on the sidewalk outside the showroom. Wil eased down beside me.

"You ever think about getting into another line of work, Brocs?"

"What, and give up all this?"

"I'm serious, man."

"Only when I have weeks like this one. How about you, want to come to work for me full time?"

"You're joking, right?"

I laughed and dug my cigarettes out of my inside pocket. I lit one and handed the pack to Wil. The lighter flared in the dark and he scooted back against the wall.

"I never been cuffed before except in training," he said.

"Not very much fun."

"It hurts like a son of a bitch."

"It can be a lot worse. They were assholes, but they weren't really rough."

I took a last drag of my cigarette and flipped it into the parking lot. Sparks skittered across the asphalt before they went dark. I got another one going and moved back next to Wil.

"Rayburn says there's a connection between Carmichael and Wilder Properties. You know anything about that?"

"No, not about any connection anyway. The guy that runs the place, his name's Otis."

"Wilder?"

"Yeah."

"Think I'll go make his acquaintance tomorrow. Want to come?"

"I think I'll pass. You're not having a very lucky week."

Anton wheeled into the parking lot behind the two Fords. Wil and I were sitting in the shadow of the building. Anton got out of the car in his pajamas and bathrobe. His hair was sticking up all over his head and he pushed it down as he strode toward the Taurus's. Wil and I stood and stepped out of the shadows.

"Jesus!" Anton yelled, grabbing at his heart. "Gave me a damn heart attack."

He stepped closer and stared at us under the lights.

"You look like a couple of commandos. What'd you do, kill the poor bastards before you took the cars?"

"Just pay up, Anton and let's get out of here. It's been a long night."

"Long night my ass, get me up at three in the morning," he mumbled as he unlocked the showroom.

"Look on the bright side," I said. "You can wake up the old lady when you get home and get some before you come back to work."

"More'n my life's worth to wake up the old bat before noon."

I laughed. Anton counted out a thousand bucks and slapped it in my hand. I separated half the bills and handed them to Wil.

"You don't have to do that, Brocs," Wil said.

"I always pay my help. Take it."

He took the money and it disappeared into his pocket.

"You trying to lure me away from the force?"

"Yeah, it working?"

"It's starting to."

We followed Anton to his car. He let us off at the truck and started to drive away.

"I'll buy breakfast," I said.

"Forget it, I'd rather sleep."

He drove off in the direction of town. Wil and I climbed into the truck and headed for Denny's. The parking lot was almost full, shift workers getting ready to head home to bed. We parked and strolled through the front entrance and the restaurant went silent. We looked at each other and started to laugh. Our breakfast arrived in record time. We ate fast and left our poor terrified waitress a hefty tip. You could almost hear the sigh of relief when we stepped outside.

"Maybe next time we should change clothes before we go out to eat," Wil said.

I pointed the truck toward the lake as the sun peeked over the hills.

Chapter 19

Wil was gone when I woke, but the coffee was still hot. I drank a cup, changed into sweats and went for a run. After a quick shower, I drove to my apartment, got rid of my burglar tools and grabbed my suit jacket. I wanted to be properly attired for my meeting with Wilder.

Baldwin was perched on a chair in the hall. I ruffled his fur as I went by. He growled and slapped at my hand. He was definitely not happy about being abandoned the last few days.

Stryker's watchdog, Morris, was lounging against my truck when I came out. He straightened and stepped aside when I got close. I ignored him while I unlocked the truck. He stood in the next parking space staring at me as I eased behind the wheel.

"What do you want now?" I asked.

"Just wanted you to know I'm still around."

"Thanks, I'll sleep better tonight just knowing that."

"Very funny, asshole."

I shot him a cheesy smile as I backed out of the lot. I don't think he was amused. It would have felt good to flip him off, but I wasn't that self-destructive at the moment.

Otis Wilder's office was located in Riker. I took Route 18 out of town, watching my rearview mirror all the way. I didn't see any cops, but I was sure they were watching me. I was running out of time; I had to find the connection between Drew and Carmichael.

I drove around Riker for over an hour before I located the street Wilder's office was on. Barnes Avenue was just an alley off of the main drag. I parked out front, pocketed my keys, and looked up and down the street. The rear bumper of a black Lincoln was sticking out from behind the building. I wandered over to check the plate. It was the right car. This was the right place. Maybe I'd get a shot at ole Lester today. The recovery fee on a forty-thousand dollar car would make up for a lot of bullshit.

I pushed into Wilder's lobby. A bell jangled as I came in and the receptionist glanced up. She was young and would have been pretty with a little less makeup. I crossed the worn linolium and stopped in front of her desk.

"Mr. Harley to see Mr. Wilder."

"Do you have an appointment, sir?"

I shifted until my jacket gaped and uncovered my gun. Her eyes widened and she scooted her chair backwards until it connected with the file cabinet behind her.

"Just tell him that Brockston Harley would like a word with him."

She swallowed and cleared her throat. "One moment, sir."

She retreated down the hall and slipped through the door at the end. A few moments later, she stepped out of the office and motioned for me to come on. I clomped down the hallway to where she waited, reached around her and knocked.

"Come in."

I turned to the receptionist and told her I'd be fine. She retreated to her desk. I twisted the knob and stepped inside. The man behind the desk was skinny with dark greasy hair and acne marks on his neck and face. He stood when I entered. "Mr. Harley, have a seat. How may I help you?"

I thumbed a business card out of my wallet and tossed it across his desk. While he read it, I settled into his visitor chair. He asked again how he could be of help.

"I'm a recovery agent."

He smiled. "Repo man."

"I'm contracted to recover a car that belongs to one of your employees."

"Who would that be?"

"Lester Crawford."

"Ah. Lester. He used to do some handyman work for me. I'm afraid he's no longer employed by my firm."

Wilder was lying. I decided to let him run with it for a while.

"Did he quit?" I asked.

He tipped his chair back and linked his fingers over his stomach before he answered. It was a funny mannerism for a skinny man. I wondered if he did it to keep his fingers still.

"No, Lester didn't quit. I'm afraid we had to let him go."

I sat forward in my chair like he was giving me priceless information.

"When was that? My latest research shows him still employed by your company."

Wilder unclasped his hands as he dropped his chair down on four legs.

"Why, just last week I believe. Bad timing for you I'm afraid." He smiled. Just a good ole boy sharing a joke.

"Yeah, bad timing." I agreed.

I got up from my chair and paced around the office like I was deep in thought. I stopped in front of the window and stared out. The black Lincoln sat outside gleaming in the sunlight. I glanced over my shoulder at Wilder and raised my eyebrows. He busied himself with a stack of papers on the desktop. He tapped out a nervous rhythm against the blotter with his right hand. I winked when he looked up at me.

"You wouldn't know who that car out back belongs to would you, Mr. Wilder?"

He stopped tapping, clasped his hands together again, and stared at me. "What car would that be, the black Lincoln? No sir, I'm sorry. I don't know who drives that."

He took a deep breath and balanced his chair on two legs, he rested his head on a grey spot on the wall behind him. He was trying to appear relaxed and failing miserably.

"I'm sure you'll be seeing Mr. Crawford again," I said. "Give him my card. Tell him to keep an eye on his rearview mirror."

Wilder stared at me for a long minute before he spoke. "I will be glad to give him the message, that is, if I ever see him again. Is there anything else I can do for you today, Mr. Harley?"

"No, that should be all."

I swung away from the window and strolled across the office. Wilder scrambled from his chair to usher me out.

"By the way. Do you happen to know Marcus Carmichael?"

Panic crawled across Wilder's face. His knuckles went white on the doorknob.

"I'm afraid I don't," he said. "Is that another repo you're trying to locate?"

I just grinned and strode down the hall. I had the answer I needed. Lester and Carmichael would both soon know that I had been here asking questions.

I sketched a salute at the receptionist as I went out. As I angled away from the curb, I saw Otis Wilder standing at the front window watching. I smirked and wondered what was going to fall out of the tree I'd just shaken.

At the cabin, I packed my stuff and Billy's laptop, and drove to town. It was time to move my operations back to Stantonville before Baldwin locked me out of the apartment. while I drove, I tried to work out a connection between Carmichael's crew and my brother. So far, the Austin-Kline deal was all we had and that could be a simple business matter. We were wandering in circles. I called Wil and told him I was going home. Then I called Rayburn to find out how his search was coming. His secretary giggled when I identified myself, then transferred me to Billy.

"Man, this Charlie thing is a dead end."

"I take it you haven't found the infamous Charlie."

"I've found a zillion Charlies, but I can't hook any of them up with any of the other players in this drama."

"Dammit, I know what I heard."

"I'm not doubting you, bro. I just don't think it's important. I'm gonna give it the rest of the afternoon, but that's it."

"Fair enough. Thanks, Billy."

I snapped the phone closed and parked in my lot. Baldwin winked down at me from the fridge as I strode in and tossed my bags. I deposited the laptop on the kitchen table and fixed myself a drink. As the bourbon burned a trail to my stomach, I dialed Melinda. She answered on the first ring.

"Hey there."

"Brocs, are you home?"

"Yeah, want to go out to dinner?"

"I'd rather stay in. How bout I see you at your place around six?"

The phone clicked in my ear. I cradled it and took a minute to ponder the pleasures of the near future. Baldwin padded into the living room behind me and parked on the coffee table as I stretched out on the couch for a nap. I was counting on not getting much sleep tonight.

A couple hours later, Baldwin was curled up in my recliner and Melinda was curled up in my lap. The stereo played softly in the background. Her clothes and mine were scattered down the hallway. The bed was a tangle of sheets and blankets and we were both pleasantly relaxed.

I had on a pair of worn gray sweat pants and nothing else. Melinda was wrapped in my robe. I sat stretched out, feet on the coffee table, head against the couch cushions, my hand under the robe, wondering if I should shower before we went out to eat. I brushed my fingers lightly across Melinda's breast. She ran her hand up the inside of my thigh. Thoughts of dinner skittered away. I brushed her lips with mine. She shrugged her shoulders and the robe slithered to the floor.

We lay together, nothing between us but a thin layer of sweat. The stereo still played, Baldwin still slept, the robe and sweats were in a pile on the floor. My stomach growled. Melinda peeled herself off the couch. I tried to pull her back and she swatted my hand.

"I'm as hungry as you are, take me out to dinner."

I dragged myself off the couch and joined her in the shower and that delayed dinner again. We eventually made our way out of the bathroom. I nuzzled her neck as she buttoned her jeans. "Darlin, you are the only good thing that's happened to me all week."

"You can tell me all about it over dinner."

I dressed and we headed to the Dragon's Claw. It was the only place in Stantonville where you could get dinner after ten. Well, except for Denny's and I wasn't sure they'd be happy to see me again.

We sat across from each other in a corner booth and ate mini egg rolls while we waited for our food. I gave her an abbreviated account of the last few days. She chuckled over the repo stories and told me I should write a book.

Our food came and we settled in to eat. We had both worked up an appetite. When we finished, I ordered drinks. Mel moved over next to me and settled in the crook of my arm.

I twined my fingers with hers and gave her hand a squeeze. She leaned her head against my shoulder. It was the first time since Drew died that I'd been completely relaxed.

"What happened between you and Halston, Brocs?"

I blew out a long breath and didn't answer for a minute. "It's not something I want to get into here. Let's go back to the apartment."

She smiled as she stood up.

"What are you grinning about?" I asked.

"I thought you'd tell me it wasn't any of my business."

I shrugged and took her hand. I was more comfortable with Melinda than anyone I'd ever gone out with. I'd been asked about my family before and never had any inclination to discuss it. I don't know what was different, maybe I just needed to talk about it because Drew was gone. Maybe, I was falling in love.

At the apartment, Melinda and I curled up on the couch. Baldwin was gone from his chair, but as soon as we got quiet, he showed up. He hopped onto the back of the couch and sat there staring at us. Melinda reached up to pet him and he ducked his head so she could scratch his ears.

"I think you've made a friend," I said.

"Two of them, I hope."

I slid my arms around her and held her close. "I hope I'm more than that."

She lay with her head cradled on my shoulder and listened while I told the abbreviated story of my childhood. I kissed the top of her head when I finished. She reached up and brushed her fingers across my face.

"Now I know why you have sad eyes."

I felt like she was staring into my soul. For the first time in my life, I didn't shy away from it.

"Your turn," I said. "Tell me about you."

"Boring stuff. I had a perfectly happy, normal suburban childhood, big house, two cars, two point three kids and a dog. Then I left for college."

"So you aren't an only child. Are you the oldest or youngest?"

I felt her tense, then she took a big breath and blew it out.

"I'm the oldest. I have a brother."

"Does he live around here?"

"You don't want to hear about this stuff."

"Fine, no family information. At least you can tell me your dog's name."

"He was Danny's dog. I never had much to do with him."

She ducked out from under my arm and hurried down the hall to the bathroom.

"Baldwin, I think I just screwed up."

I was trespassing in her personal space. I knew the drill. I'd done it before myself, dozens of times. If she ran true to form, the next time I called, she would be busy, or she'd make the date and stand me up. It was funny, I finally found someone I could open up to, and she wouldn't talk to me. And instead of recognizing the signs, I'd just kept pushing until she bolted. Dammit. Guess I'd try a little damage control when she came back.

I took our empty glasses to the kitchen, then settled again on the couch. Melinda joined me, but the ease between us was gone. I laid my arm along the back of the couch and ran my fingers through her hair.

"Mel, I really care about you. If there's something you don't want to talk about, it's okay. I understand."

"No, you don't understand, but that's okay for now."

She relaxed by my side and I pulled her down on the couch. We lay together not talking, Melinda still not totally at ease. I started thinking about my meeting with Wilder. I wasn't sure why I'd made him so nervous. He must have thought I knew more than I did. Melinda shifted in my arms to look at me. "You got so still, I thought you were asleep."

I shook myself back to the present. "Nah, just thinking. Had an odd encounter today."

"With?"

"Otis Wilder."

"He's a nasty piece of work."

"You know him?"

"Sure, we do a lot of business with Wilder Properties. They buy a lot of rentals, mostly office buildings."

"Rumor has it that Carmichael is tied up with them somehow. Know anything about that?"

"Not offhand, but I can check into it. Is this about Drew?"

"I'm not sure what it's about yet."

"I'll see what I can find."

"Be careful who finds out you've been asking."

"No one will find out."

We lay together a while longer, just holding each other, but Mel never did really relax again. Finally, she scooted out of my arms and sat up. "I really need to go, I've got an early day tomorrow."

I wanted to ask her to stay, but something held me back. I walked her outside to her car trying to figure out how to undo the damage my innocent question seemed to have wrought.

"I'll talk to you tomorrow, Brocs."

I hoped she meant it. Mel must have read my mind. She brushed the hair off my forehead and kissed me softly. "Stop worrying, I'm not going to run away."

I stared across the parking lot as she drove away and smiled. Maybe, just maybe, my luck was starting to change. I strolled back into my building and stopped just inside. My shoulders drooped in frustration when I saw who was waiting there. Detective Stryker.

I sighed. "Don't you ever sleep?"

"I could ask the same about you. Course, if I had that around, I wouldn't be doing much sleeping either."

I lunged forward. Stryker backed up until he was against the wall. I pressed in until we were nose to nose. It took all my restraint to keep my hands at my sides. I wanted to strangle him. "Don't you say one word about Melinda. Do you understand me?"

Our eyes were locked and I was close enough to hear him breathe. He dropped his gaze. "I'm sorry, that was completely out of line. I apologize."

I stepped away still breathing hard and Stryker's muscles relaxed. We stood silent in the entry of the building while I got my temper under control.

"What the hell do you want?"

"I'd like to have another look at your apartment."

"Christ, it's almost midnight."

"I'm aware of that."

I shook my head. "You're a real pain in the ass, detective."

I didn't have to let him in, but I didn't have anything to hide. The sooner he figured that out, the sooner Drew's killer would be found. The sooner I'd have him off my back. I motioned toward the stairs and he trudged up behind me. Baldwin hissed when Stryker strode in behind me. I smiled and tossed my jacket over the chair.

"Are you searching for anything in particular? I asked. "Can I help you find something?"

"No, thank you."

"I'd really appreciate it if you didn't make quite as big a mess this time."

A smile flashed across Stryker's face. I poured a drink, and took Baldwin's spot in the recliner. The robe and sweat pants were still on the floor. The bed was still a tangled mess. I sipped my bourbon and waited for Stryker to finish.

Stryker took in the clothing on the floor but didn't comment. If he had, I would have knocked the shit out of him. All in all, I was disappointed. I would have enjoyed popping him.

He smoothed a pair of latex gloves over his fingers and strolled along the shelves of books, sliding one out at random, flipping the pages, pushing it back into place. He paused at the criminal justice books. They were worn and used. He took one down, glanced through it and smiled before he replaced it and turned toward me. "I'm afraid you've gotten Wil Pinkerton into a bit of trouble at work."

"Wil Pinkerton is an outstanding cop. If you guys don't recognize it soon, I'm going to hire him away from you."

"You're assuming you'll still have a business."

"I'm assuming you're chasing your tail or you wouldn't be wandering around here scrabbling for evidence in the middle of the night. You don't have a clue who killed my brother, do you?"

"I have a gun with your fingerprints."

"Then why haven't you arrested me?"

"There are some other issues that need to be dealt with first."

"That's bullshit, Stryker."

He turned away and continued to page through my books. I slumped in the chair.

"So, tell me about your investigation, Mr. Harley."

"I've asked a lot of questions."

"And?"

"And I've created a lot more questions."

"But no answers."

"Not yet. But I haven't wasted a lot of taxpayer money and manpower watching the one person in this town that would never have harmed Drew Harley."

"So, who would have killed Andrew Harley?"

"I won't know that until I know why."

A small smile touched the corners of his mouth briefly and disappeared. It stayed longer in his eyes, but it died there too.

"Stryker, what possible motive do I have for killing my brother?"

He turned away from the shelves and looked me in the eye. "Jealousy, Mr. Harley. It's one of the oldest motives in the world."

"What was I jealous of?"

"His life."

"You can't prove that."

"Hmm."

He turned away and I stared at the floor.

"You know something, Stryker. You were the only cop who ever busted me that wasn't a total prick. You didn't treat me like a second-class citizen. You treated me like the dumb, confused kid I was. I always thought, or hoped anyway, that my dad was that kind of cop. What happened to you?"

Stryker glared at me in silence. A shadow passed across his face before he turned and moved toward the entry. He snapped off his rubber gloves before he stepped out into the hall.

"Goodnight, Mr. Harley."

Chapter 20

My phone rang at eight the next morning. I was awake, but not up. I snagged the receiver prepared to tell Nick to go fuck himself. It wasn't Nick. It was Detective Stryker.

"Good Morning, Mr. Harley."

I swallowed a groan. "What now, Stryker?"

"I'd like to see you this morning. Could you meet me somewhere?"

Shit. "When and where?"

"You name the time and place, Mr. Harley, and I'll be there."

"I'll meet you at Doc's around nine."

"Very good."

The phone went silent in my ear. I cradled it and got dressed. I made sure Baldwin had food and water and had almost made my escape when the phone rang again. I snatched up the receiver. "Talk fast, I'm on my way out."

"It's Melinda."

Muscles that I hadn't known were tensed relaxed at the sound of her voice. "Hey, good morning. My day just improved a hundred percent."

"There was a car in your lot when I left last night that looked suspiciously like an unmarked police car. Wanted to make sure you weren't behind bars."

"Not yet, but the day is young. I'm on my way to meet Stryker now."

"I found out something about Wilder for you."

"Already? You work fast."

"So I've heard."

"So, tell me about Wilder."

"Wilder doesn't own the business. He manages it for a guy named Glen Austin. I couldn't find any connection with Carmichael. Sorry."

I smiled to myself, but didn't explain the connection.

"You did great, Melinda. Thanks."

"Oops, Halston's here, gotta go."

I hung up the phone and continued outside. The weather was clear and almost warm. I walked to the truck, then looked at my Harley and decided I really needed to ride today. I straddled the bike while it warmed up and let my mind wander. I didn't want to meet with Stryker. I just wanted to take off. Ride into the mountains and disappear for a while. The rumble of the engine shoved my unpleasant thoughts to the background. It was too nice a day not to try and enjoy it.

I took the long way to Doc's, but Stantonville's not that big and I arrived outside the restaurant way too soon. Stryker's car was parked in the lot when I rode in. I stopped next to it and shut off the engine. In the sudden quiet, I pushed the kickstand and stared off down the road. The need to get away from everything was almost a physical ache. With a sigh, I eased out of the saddle and ran my fingers through my windblown hair. I was startled by a voice close behind me. "I get that urge, too. Never had a bike, though."

I turned toward the speaker. Stryker was slouched against the side of the building, hands shoved deep into the pockets of his Dockers. His face was strained and dark circles ringed his eyes. It didn't appear that he'd slept much the night before. I checked the parking lot to see if he had reinforcements in place. I didn't spot anyone else. "You here to arrest me?"

"No, just to talk."

I checked once more, not sure whether to believe him. I still didn't see any other cops. With a shrug, I pushed into Doc's. Stryker followed me to a booth in the rear and scooted onto the seat facing the back of the room.

"You like your eggs scrambled?" I asked.

"That's fine."

I held up two fingers to Doc, he gave me nod and turned to the grill.

"You come in here often?" he asked.

"I don't like to cook."

Stryker's expression relaxed, and he settled back into the booth.

We sat without talking. Doc brought orange juice and coffee. A few minutes later he returned with two plates, scrambled eggs, toast, and sausage. We ate, still without talking.

I tried to read something in Stryker's face. It was closed. So far, he hadn't given me a clue as to why we were here. I ate and wondered if he was going to spring some new evidence on me, like he did with the gun the last time we met over food. I finished eating and pushed my plate away. Stryker was still deeply involved with his breakfast and still silent. I studied him over my coffee cup. Something was different with him today, but I couldn't determine what. I lifted my coffee cup and found it empty. Stryker laid his fork across his plate. I caught Doc's eye and tipped my coffee cup. Doc topped off our coffee and took away the empty plates. I waited for Stryker to speak. He stirred in sweetener and sipped his coffee, apparently in no hurry to start. I shifted on the vinyl seat and stared toward the front windows. This was Stryker's game, if he wanted to sit and not talk, I wasn't going to argue. He finally placed his cup carefully on the table and met my gaze.

"You're right about me," he said. "I wanted it to be you. I wanted the answer to be easy and I didn't look anywhere else."

I hunched forward and started to speak. Stryker held up his hand. "You were so cocky when I busted you as a kid. So sure you weren't going to jail. I hated that and I hated that there was nothing I could do to keep you locked up. When I realized who you were, I wanted to get even."

I stayed silent, so he continued. "Your .22 with your fingerprints was found with your brother's body. It was meant to look like a suicide. I believe the killer assumed the gun belonged to your brother. That's where he made his mistake. Your brother's fingerprints are not on that gun. Only yours. That presented me with an open and shut case except for one thing. There are smudges, probably made by latex gloves, on top of your fingerprints."

I nodded.

"You already knew that didn't you?"

I gave him a noncommittal shrug.

"You know, Wil Pinkerton could be fired for passing you that information."

"You aren't going to turn him in."

Stryker fiddled with the handle on his mug and stared into its contents before he answered. "No, I'm not going to turn him in. He's a good cop."

Stryker went silent. Doc came around and warmed up our coffee. Stryker fiddled with the sweetener packets, but didn't add them to his coffee. Then he spoke.

"Mr. Harley, I've spent a great deal of time watching you and talking to you. I learned something, but I chose to ignore it until now. I learned that if you were going to kill someone, you wouldn't make a stupid mistake. You are not a stupid man. You also aren't the screwed up kid I busted all those years ago."

I sipped my lukewarm sludge and slouched down with the cup cradled on my chest. The knots of tension in my shoulders diminished a little as I waited for him to go on. When he continued, he didn't meet my eyes and his voice was so soft it barely reached across the table. "You were right, what you said last night. I'm not the cop I was back then. Politics and lawyers have soured me on the system. I watch thugs walk with a slap on the wrist after we've spent months bringing them down." He glanced up and met my stare. "That's not an excuse, just an explanation. I probably should get out, but I'd like to retire with my pension."

He shrugged gave me a self-deprecating grin. I parked my elbows on the table. "What do you want from me?"

"I've put myself behind the eight-ball. Now I have to play catch-up. I thought maybe, since you have some interest in seeing justice done in this case, and have spent some time working on it, that perhaps we could work together."

"Off the record of course."

"Well, yeah, off the record."

I stared at the coffee cooling in my cup. I swirled it around and then pushed it aside.

"I told you last night that I'd asked some questions and all I had for my time were more questions. I have a lot of things that seem to be connected, but none of them connect with Drew. I'm afraid I won't be a great deal of help."

"Give me what you have, let me play with it, see if I can make a connection you haven't."

"And for that I get what?"

"Hmm. That's the question isn't it? Me off your ass for one thing, I guess."

I picked up my mug, curled my lip at the greasy dregs there and put it down.

"Let me think it over. I'll call you."

"Soon, Mr. Harley."

I smiled. "Call me Brocs."

Stryker stood when I got up to leave and we shook hands. I could feel his eyes following me as I wove my way between the tables and out of the restaurant. I stopped next to my bike and took a deep breath. The sense of impending doom was gone. I dialed Melinda's cell phone to share the good news.

"Hey, Mel," I said when she picked up.

"Oh, hi, Brocs."

Okay, that wasn't the most heartfelt greeting ever, but I pressed on. "I got some really good news just now, got time to grab a cup of coffee somewhere?"

I could hear voices in the background and Melinda speaking to someone else, then she came back on. "What was that?" she asked?

"I said I have some really good news, wondered if we could grab a cup of coffee somewhere so I could share it."

The voices in the background were back and it was a long time before she answered. I straddled the Harley and waited.

"Okay, sorry about that. Um, you said coffee, sure, where do you want to meet?"

"How about Denny's in half hour or so?"

"Right, okay. I'll catch you there."

I punched the 'off' button and dropped the phone in my jacket pocket. To say she sounded less than enthused to meet me would have been an understatement. I fired the bike and killed a little time riding around town, then parked at Denny's and went inside. Mel's car wasn't outside, but it had only been twenty minutes. I got a table and ordered coffee. Ten minutes went by and Mel still wasn't there. I got a refill and ordered a piece of pie. I finished the pie and the better part of a pot of coffee before I looked at my watch again—forty minutes had passed. I'd read the menu six times, the backs of the sugar packets and the ingredients in the non-dairy creamer. Mel wasn't going to show.

Face it, Brocs old buddy. You blew it last night. The only reason she called this morning was because she'd already promised to find out about Wilder for you. I scooted out of the booth and tossed the tip money down next to my pie plate.

I paid my bill and went back to my bike. I dialed Mel's cell phone, but it went straight to her voicemail. I didn't leave a message. There wasn't any reason to. What was I going to say?

I stared down the road and sighed. The weather was perfect. I had a motorcycle. So I didn't get to share my good news, I could still celebrate. I climbed on and rode out of town. Stryker and I were on the same team now. I hoped it wasn't too late to find Drew's killer.

I rode over the hill roads Billy and I had traveled the other day. No real destination in mind, just enjoying the weather and the feeling of no longer having an ax hanging over my head. I took a twisted route towards Billy's house, getting ready to head home, when I realized how close I was to Marcus Carmichael's place. It was just after noon and the place looked quiet, not deserted, but nothing much going on. Maybe it was time for a visit with Marcus.

I turned around and headed back to town to change into my leathers. They were better for intimidation than jeans and I wanted every advantage when I went to face Carmichael. The sun was warm on my black jacket as I rode around Cedar Lake for the second time that day. I parked the bike off the road and fished my phone out of my pocket to call Wil.

"I'm going to try and talk to Marcus Carmichael," I said when he answered. "I'm at his place on the lake now."

"So?"

"So, if I don't show up at home tonight, you might send in the Marines."

"You think it's a good idea to go in there the way your week's been going?"

I ignored him and went on. "Pass along a message to Stryker for me."

Now I really had his attention. "You want me to give Stryker a message from you?"

"Yeah, tell him where I am, then tell him I'm going to give the tree another shake and see what falls out."

"Anything else?"

"Tell him if I make it home tonight, I'll meet him in his office tomorrow."

"Right. You sure you know what you're doing?"

"I hope so, bud."

I clicked off my cell phone and stowed it in the inside pocket of my coat. My 9mm was under my shoulder. My .22 was in the pocket of my jeans, undetectable I hoped, under my leather chaps. If everything went well, I wouldn't need either one. I fired the bike and idled up to the gates of Marcus Carmichael's fortress.

I pushed a call button on the box outside the entrance. Video surveillance cameras swiveled in my direction. I ignored them. A man strode out of the guardhouse halfway up the drive and stopped just inside the gates.

"What do you want?" he asked.

He was about my height with the hulking shape of a serious body builder. I wouldn't want to take him on one on one. He had arms the size of my thighs.

I stepped toward the gate and stopped two feet away. The cameras followed to keep me in sight.

"I'm here to see Carmichael," I said.

"What's this about?"

"That's between him and me."

"That ain't gonna get it, bub."

"It's all you're getting."

He took a couple of steps away from the gate and spoke into a radio, his gaze never left my face. I stood relaxed, watching him from half closed eyes. He holstered the radio and came to the gate.

"Take the drive up to the house, park at the steps."

I nodded, mounted the bike, and fired it up. When the gates opened, I rode through and parked behind a Cadillac Escalade and a little BMW like Billy's that was almost hidden by the bulk of the SUV. Another guard met me at the foot of the stairs and led me up to a porch that ran along the entire front of the house. Holding it up were columns that wouldn't have been out of place in the Deep South. I trailed the guard toward two heavy oak doors with hand-carved relief work across the top and down the sides. A battering ram would have a tough time getting through them. They opened onto a marble-floored foyer the size of my apartment. Potted trees and plants dotted the entryway. A waterfall trickled into a rock-lined pool. I expected to hear birdsong. A skylight above patched the shining floor with pools of light. We stepped inside and I glanced around trying to locate the surveillance cameras. They were well hidden, probably in the trees, but I was sure they were there. Carmichael was probably watching me right now.

"You packin?" the guard asked.

"Sure," I said.

"Gotta have it, dude."

I started to reach under my jacket. He brushed my hand away, and lifted my nine from the holster under my arm. He turned it over in his hand, nodded his approval and placed it carefully into the drawer of the hall table. His admiration for my piece made him careless, I guess, because he didn't pat me down. I still had the .22. Of course, he didn't need to be too careful. He had plenty of help. My earlier perusal of the hall assured me I wouldn't live to tell about it if I got into a firefight with my pocket gun. There were three more thugs I could see, no telling how many more hidden away. Carmichael was awfully paranoid for an honest citizen.

"This way," the guard said.

I trailed him down the marble hallway. The walls were lined with scowling portraits. I wondered if they were actual family members or if Carmichael just picked them up at an art auction. We stepped into a book-lined study. As I walked in, there was movement behind Carmichael's desk as someone ducked through the door behind him.

"He's here, Mr. Carmichael."

"Fine. Leave and close the doors behind you."

"Yes, sir."

The guard pointed toward Carmichael. I moved into the room as my guide retreated. I resisted the urge to check if I was now locked in.

Carmichael sat enthroned behind a desk that made Rayburn's look like a child's toy. A door behind his desk appeared to lead to a bathroom. Unless I missed my guess, another thug was hunkered down in there listening to our conversation. Carmichael stood as I came forward and motioned for me to sit. We locked eyes. His were blank, nothing showing, the ultimate poker player. I tried to match his look and held it until he turned away. Then I sat.

"What can I do for you, Mr. Harley?" he asked.

I didn't ask how he knew my name.

"First you can tell me what I'm supposed to call you. Marcus, Glen, Bailey?"

He rearranged his face into a semblance of a smile. "I see you've been doing your homework, Mr. Harley."

I sat silent and waited for him to continue. He straightened the already neat papers on his desk. I slouched in my seat, crossed my ankles and watched from beneath hooded eyes.

"You may call me Marcus," he said.

I nodded.

"Now, what brings you here, Mr. Harley, or may I call you Brocs?"

"Mr. Harley is fine."

Carmichael stiffened in his chair. I grinned to myself. We were playing a juvenile game of one-upmanship. So far, I was ahead.

"Tell me what you know about the death of my brother."

Carmichael's features composed themselves into an expression of sadness. It wasn't any more sincere than his smile.

"Very sad," he said. "Drew was a wonderful man. It's always such a shame to see a young man take his own life. I understand he had just gotten engaged. I called your father and gave him my condolences."

I clamped down on my anger and stayed relaxed in the chair.

"Tell me about a man named Lester Crawford."

Carmichael's eyes widened briefly, then went back to normal.

"Lewis Crawford, did you say?"

"Lester."

"Lester Crawford. Hmm. That name doesn't ring any bells. May I ask what this is about?"

"I understood he was an employee of yours."

"He may have been. I have a great many employees. I don't know them all."

"I believe he worked for Otis Wilder."

Some of the tension went out of his shoulders when I said that.

"Well, he couldn't have been an employee of mine then, could he? May I offer you a drink, cigar, cigarette, Mr. Harley?"

"No thanks. What's your connection with Halston Harley?"

"Your father?"

"Halston Harley is not my father."

"Oh, that's right. Forgive me. I forgot that was a sore spot with you."

His expression told me that he knew very well how I felt about Halston Harley. How the hell did he know that? Score one for the bad guys.

"We do some business with Harley Real Estate. We do a great deal of real estate business and I try to spread the wealth, so to speak." He raised his hands in a gesture of benevolence. His face rearranged into what passed for his smile. I stood from my chair and glared at him until he turned away.

"Tell me what happened to my mother," I said.

He checked his watch, then stood and held out his hand guiding me toward the door. Tension corded the muscles in his neck and pulled his face into a grimace. "I'm sorry, Mr. Harley, I have another appointment. I hope I've been able to help with your inquiries."

I ignored his hand and stepped away.

"I hope so too."

I turned and stalked across the office.

"Mr. Harley."

I stopped and turned around.

"You should be careful…about sticking your nose into other people's business. It could be unhealthy."

It wasn't the voice from the phone, but the message was similar. Close enough that fear ran its cold fingers up my spine. I kept my face blank. Now I knew who the players were. I just needed to get out of here alive and find out what game we were playing.

"I'm sure we'll talk again, Carmichael," I said.

"I doubt it. I hope you find whatever it is you're searching for."

"Oh I will. I have no doubt about it."

I pushed out of the office and clattered down the marble hall. My footsteps echoed off the walls. The guard removed my gun from the drawer and handed it to me as I drew even with him. I rammed it under my arm and stepped outside. The sun was low in the western sky, just a smudge of orange and purple through the trees. I stood for a minute and let my eyes adjust to the soft light. Behind me, the guard remained on the porch until I started down the stairs.

My bike was still parked where I left it. The Escalade was gone, but the Beamer was still there. My phone rang inside my jacket pocket. I ignored it and gave the Harley a quick once over before I threw my leg across. I didn't really think they'd do something to the bike. That was too obvious. I didn't actually think they'd do anything today, but I had no doubt I'd be hearing from Carmichael soon. The message tone sounded on my phone before I started the engine. I ignored it as well and idled to the gates. They swung open. I rode through and I decided to take the long route home.

Chapter 21

My headlight threw shadows across the road as I wove the bike through the hills. I mulled over what, if anything, my visit with Carmichael had accomplished. Maybe all I had done was to let him know how little information I really had. I ran through the conversation and decided it had mostly been a waste of time. It confirmed my suspicions. Carmichael knew something about Drew's death and maybe about Mom's as well, but I hadn't learned anything concrete. I still had no proof and now Carmichael knew I suspected him.

I checked my rearview mirror. Headlights glowed behind me in the distance. The road twisted and turned its way to the top of the ridge before dipping down to the valley below. Guardrails circled the corners to keep foolish drivers from landing in the tops of pine trees. I checked my mirrors again. The lights were still there. I was relaxed, riding slow and careful, in no real hurry to get home. I kept my eyes peeled, watching for gravel in the corners and enjoying the night, the twisty hill road and the ride. I scanned my mirrors. The lights behind me had moved closer.

I felt a slight squiggle of concern, but shook off my paranoia. I was letting my imagination get the best of me. I leaned into the next corner and the lights disappeared. The road fell off into a long hill with an escape ramp for trucks. At the bottom, I turned again and started up the last big incline before the road dropped into the valley.

When the road straightened, I checked my mirrors. The headlights were closing in fast. It wasn't just my imagination. A surge of adrenaline raced through my system. I clamped my hands tighter on the grips and pressed my feet down hard on the pegs to keep them from shaking. I took a couple of deep breaths and wished I were wearing a helmet.

The headlights grew larger. I could hear the car engine over the cackle of the bike as it tucked in close to my rear wheel. I looked ahead for an escape route. Nothing, no one ever needs to escape on the uphill side.

"Shit."

I picked up my speed. I couldn't ride any faster on that road. My bike wasn't built for it. I could see a turn coming up. If I could make it around that corner, I could hammer it down the other side. If I reached the valley, I knew I could lose them.

I leaned into the curve and accelerated. I could feel the bike wiggle beneath me as I lost traction. The car gently tapped my rear wheel. The little wiggle got out of control. I popped up out of my lean to keep from losing the bike and getting run over.

The guardrail rushed toward me, the tops of the pine trees rising above it. I kicked away from the Harley as the front wheel smacked the barrier. As the back wheel leapt off the road, I pushed off and rolled into a ball. The rear of the bike catapulted me over the guardrail.

I tucked my head inside my arms. Tree limbs grabbed at me as I fell. The pine boughs slowed my fall and with a last crunch, I fell free of the branches. I hit the ground with a thud. My breath whooshed out and I lay on my back, trying to remember how to inhale.

I stared up into the tree above me. The branches swam in and out of focus. To my left, further down the hill something was burning. My bike.

I closed my eyes. When I opened them, the branches above my head were still. My lungs seemed to be functioning again. I took a deep breath and felt a stab of pain on my left side. Cracked rib maybe. I rolled to my right side. Pain radiated out from my ribs. I waited for it to subside. I tried to sit and let out a groan as I sagged to the ground on my back.

I bent my knees and waited for the waves to recede. As they eased to a dull throb, I ran an inventory. Arms and legs still seemed to be attached and in somewhat working order. I turned my head slowly from side to side. Neck was sore, but didn't feel broken. I twisted slightly. My ribs twinged. I held tense against the onslaught and rolled quickly into a sitting position.

It was awful. I sat, arms draped across my knees, head down and didn't move again until the worst had passed. I made another inventory of injuries—lots of bruises and scrapes. Blood ran down my face from a cut on my forehead. I wiped my eyes clear. A cut on my thigh looked like it might need stitches. My jeans were sticky with blood beneath my leathers. I flexed my arms and fingers. The pain was intense, but not sharp. Abused muscles, not broken bones. I squinted up through the tree and followed the path of my crash marked with broken branches. I felt damn lucky to be alive. I said a heartfelt thank you to the makers of my leathers and pushed to my feet.

When I stood, my vision darkened. I hunched against the trunk of the tree I'd just fallen through and willed my knees not to buckle. My stomach lurched. I bent over and threw up. Not much there, I hadn't eaten since breakfast. I gagged a couple of times, then spit and concentrated on keeping my stomach quiet. When it quit rolling, I straightened and tried to get my bearings.

I was almost to the valley floor. The highway was about a quarter of a mile away. My bike still smoldered off to my left. I said goodbye to the Harley and moved toward the road. The going was slow. My mashed and torn muscles didn't want to cooperate. I shuffled toward the highway until my knees would buckle. When that happened, all I could do was breathe, wait for my strength to return, and stumble back to my feet. The quarter mile hike took over an hour.

I made it to the highway and wondered if I could thumb a ride. I looked at my torn, bloodstained clothes, and decided it wasn't likely. I stayed in the shadows and moved down the road until I could see a mile marker. When I was sure of my location, I searched for a place to wait. A pile of rocks stood off to my right and I stumbled toward them. In the dark, facing away from the road, I sank to the ground. Slumped against the rocks, I waited for my quivering muscles to still and my breathing to return to normal. I felt secure in the darkness. I needed to call Wil if my phone was still in one piece. I closed my eyes just for a minute.

When I opened them again I guessed a couple of hours had passed. The moon had moved across the sky. My leathers were wet with dew and I shivered with cold and shock. I couldn't remember whether or not I called Wil before I passed out. I fumbled at my jacket pocket for my cell phone, glad to find it still there. I worked it out and prayed that it wasn't broken. I patted my shoulder holster and found it empty. I felt in my pocket for the .22. It was there, but I'd have to roll onto my side to get it out. Just the thought of moving sent an ache through my whole body. I left it where it was.

The cover on my cell phone was broken. I pushed the 'on' button, expecting nothing. To my surprise, it lit up. I shuddered with relief and dialed Wil at the office. He didn't pick up. I tried him at home. Nothing.

"Come on, Wil," I whispered.

I dialed his cell phone and he answered before the first ring finished.

"Brocs?"

"Hey, Wil. Mind giving me a ride home?"

"Where are you and where the hell have you been?"

"Tell you when you get here."

"What's wrong? Brocs, what happened?"

"Just come get me."

I told him where I was waiting, then sagged against the rocks and closed my eyes. The adrenaline had left my system. My teeth chattered with the cold. Every torn and crushed nerve ending clambered for my attention. I tried to think of something else. Melinda came to mind. I tried to pursue that, but I fell asleep or passed out. I woke when someone called my name. "Harley! Jesus, Brocs. Wake up."

I squinted through swollen eyes and grinned. Wil knelt next to me. Dean Stryker was standing behind him.

"Well, Mr. Harley. You shook the tree. What fell out?" Dean asked.

"Just me." I answered.

"Jesus, Brocs," Wil said. "You should have told me to bring an ambulance."

"It's not as bad as it looks."

"Man, you haven't seen how bad you look."

"Just give me a ride home."

"I'll give you a ride to the ER."

Dean and Wil helped me to my feet. That amount of movement was too much. I jerked away and hunched against the rocks until everything settled down again. Between them, I hobbled to the car. I lay down on the backseat and closed my eyes. Wil covered me with a blanket from the trunk. Dean took his place behind the wheel and started the car. Wil sat beside him and turned around to watch me, apparently to make sure I didn't die before we got to the hospital.

"Brocs," Dean said.

"Yeah."

"I'm thinking Melinda's going to be a bit disappointed in your physical condition."

"I don't think she'll care one way or the other."

He and Wil traded looks. I didn't offer any more information. I didn't have the energy. I hobbled into the ER between my rescuers. The nurse behind the desk went pale and motioned wide-eyed for us to follow her. We made it to an exam room and I crumpled onto the bed. I closed my eyes and waited for relief. Wil stood next to me. I took a deep breath and looked up at him.

"Don't let them cut off my leathers."

"I'm not too worried about your damn leathers, Brocs."

I reached down and started to unzip the right leg. The muscles in my abdomen cramped and left me breathless. I clenched my teeth and hunched over until they relaxed. When the cramp had passed, I slumped exhausted against the pillow.

Wil stood over me, his face ashen. "You just stay still," he said. "Don't do that again."

I nodded. He unzipped my chaps and folded them over his arm. I motioned for Dean. He came over and I pointed to my right pocket. He reached inside, worked out my .22 and dropped it into his coat pocket. I lay still for a minute, gathering my strength, then sat up very slowly. Wil eased off my jacket, unbuckled the shoulder rig and folded it inside my coat. I slumped against the pillows, gritted my teeth and fought back waves of nausea.

"What happened to your nine, Brocs?" Wil asked.

"Lost it when I crashed."

"Want me to try and find it?"

I shook my head, eyes closed.

"Can you tell us what happened?" Stryker asked.

My muscles went into another spasm. I grunted and tried to keep breathing until it stopped.

"Later," I whispered.

The longer I lay there, the worse it got. The slightest movement sent my muscles into contraction. I stayed still and didn't even think about moving. Wil worked off my boots and set them on the floor with my leathers folded on top. After a wait that seemed like hours, the doctor arrived.

"What happened to you, Mr. Harley?" he asked.

"Motorcycle crash," I mumbled.

"Looks like you fell out of a tree."

"Fell through one."

The doctor went silent for a minute. "You crashed in the hills?"

"Uh huh."

"You are a very lucky young man. Those your leathers?"

"Yes."

"Probably saved your life."

I closed my eyes. The doc ran Wil and Dean out of the room and sent me to x-ray. To his surprise, I didn't have any broken bones. Lots of lost skin, a few punctures, but nothing broken, not even a rib. He sewed up my cuts, medicated, and wrapped the rest and advised me to spend the night in the hospital. I declined and waited for Wil to help me out to the car. He came in a few minutes later with my gray sweat pants and my tennis shoes. I struggled into them, shrugged on my jacket and hobbled to the car.

"You want to go home or to the lake?" Wil asked.

"Home tonight, the lake tomorrow."

"You won't be able to move tomorrow."

"Home. Take me home."

Stryker drove to my apartment and parked next to my truck. Wil helped me out of the car and they mostly carried me up the stairs. Baldwin greeted me with a growl. I ignored him as Wil helped me down the hall to my room. I let my jacket slide off my arms to the floor and sank onto the bed. I closed my eyes and waited for the ache to pass. When I opened them again it was daylight.

"Hey, Brocs."

It was Wil. I rolled my eyes toward his voice. It was too hard to move my head.

"You want something to eat or drink?" he asked.

"Bourbon."

"With pain pills?"

"With more bourbon."

Wil laughed and disappeared from the doorway. He came back with a glass. I managed after about ten minutes to reach a sitting position. Will shoved a couple of pillows behind me and I sagged onto them.

"That was probably more trouble than it was worth," I said.

"Beats drinking through a straw."

I grinned and swallowed the drink.

Wil left, filled my glass and brought it and the bottle in and placed them on the table next to the bed.

"Stryker wants to talk to you," he said.

"He can wait till tomorrow."

"Melinda's here."

"Mel's here?" I asked in surprise.

"Of course."

"Take her out to dinner or somethin'."

Wil smiled and left the room. I finished the bottle of liquid painkiller and went to sleep. Sometime during the night, I dreamed of Melinda. Even felt the soft touch of her fingers against my brow. I woke expecting to see her face, but I was alone. I moved to sit up and let out a groan. My head throbbed. I had a hangover, side effect of the world's oldest painkiller. Wil brought me a drink. I swallowed it and lay back against my pillows. My stomach settled as soon as the whiskey hit it.

"I need to take a piss."

"You need a hand with that?"

I grinned and raised an eyebrow at Wil. "I think I can handle it."

"That's good. You don't get up soon I might steal your girl."

As he left the room, I heard him tell somebody that I was going to be fine. I limped into the bathroom. The face that stared out of the mirror wasn't pleasant to look at. I took a leak, brushed my teeth, and decided things might be improved by a bath. I soaked away most of the blood and pinesap and let the hot water loosen my sore muscles. When I got out I didn't feel much better, just cleaner, and I didn't smell like Pine Sol anymore. I found a clean pair of sweats, and a soft, almost worn out tee shirt. I thought about putting on socks, but decided it hurt too much to bend over that far. Finally dressed, I shuffled slowly to the living room.

Melinda was sitting in the recliner with Baldwin on her lap. Wil was on the couch. He stood and I took his place. Wil moved to the floor against the coffee table. Melinda watched me with concern as I settled on the sofa. I gave her a small wink. She asked if I felt as bad as I looked.

"Worse, I think."

She got up and perched on the edge of the seat beside me. Wil rose and disappeared from the room. Melinda traced the bruise on my face with light fingers and followed it with a soft touch of her lips.

"You scared me silly," she said.

"I didn't think I'd ever see you again?"

"What?"

"When you didn't show up at Denny's the other day, I thought I'd pissed you off—you know, asking about your family and stuff."

"I had to see...someone, it took longer than I expected. I did leave a message on your phone."

That was probably the message I got as I was leaving Carmichael's.

Melinda bent and touched her lips to mine. My pain disappeared. I deepened the kiss and shifted to pull her close. Agony shot through my ribs and I froze with a grunt.

"Bad idea. Sorry."

Her lips twitched. Before she could speak, her cell phone went off. She checked the readout and pulled away. "I need to take this."

She walked across the room to take the call. She was only on the phone a couple of minutes and all I caught were the last four words. "I love you too."

Ouch, a direct shot to my heart. As she came back to my side, I tried to pretend I hadn't heard.

"You gonna live till tomorrow?" she asked.

"Pretty sure."

"I've gotta run, how 'bout I come to see you then?"

"Sure, whatever."

She kissed me on the forehead and stood to go.

"Mel," I asked. "Were you here last night? In my room?"

She nodded.

"I thought I dreamed you."

"I'll see you tomorrow, Brocs. Try to stay out of trouble."

She stopped to speak to Wil before the door closed behind her. Wil took her place in the recliner after she'd gone.

"That woman is truly fine," Wil said with a grin. "You just take as long as you need healing up. I'll be glad to stand in for you."

I had a sneaking suspicion someone else already was. It was a measure of how bad I felt that I didn't pursue that line of thought.

"Annie was all set to come over here and take care of you. I convinced her Mel and I could handle it and she didn't need to give Ronnie any more reason to hate you than he already has."

"Ronnie doesn't have anything to worry about from me. Especially right now."

Will laughed. I just closed my eyes. When I opened them again, it was dark and I was alone. I gave some thought to getting up and going to bed, decided it was too much trouble and went back to sleep.

Wil greeted me the next morning, followed by Dean Stryker. They put a box of donuts on the coffee table, made a pot of coffee, and brought an extra chair into the living room. Stryker sat down across from me as I shifted to an upright position.

"Morning," I said. "Make yourselves at home."

Wil sank into the recliner and bit into a donut. "Don't mind if I do."

"I think I'd like to hear how you came to fall off a mountain, Brocs," Stryker said.

Chapter 22

ammit, Brocs," Dean said when I'd finished. "Why didn't you tell me about the phone call before?"

"I tried, the day of Drew's funeral, when we met at the restaurant. You weren't inclined to listen. After that I didn't figure you'd believe me."

He silently swirled the coffee in his cup. "I probably wouldn't have," he said.

He at least had the good grace to look ashamed.

"I would have believed you." Wil said softly.

I winced against the cushions. "I was trying to keep you out of this mess, Wil."

Wil shook his head and snagged the last donut out of the box. I picked up my coffee cup, found it empty and put it down again. I felt better today, but it was a fleeting thing and my energy level was starting to drop.

"What I don't understand," said Dean. "Is why you made the connection between your brother's apparent suicide and your mother's death?"

"I can't really explain it. Just a hunch I guess."

"Hunches are usually based on a fact. Not necessarily one that makes any sense, but a fact nevertheless. I've heard your story. I still don't have the key."

"I don't know, Dean. I can't explain it."

"Try."

I sighed, shifted my position and looked out the window. Wil must have read something in my expression. He took my coffee cup, fixed me a drink instead and put it on the table at my elbow. I picked it up and swallowed half of it. I swirled the ice in the glass and stared into the amber liquid. There weren't any answers there. The glass clinked as it settled against the table top. Dean was sitting forward in his chair watching me. I stared at the hands in my lap and tried to come up with a way to talk about my dreams without sounding like some New Age spacer. I couldn't, so I just started talking.

"I've been having dreams since Drew died."

Dean cocked his head and gave me a funny look. He started to speak, stopped himself, and waited for me to go on.

"Except they're not really dreams," I continued. "They're more like memories."

"I'm not following you, Brocs. Start at the beginning."

I closed my eyes and rubbed my hands over my face. "I don't want to get into all that."

"Brocs, if we're going to figure this out I need to know what you know."

The thought of going through my childhood with a stranger was distasteful. I didn't talk about it with my friends. I hadn't even told Melinda all of it. I finished my drink and rolled the empty glass between my hands. I'd been over and over my dreams and my memories and didn't have a clue why I thought Carmichael was involved in Mom's death. I glanced at Stryker. He wasn't going to let me out of this. I stared past his shoulder and tried to figure out where to begin. Finally, I sighed, and started talking.

I'd already told him about Halston's feelings when he found out Mom was pregnant. I hadn't told him about getting knocked around when Mom wasn't home. About the broken arm that supposedly happened when I fell out of a tree—that actually resulted from a push down the cellar stairs. Or the concussion I got when I 'accidentally' fell off the roof helping Halston hang storm windows. Those were easier to deal with than watching Halston introduce Drew as "my son" and completely ignore me. Without Drew, I don't think I could have stood it.

I went through the dreams that started after Drew died. Trying to tie all the disjointed memories into a complete story. That's where I found the seeds to my hunch.

"Carmichael was at Mom's funeral. That must be why I tied them together."

"That's pretty weak, Brocs.

"Dammit, you wanted to know where the hunch came from. I just told you. I can't help it if you don't think it amounts to anything."

I was exhausted, at the end of my endurance. All I wanted to do was go to bed.

"Go home," I said.

Wil laughed. Dean looked taken aback and stood up from his chair. "I'll be over in the morning," he said.

I flapped a hand at him as he went toward the door.

"You want something to eat before I get out of here, Brocs?" Wil asked.

I shook my head. I just wanted to sleep. Wil followed Stryker out. I struggled up from the couch and shuffled down the hall to my bedroom. Baldwin hopped up in the window and stared down at me.

"I don't have enough bourbon to kill the ache, bud."

He blinked like he understood, then rolled onto his back and started licking his butt. I envied his flexibility. Since I couldn't occupy myself that way, I closed my eyes and concentrated on relaxing my muscles one by one. Eventually I fell into a restless sleep.

Pain roused me a couple of hours later. It was after nine and I wondered if Melinda had called while I was zonked or if she'd come over and I'd slept through the visit. I climbed out of bed and went to the kitchen for Tylenol. My stomach growled and I searched through the refrigerator for food—nothing there that didn't have to be cooked. I wasn't hungry enough to go to that much trouble. If I ate tonight, it was going to have to be delivered. I snagged the phone off the counter and punched in Melinda's number.

"Hey, Mel. It's Brocs."

"Oh...hi."

That was a rather lukewarm reception, but I plowed on anyway.

"I was thinking about ordering a pizza, want to come over and join me for dinner?"

"I...uh..."

"Mel, what's wrong?"

"Nothing...Um, this is a really bad time, I gotta go."

The phone clicked and I stared at it trying to figure out what that was all about. Melinda had sounded scared... upset...I wasn't sure what it was, but I was going to find out. The phone clattered on the table and I shuffled to the bedroom. Baldwin watched from his spot on the windowsill as I struggled into my clothes.

I reached in the bedside table for my nine, remembered it was lost and went to the dresser for my . 22.

"Shit." Dean still had it.

I picked up my keys and made my way carefully down the stairs of my building and out to the truck. The effort was excruciating. I felt as if I was moving in slow motion. I had to rest against the truck to gather enough energy to climb inside.

Finally, I drove into the parking lot of Melinda's building. I swore as I limped up her stairs. In her hallway, I paused to catch my breath before I rapped on the door.

She pulled it open on the safety chain. Her eyes widened in surprise when she saw me standing there. She tried to slam it closed, but I managed to wedge my boot in first. She stepped away from the opening and I couldn't see her face.

"Melinda, what's wrong?"

"You shouldn't be here. Why did you come over?"

"I...you sounded odd on the phone, I was worried. Mel, what's wrong?"

"Just leave, okay. Just get out of here."

She shoved against my foot and it took all my diminished strength to keep it there.

"Dammit, Brocs. Just go. I don't want to see you anymore, okay? Just get out of here."

I stepped back like I'd been slapped and the door slammed shut. I heard the bolt slide home in the lock as I stared in confusion. I knocked again, but she didn't open up.

"Come on, Mel, let me in," I called.

The apartment across the hall opened and a woman's gray head poked out.

"You'd better get out of here young man or I'm calling the police."

I slumped and turned toward the stairway. When I looked over my shoulder, the neighbor was still watching to make sure I left. I hobbled down the stairs and sat in my truck trying to puzzle out what had just happened. I'd been dumped before, but I'd usually known it was coming or at least what I'd done to screw things up. When I realized what must really be going on I felt like an idiot. She was with another guy. I'd just made an ass out of myself rushing across town to interrupt her date.

I turned the key in the ignition and drove home on autopilot. My hunger pains from earlier had been replaced by a hollow empty feeling that food wasn't going to dispel. I parked in my lot and sat for a long time. I wanted Melinda in my life. Maybe not forever, it was too soon to know that, but I didn't want it to end before we had a chance to find out. I gathered my strength and cursed my sore weak muscles as I climbed another set of stairs. Eventually I made it inside. I poured a glass of bourbon and took a sip. It tasted like shit. I dumped the rest down the drain. I hobbled into the living room and slumped into the recliner.

The revelation I'd had in Mel's parking lot was wearing thin. She may very well have been dating someone else. I had no claim on her. But it was out of character for her to promise to come over and then make another date instead. She'd sounded frightened on the phone and she acted frightened when she opened the door and saw me in her hallway. Something was wrong. It wasn't my imagination.

I fumbled my cell phone off my belt and started to call Wil, changed my mind, and punched in Dean Stryker's number instead. As it rang, I checked the clock and hoped he wasn't already in bed. He answered on the second ring.

"Dean, this is Brocs. I think we have a problem."

"Okay."

"Mel was supposed to stop over tonight. She hadn't come when I woke up, so I gave her a call and she brushed me off."

"Alright, I assume there's more."

"She sounded odd. Scared maybe, so I drove over to her place. She wouldn't let me in, couldn't wait to get rid of me."

"Hang on."

I heard Dean say something in the background, then he came back on the line. "I'm gonna change phones, give me a sec while I go to my study."

I waited, heard Dean lift the extension, then the click as the other phone was hung up.

"Okay, without sounding like an asshole here, what makes you think she didn't just have another date?"

"That's what I thought at first, but she wasn't embarrassed, Dean. She was scared. I'd swear it."

Dean was quiet for a minute. I cradled the phone on my shoulder as I hobbled to the fridge for a beer. I twisted the top off and sat down at the kitchen table before he spoke again.

"Brocs, are you sure you're not reading more into this then there really is?"

"I don't know, maybe. I don't think so." I took a long pull from the bottle and tried to order my thoughts. You weren't here yesterday, but before she left..." I paused and rubbed my temples. "Dean, I think somebody's pushing her, threatening her to get her to stay away from me."

It sounded lame even to my ears, but Dean went with it. "You think they were there when you called?" he asked.

I hadn't thought of that. "I guess they could have been. I don't know. Can you run a background check? Find out what somebody could use against her that would scare her away that fast."

"You think Carmichael got to her?"

"Something happened, Dean. Yesterday we were more than friends. Tonight I got the heave-ho. Hell, I haven't been mobile enough to piss her off. I have apparently got Carmichael worried, though."

He sighed into the phone. He wasn't convinced, but he did promise to see what he could find out tomorrow. I switched off the phone and went back to the recliner. I tipped it back and Baldwin curled up on my lap. I rubbed his ears while he purred softly.

Dean might not believe me, but now that I'd had a chance to think about it, I was sure Carmichael had threatened Melinda somehow. It's the only thing that made sense. I wished I knew her better. Without knowing more of her background, I had no way to speculate on what he'd threatened her with. We just hadn't had a lot of time to get to know each other yet.

Baldwin shifted on my lap and I rubbed his tummy. He purred louder. Was this just the first round of the battle? Would Carmichael make his way to all my friends? Who would be the next to cave? I wondered if that's what it had been like for Mom, a smaller and smaller circle of friends until she was alone, with no one to turn to. I pushed Baldwin off my lap and went into the kitchen for another beer. He sat across the table from me while I drank. I finished the beer and picked at the label. What I wouldn't give right then to get my hands on Marcus Carmichael.

"Bastard!"

I swiped the bottle off the table. Baldwin shot out of the room. It clattered off the cabinet and bounced across the kitchen floor without breaking. I picked it up and dropped it into the trash. It fell onto the used coffee filters at the bottom of the bag and shattered. I laughed. It was better than crying.

Baldwin was sitting on the windowsill when I went back to bed. At least they couldn't turn him against me. He hopped down and curled up on my pillow. I dropped off to sleep with his purrs rumbling my ear.

◾ ◾ ◾

I was walking down the hall when I heard voices coming from the study. I stopped and leaned against the wall beside the door where I could hear without being seen. A woman cried softly. A deeper voice mumbled something to her. I edged closer and peeked inside the room. Mom was sitting in a chair crying into her hands. Halston paced around her.

"Marilee, you've got to understand. I was desperate."

His voice was pleading. Mom still cried into her hands. He sank to his knees beside her chair and put his hand on her shoulder. She jerked as if he'd struck her.

"Please, Marilee. Please understand. I love you more than anything else in the world."

Mom lifted her tear-streaked face to him.

"I loved him. Didn't you understand that? I still love him. Every day I look at Brocs and see him in front of me and I still love him. How could you have done this to me? I hate you."

She never raised her voice. The softness of her speech carried a finality that yelling wouldn't have. Halston jerked to his feet. Without realizing it, I'd crept closer as she spoke. Halston glanced up as he rose and saw me in the doorway.

"That little bastard ruined everything. You'd love me if it weren't for him. Get out," he yelled at me. "Get out of my sight."

I looked at Mom's tear-stained face.

"Mom?"

"Go sweetheart. Go out and play."

"But, Mom."

"Brocs, everything's okay, honey. You need to go out and play now."

I walked out the door and started down the hall. Everything turned dark. I was in an endless tunnel and someone was chasing me. I ran and cried out for help, but no one was there. The footsteps behind me grew louder. I ran faster and faster, but they kept getting closer.

"Mom," I shouted. "Mom, help me."

As fingers grasped my shoulder, I screamed.

◼ ◼ ◼

"Brocs. Wake up. Wake up. You're having a bad dream."

I blinked my eyes and looked up at Wil. He was shaking my shoulder. The sheets were wet with sweat and I trembled at the memory. I rubbed my eyes.

"You okay?" he asked.

I took a deep breath and nodded. Wil looked relieved. I sat up and ran my hands through my hair. There was something I needed to remember. I tried to get it back, but it stayed just out of reach. Wil backed out of the room. I heard coffee-making sounds coming from the kitchen as I showered and dressed. When I came out of the bathroom, I felt human for the first time since the crash. I walked into the kitchen and straddled a chair. Wil set a coffee cup on the table in front of me.

"Another one of your memory trips?"

"No, I think this one was just a nightmare."

I wasn't ready to share. I didn't know yet what it meant.

"That crash you had would be enough to give anyone nightmares."

I didn't tell him it hadn't been about the crash. I sipped my coffee and tried to bring back the images. They were gone.

"I'm going in to the office. See if I can make enough to pay the ER bill."

"You ready to go back to work?"

"Yeah. I'm fine."

Wil raised an eyebrow at that. I ignored him.

"What are you doing here this morning?" I asked.

"I called and you didn't answer the phone, so I came over. When you didn't answer my knock, I unlocked the door and came in. Buddy, you were sleeping hard. I didn't think I was ever going to wake you."

I put my coffee cup in the sink and rinsed it out. I noticed my nine-millimeter laying next to the sink. It had a couple of nicks in the finish but it was clean and oiled.

"I didn't think you'd find this in a million years. Thanks, Wil."

He just shrugged.

I picked it up, released the clip, popped it back home and rammed the slide back to chamber a round. Everything seemed to be in working order. I put it on the counter and turned to Wil.

"What'd you need this morning?"

"I just wanted to check in. See if you needed anything."

"I'm fine, a lot better today."

"Okay then. I guess I'll head to work. Stryker called just before I left to come over here. He wants to talk to you. Said he got the information you needed. Drop by the station as soon as you get a chance."

"I'll do that."

Wil slipped out and I moved to the recliner and cleared my mind. I tried to bring back the dream, but it was no use. There was something important there, I was sure of it. I wasn't going to get it back right now. I'd just have to wait until it came on its own. I found my jacket and keys and headed outside. I stopped at the empty parking space next to the truck. I missed my bike.

Chapter 23

The office hadn't changed since the last time I'd been there. Maybe a little more dust. My machine showed twenty-two messages in blinking red numbers. I tossed my jacket onto the couch and sat down behind the desk. I found a yellow legal pad in the right hand drawer, hit the message button on the machine, and made notes on the skips. There were only six messages. Thirteen were hang-ups. Three of them were from Rudy Macklin. I called Rudy first.

"Rudy, Brocs Harley."

"Brocs, I heard about your little trip down the mountain. How you doing?"

"I'm fine. A little stiff, but I'm okay."

"Hey, that's great. Look, I'm glad you got in touch. That Lincoln I had you after turned up on the lot a couple of days ago, so just bill me for the time you've got in on it and I'll send you a check."

"Just turned up on the lot, huh?"

"Yeah, never had that happen before," he said with a laugh. "I guess if you live long enough you'll see everything, won't you?"

"I guess so, Rudy."

My mind went into overdrive. I'd never actually seen the car that booted me off my bike.

"What day did it turn up?" I asked.

"I don't remember exactly. A day or two ago I guess, why?"

"I just wondered. Thanks for calling, Rudy. Get in touch if you need me."

"I will, you can count on it."

"Hey, Rudy?"

"Brocs, sorry. I've got all hell breaking loose out here today. I've got three salesmen out with the flu. I'd better get out to the floor."

The phone went dead in my ear before I could even say goodbye. Rudy walked that car lot a dozen times a day. There was no way he didn't remember when the Lincoln turned up. I felt my inner circle drawing in. I suspected I knew what car had booted me over the guardrail. I shrugged into my jacket and drove over to Rudy's lot to take a look.

There wasn't a single customer on the lot when I arrived. Guess the rush was over. I counted six salesmen playing poker next to the coffee machine. I parked the truck and started trolling through the lot. There's not a car salesman in the world that can resist accosting a window shopper. I paced up and down the rows of cars, glancing toward the poker game from time to time. Not a single salesman moved. If I needed any more proof that my enemies had gotten to Rudy, there it was.

I meandered away from the new cars and started up and down the aisles of the used car lot. I spotted the Lincoln at the end of a row and headed that way. Rudy intercepted me before I got to it. "Brocs, what brings you down here? You in the market for a new car?"

"Just browsing. Never know when I might spot something I can't live without."

I sidled past Rudy and headed toward the Lincoln again.

"I got something on the showroom that might interest you," he said.

"I'm fine out here."

"Brocs, please. Come into the showroom with me."

I looked Rudy in the eye. His fear was obvious. I thought I'd push a little bit and see what happened. "Mind if I take a gander at that red Mazda." It was parked right next to the Lincoln. "Hey, look at that. Is that the Lincoln I've been trying to find?"

Rudy stepped in front of me and blocked my way. "Brocs, you don't understand what's going on."

I stepped back a pace. "Actually, I think I do."

"I can't let you see that car, Brocs."

"You got a daughter, Rudy?"

His face lost all color. I thought he was going to pass out.

"Please leave now, Brocs."

"Yeah, been nice working with you, Rudy." I turned and strode to the truck. Once behind the wheel I glanced across the lot. Rudy was leaning against a van. I guess he was gathering up his strength before he went inside. I waited until he opened the showroom door before I started the truck. As he made his way across the room to his office, I drove down the aisle and stopped in front of the black Lincoln. A black smudge of rubber streaked the right side of the shiny chrome bumper. A small scratch marred the chrome just beneath it. That was the only evidence of the Lincoln's brush with my Harley. Lester Crawford had pushed me off the mountain with the Lincoln. Lester was Marcus Carmichael's problem solver. I was Carmichael's latest problem. They hadn't scared me off with a direct hit so now they were working from the outside in.

I dropped the truck into gear and drove away. Rudy came out of his office and watched from the window of the showroom as I drove off the lot. I waved and turned toward the police station. Stryker was in his office with another detective when I arrived. I left a message for him to meet me at the Dragon's Claw and went to get some lunch.

I ordered for two and was munching an egg roll when Stryker entered. He scooted into the booth across from me and picked up the other egg roll. The waiter brought the rest of our food and Stryker started to eat.

"Wil said you had another dream."

"Just a nightmare. Not sure if it has anything to do with this."

He nodded and we ate in silence for a while. Dean finished his lunch and fiddles with his tea glass.

"I found out about Melinda," he said. "You were right."

I stopped eating.

"She has a brother, Danny, he's nineteen now, I think. When he was eleven, he was in an automobile accident. Their parents were killed; he suffered a brain injury. Melinda has pretty much raised him since their parents died. It hasn't been easy. There've been years of therapy and he'll never be completely over it, but last year he moved into one of those communal living programs that help adults with mental impairment live on their own. From what I could find out, he's doing very well. He has a job. I think if he were threatened, Melinda would back off. He's like a son to her."

I pushed my plate away and absorbed what Dean had told me. The "I love you" phone call made sense if she was talking to her brother. If she thought Danny was in danger, she'd drop me in a heartbeat.

"Thanks, Dean. I don't guess there's anything the police can do?"

"Not unless she asks for our help."

"She won't do that. They'd kill Danny before you guys could do anything."

Dean nodded in agreement. I picked up my fork, but I wasn't hungry anymore. I left it on my plate and slouched against the seat. "I know who pushed me off the mountain," I said.

Dean stopped fiddling with his glass and waited for me to go on.

"Lester Crawford. He works for Carmichael. I think he's Carmichael's fixer."

"You have evidence?" Dean asked.

I shook my head and we both went silent.

"I lost my best client today, Rudy Macklin. They threatened his daughter. Carmichael's running scared. He thinks I know more than I do, and I'm afraid someone I care about is going to get hurt because of it."

"Maybe you know more than you think."

I motioned for the waiter to refill my glass and drummed my fingers on the table top.

"I've told you everything I know, Dean. I have nothing on Carmichael. Nothing I can go to the cops with. I'm no threat to him."

"Maybe you're going at it from the wrong direction."

I rested my elbows on the table and waited for him to continue.

"Maybe you're on the wrong track. I don't think Carmichael would have had to kill anyone to keep the money laundering operation going."

"What else could it be? Drew wasn't any kind of a threat to Carmichael or Austin-Kline."

"Think about this. If Andrew found out Halston was laundering money through the business would he confront the old man about it?"

I started to answer and he held up his hand.

"Think about it for a minute."

I stared off into space. Stryker watched in silence.

"No, he wouldn't have confronted him," I finally answered. "He would have quit and come to work for me."

Stryker nodded in agreement.

"What about your mother?"

"What do you mean?"

"Would she have left Halston if she found out his business was dirty."

"Of course she would have."

"Stop thinking with your heart and think with your head, Brocs."

I closed my eyes and thought about Mom.

"What are you getting at, Stryker?"

"Your mother married Halston Harley because she didn't want to face life as a single parent. Granted, in those days it was a big deal, but it leads me to believe that she wasn't very confrontational."

Something glimmered in the shadows of my mind. I closed my eyes and tried to bring it forward, but it skittered away. I sighed in frustration.

"What do you think is going on, Dean?" I asked.

"I don't know. If we knew why your Mom wanted out of her marriage, we might have some idea."

"Shit, Dean. There's no one around that even knew my Mom back then."

"I think you've got the information, Brocs."

I shook my head. "I don't have any idea."

"It's there, you just need to bring it out. Would you consider getting hypnotized?"

"No. That doesn't work unless you believe in it. I don't."

"Have you ever talked to a therapist?"

"No and I'm not going to start now."

"It was just an idea."

"Forget it."

Stryker checked his watch. "I've got another meeting. Keep thinking about it and I'll talk to you later."

I trailed him out, angled behind the wheel of my truck, and drove up to the cabin. Sun glinted off the water. I rooted through the fridge for a beer and wandered down the trail to the dock. It was warm by the water. I peeled off my shirt, cracked open the beer, and sat down with my back against a corner post. A hawk circled high overhead searching for dinner as I stared across the water. A soft breeze rippled the lake. A fish broke the surface and rings radiated out toward the shore. I relaxed and closed my eyes.

"Help me out here, Drew," I whispered. "I don't have a clue what's going on."

I could feel Drew with me there. His presence was so strong I could almost touch it, but he wasn't talking. A rock clattered down the path behind me. I grabbed my gun and threw myself onto my chest. My muscles screamed in protest as I hit the dock. I ignored the pain and glared down the barrel at the intruder.

"Jesus, Brocs. Don't shoot."

It was Billy Rayburn. I let my head sink to my arms and the gun go limp in my grasp. Jesus, I just drew down on one of my best friends. I got up from the dock and brushed sand off my chest. Rayburn watched as I shoved the nine into the holster and pulled my tee shirt over my head.

"What are you doing here, Billy?"

"I was looking for you. You didn't answer your phone. I took a shot and decided to see if you were up here."

I crunched up the path. Billy fell into step beside me. We climbed the porch steps and sank into chairs.

"So, what's up, Billy?"

"I...Uh..." Billy fiddled with the tail of his suit coat, his eyes glued to the floor between us. "Look this thing with

Carmichael has spilled over onto me. I just can't deal with it."

"What do you mean?"

"It's just the thing with Manny, and then your crash."

"I'm not following, man."

"Look, it was just money, no one was supposed to get hurt. Carmichael said no one would get hurt."

"Carmichael, said?" Sick realization settled in my gut. "You've been talking to Carmichael?"

"I...he just wanted some information. I didn't think it would be a big deal."

I jumped to my feet and started pacing across the porch. Billy scooted away as I stopped in front of him.

"Let me get this straight. You were feeding information to Carmichael? About what we were doing?"

"He's got me by the balls, dammit. What was I supposed to do?"

"So all along you've been telling him what we were looking into, and he was dribbling out little bits and pieces that weren't going to lead us to shit. Is that what was going on?"

"But he promised that no one would get hurt. He just wanted to drag it out long enough for you to drop it."

I spun away and leaned against the porch. My knuckles were white where I gripped the top rail.

"So you told him Wil was going to see Manny and pick up the files Drew left there."

"Brocs, you gotta believe me, he promised no one would get hurt. I swear."

I spun around and glared at Billy. "So how'd he explain what happened to Manny?"

"He said it was a mistake, a mix up. It wasn't supposed to happen like that."

"And you believed him?"

"I didn't have any choice, Brocs. He could ruin me."

"He almost killed me, Billy."

"That wasn't supposed to happen."

I couldn't believe I was having this conversation with one of my closest friends. I would have trusted Billy Rayburn with my life.

"So you're telling me you're still in his pocket."

"I'm in too deep with Carmichael to get out, I don't have any choice."

"Well how about turning the tables, what's he got planned next?"

"I don't know, maybe something to do with Wil."

"Any idea what?"

"I can't say anymore, I've already said too much."

My mind was racing, trying to figure out a way to protect Anne. I wasn't worried about Wil, they wouldn't go after him up front. Carmichael would try to get at him through Annie. I stepped off the porch and went to the truck. Billy came down the stairs behind me and shuffled across the drive. When he got to my side, I handed him the key I'd just slipped off my ring.

"What's this?" he asked.

"My key to the cabin."

"You don't...I...Shit, Brocs, I'm sorry."

"I don't want to hear it, Billy. Just do this one thing for me. When you talk to Carmichael in the morning, you tell him something to make him believe that Wil and I are on the outs. I don't care what you say, or what you do, but you make sure he doesn't have any way to get at Wil or Annie."

"I may not even see Carmichael tomorrow."

"You'd better. If something happens to Anne because of you, Carmichael will be the least of your worries."

Bill stepped away from the venom in my voice. I just slid behind the wheel, backed around his BMW and drove to town. Little pieces were starting to fall into place. That wasn't a BMW like Billy's I saw at Carmichael's place, it was Billy. He was probably the one hiding in the bathroom in Carmichael's office listening in the night I got run off the mountain. That sonovabitch! It was all I could do not to turn around and beat Billy Rayburn to a bloody pulp.

The bastards had cut off all my lines of communication. First Melinda so I couldn't get to Halston, then Rudy to cut into my business, and now I find out Rayburn was in his camp all along. Wil would be next unless Billy could convince Carmichael to leave well enough alone. I didn't have a lot of faith in that.

Chapter 24

Fear for Wil and his sister Anne crawled up my spine. Wil would be next on Carmichael's list, Billy as much as said so. I had to stop it before it happened. I grabbed my cell phone to call Wil and it was dead, so I parked at a pay phone outside of Walgreen's. He didn't answer, so I left a short message asking him to meet me at the End Zone and a quick explanation, then I paged him and waited. When he didn't call after ten minutes, I dialed Dean's office. I tapped my foot impatiently as I waited for an answer. When Dean picked up, I let out a sigh of relief.

"Dean, I need your help."

I heard a sharp intake of breath.

"Where are you? Are you okay?"

I closed my eyes and tried to relax before I spoke again. "Not that kind of help. I'm okay for the moment."

"What's going on?"

"Billy's wrapped up in this some how. With his help, these bastards are putting the squeeze on everyone. I'm running out of friends. I need your help before they cut me off from everyone. I can't get to these guys alone."

"How's Billy involved?"

"I don't know, I don't have any proof, but I know he's been feeding Carmichael information all along. That's how they knew about the papers at Luigi's. It's probably how they knew to lean on Rudy and Melinda. Sonovabitch, I can't believe Billy would do this to me.

"I doubt if he had much choice, they probably threatened to kill him if he didn't help. That still makes him an accessory to murder."

"Christ, Dean. I hadn't even thought of that."

"I'll get someone looking into Billy's involvement, what else do you need from me."

His voice was calm. I stretched the tension out of my shoulders and tried to match his tone.

"First I need you to get in touch with Wil. I left him a message, but I need to make sure he understands what's going on. Have him meet me at The End Zone around nine. It's a sports bar down on Ninth Street. Tell him he and I need to have a very public fight. It's got to look real. Tell him not to pull his punches."

"What's that going to accomplish?"

"If Wil and I get into it, I hope Carmichael will hear about it from Billy. If they think Wil's no threat, maybe they'll leave him alone."

"Brocs, I don't think that's necessary. He's a cop. What can they threaten him with?"

"They won't threaten him. They'll threaten his sister or her kids. I'm not going to let anything happen to Anne."

"Okay, what else?"

"I need a bolt hole. I need to become invisible until I figure out what's going on."

"Let me work on that. I'll get back to you."

"Thanks, Dean."

I hung up the phone and drove to the apartment. Baldwin greeted me and dropped a dead mouse at my feet. I didn't show my usual interest in his catch. He swished his tail back and forth and stalked around the living room chattering to himself while I poured a drink.

I turned on the stereo and sank into the recliner. What the hell was going on here? What Stryker had said at lunch made sense. Neither Mom nor Drew was confrontational. Mom probably didn't have any information at all about Halston's business. If Drew found out he might have told me about it, but he wouldn't have gone to Halston. He would have quit and come to work at H & H. I fell asleep without coming up with a solution. No dreams or memories enlightened me while I slept. I woke in the dark, stretched the crick out of my neck and went downtown to the End Zone. I was at the bar nursing a beer when Wil strode in. He squeezed onto the barstool next to me, ordered a beer and gave me a dirty look.

"What's your problem?" I asked.

"You're a real prick."

I covered my grin by taking a drink.

"Don't you have anything to say for yourself?" he asked.

I shrugged my shoulders. I wasn't committing myself to his argument until I knew what the subject was.

"Don't ignore me, Harley. I'm trying to talk to you."

He wasn't giving me much to work with. I thudded the beer bottle down on the bar and spun on my stool until we were face to face.

"So talk, I'm not stopping you."

"I want you to fuckin leave my sister alone."

My eyes widened in surprise. Wil was good, he was acting really pissed.

"What the fuck are you talking about?"

"I'm talking about Annie. Leave her alone. She's got enough problems without you fucking up her life."

I didn't have a clue what Wil was getting at, but I decided it was perfect for my plans so I played along.

"Look, Pinkerton. Stay out of it. What's going on between me and Anne is none of your goddamn business."

"I'm making it my business."

"Piss off."

"Fuck you."

"No, man. I like Anne better."

I never saw the punch coming. He brought it up from somewhere near the floor. When it connected with the side of my head, lights exploded behind my eyes. I came off my barstool and landed in a heap on the floor. I stayed put, letting my senses come back. The floor smelled like stale beer. I wrinkled my nose and rolled to a sitting position.

Wil stood a few feet in front of me, face flushed, breathing hard, fists clenched at his sides. I launched myself from the floor and caught him just above the knees. He crashed to the hardwood with me on top of him. He landed another punch and blood dripped from my nose onto his shirtfront. We scrabbled around among peanut shells trying to land blows. I caught Wil in the nose. He bucked underneath me and tried to land a head butt. I dodged and took it as a glancing blow. Good thing or I'd been out for a week.

Hands grabbed at me from behind and jerked me off the floor. I struggled to get away. I was having a hard time remembering that this fight was fake. Wil's anger seemed too real. He scrambled to his feet and landed a blow to my kidneys before someone drug him away. The bouncer propelled me outside.

"Bastard," I whispered as I went by Wil.

"No, that would be you, Harley."

I dropped my head. That was a blow below the belt, something my friend Wil would never say. The bouncer pushed me out and I stumbled onto the sidewalk in the dark. Blood dribbled over my upper lip. I sniffed and crumpled the tail of my tee shirt against my bleeding nose to stop the flow.

"Don't come back in here until you cool off," the bouncer said.

I nodded and scuffed down the street. Wil stalked out as I moved away.

"I'm warning you, stay away from Annie."

I ignored him and kept walking. That hadn't been a staged fight. That had been real. I wondered if Dean had told him what I needed or if Carmichael had already gotten to him. There was no way for me to find out now.

I washed the blood off when I got home and tried to call Dean. He wasn't answering any of his numbers. I didn't leave a message. I took my newest headache to bed and tried to get some sleep. The fight ran over and over in my mind. What would make Wil think I'd do anything to hurt Annie? It was after midnight before sleep claimed me.

I jerked out of a sound sleep and sat bolt upright. Something was pounding against the walls. In the dark, the pounding noise seemed to surround me. I shook my head, trying to get my brain into active mode. The noise grew louder. Realization finally arrived. Jesus, they were going to knock the hinges loose. I struggled into my jeans, stomped down the hall, and jerked the door open. Dean Stryker was standing there with two uniforms. Several of my neighbors were standing in the hall in their nightclothes trying to find out what the noise was all about. Stryker grabbed my arm and snapped his handcuffs around my right wrist.

"You're under arrest for the murder of Andrew Harley."

Before I could respond, he twisted me around and snapped on the other bracelet. I stood in stunned silence as he read my rights.

"What the hell is going on?" I finally asked.

Mrs. Chancellor from next door grabbed Stryker's arm before he could answer. He jerked away and swung toward her. "What?" he snapped.

She gave him the full force of a glare honed by years of teaching junior high school boys how to diagram sentences. Even though her head barely reached his shoulder, Stryker didn't have a chance. I would have laughed if the situation were less serious.

"Um, I apologize, ma'am. How may I help you?" he mumbled.

"What are you doing with this young man?"

"It's a police matter, ma'am. I'm afraid I can't discuss it."

"I've seen you over here. You've been harassing Brockston ever since his brother died and I think it's shameful."

"Uh, yes ma'am. I mean, no ma'am. There hasn't been any harassment, just normal police work."

I snorted in disgust.

"Peters, get him out of here," he snapped at one of the uniforms standing outside my apartment.

Peters spun me away from the altercation and pushed me down the hall. Mrs. Chancellor started back in on Stryker as I stumbled out of the building. Peters handed me off to a different cop stationed at the entrance. My new escort shoved me across the lot and deposited me in the rear seat of Stryker's unmarked car. Stryker appeared a few minutes later with Mrs. Chancellor hurrying along behind him. "You should be ashamed of yourself", I heard her tell Stryker as he opened the car door.

"I'm going to call your chief," she said, as he closed her out. She was still scolding as he dropped the car in gear and sped out of the lot.

"Jesus," Stryker mumbled.

"What the hell's going on here?" I asked. "You know I didn't kill Drew."

"Save it, Harley."

I ground my teeth in frustration and leaned forward to keep the weight off my cuffed wrists. Carmichael must have gotten to Stryker. I didn't think that would be possible—had never even considered it. Shit. I was in nine kinds of trouble now.

Stryker dragged me past the front desk, down the hall, and pressed me into a chair. A uniformed officer typed up the report. Stryker sat across the desk and pinned me in place with his cold cop stare. What in the hell had I done in the last two days to piss off the two people I needed most right now? When the officer finished with the bookkeeping details, he nodded at Stryker.

"Do you have a statement to make, Mr. Harley?" Stryker asked.

"Not without my attorney."

He turned toward the officer. "That will be all, Simons. I'll take it from here."

Officer Simons scooped the paperwork off the printer and handed it to Stryker. Stryker pushed me down another hallway, shoved me into an interview room, and told me to sit. I sat. I didn't have a lot of other choices at the moment.

An officer brought me a phone and unlocked the cuffs long enough for me to call Marshall Levinson. He was my attorney once upon a time, but I hadn't spoken to him since Stryker busted me for car theft. I hoped he would remember me. He was out of the office. I left a message with his answering service and prepared to wait. I tried to think of someone else I could call. Nick would probably go my bail if I agreed to work free forever. Probably not worth it, at least not yet.

I slumped at the scarred wooden table waiting to find out what was going on. I thought Stryker would come back, but he didn't. An officer came and took the phone away. I watched the clock tick off the minutes. My attorney didn't show, Stryker didn't show, no one else came in. I needed to take a piss.

My hands were numb from the bracelets, my ass was numb from the hard chair and my head was pounding from the beating I'd taken from Wil Pinkerton. An officer arrived and escorted me to the toilet, then stuck me in the same depressing room. That was the only contact I had in three hours. By five a.m. I was past anger. All I had left was exhaustion.

At that hour of the morning there's not much going on at the Stantonville PD. The shift is down to a skeleton crew. All the uniforms are out in their cruisers and there are only a handful of people in the building. I was slumped half asleep when Stryker slipped inside. He unlocked the cuffs, held a finger to his lips and lifted me to my feet. I stumbled out of the room, my muscles cramped from inactivity. He guided me to his office through the back hallway. We didn't pass another soul. When we were inside the office, he pointed to a chair, checked up and down the hallway, then clicked the lock and walked toward me. I sat and tried to rub some feeling into my wrists. My anger was starting to blossom.

"What the hell was that all about?" I asked.

Stryker grinned. "You said you needed to disappear. Well, you just did."

My anger was turning to confusion.

"What are you talking about?"

"I just finished redoing the paperwork that Officer Simons started earlier. Brockston Lee Harley was arrested for the murder of his brother, Andrew Harley. While in custody, he proved unmanageable and will be held in solitary confinement, away from the jail population until his arraignment hearing. I'm making an announcement to the press in about an hour. Your name will not be mentioned. I'll just say we have a suspect in custody. But, if Carmichael has eyes inside the department the paperwork appears legit. He'll know you're here, but there's no way for him to check who's actually being held in solitary."

"Jesus, Dean. You could have told me what was going on."

"It wouldn't have looked real."

"Shit!"

Stryker smiled.

"What did you tell Wil?" I asked.

"I never got a chance to talk to him, just left a message that he was supposed to meet you, why?"

"He met me alright, beat the shit out of me while he was at it."

"Well, that's what you were after isn't it?"

"Stryker, you don't understand. He was furious. He thinks I did something to Annie."

"Let me try and get in touch with him, find out what's going on."

Dean left the office to call Wil. I paced around the office and wished I had a cup of coffee.

Twenty minutes later, Dean returned with an eight-by-ten envelope. He handed it to me and I lifted the flap and slid the contents out. It was a series of pictures showing me holding, kissing and then undressing Wil's sister.

"What the hell is this?"

"Someone left those with Annie's husband yesterday. He came home and went ballistic on her. She called Wil. Wil came after you."

I looked closer at the photos. They were decent fakes. At first glance, they looked real, but the lover's weren't Annie and I. They just had our heads.

I threw the photos on Stryker's desk. "I would never do that to Annie. I wouldn't hurt her for the world. Wil should know that."

"I think, after you two had your altercation, Wil took another look at the photos and decided to have our lab guys check them out. They told him they were fakes. Then he started to wonder if this was something Carmichael cooked up to try and get at you. He went back and talked to Annie and his brother-in-law—tried to straighten things out with them. I take it that didn't go very well. Anyway, by the time he got around to catching up with you, I had you on ice. Needless to say, he was glad to get my phone call."

I sighed and rubbed my hands through my hair. "This shit can't go on much longer, Dean."

"He's running scared, Brocs. That means we're getting close."

Exhaustion settled over me like a blanket. I just wanted to go somewhere and sleep for a while.

"How do I get out of here and where am I going to stay?"

"Think you can pass yourself off as a navy fighter jock?"

"I guess."

There was a knock at the office door and Stryker smiled. "Good, that's the guy coming in to give you a haircut."

Stryker's barber gave me the military special. After he left, Dean handed me a set of Navy whites and left the room while I changed. The uniform was a perfect fit. The shoes were a little tight, but not too bad. As I finished buttoning up the shirt, Stryker knocked and strode in. I turned to face him and he stopped abruptly. The color drained from his face, and he swallowed hard as he stared at me. His hand trembled as he pushed the door closed behind him.

"My God," he whispered. "You really do look just like Charlie."

Charlie again.

Stryker slumped in his desk chair. I could see tears pool in his eyes. I didn't know what was going on. I leaned against the office window and stared out to give him a minute. The sky was bright in the early morning sun. Cars were starting to move on the streets. My eyes were gritty and dry. I felt like I hadn't slept in a week. When I turned away from the window, Stryker stared down at a framed photo in his hands. I sat across the desk from him. He handed me the photo. A navel officer smiled from the frame. The tag on his uniform said Stryker. I glanced down at the tag I was wearing. The name was the same. When I glanced up from the photo. Stryker was staring at me.

"That photo is of my son Charlie. He died in an automobile accident two years ago. He was just a few years older than you."

I stared at the photo. It was a little like peering into a mirror. Charlie Stryker and I could have been brothers.

"I...I can't do this, Dean. I can't wear your son's uniform."

"It's the easiest way I came up with to get you out of here, unless you'd like me to lock you in a car trunk or something."

"Shit!"

"What was your father's name, Brocs?"

I looked at him in bewilderment. "What?"

"The first time we talked you told me Halston Harley wasn't your father. What was your dad's name?"

"Lee Weston." I glanced down at the photo in my hands, then up at Dean. "His name was Lee Weston."

A small smile flickered across Dean's face.

"That explains a lot. I thought you resembled Charlie. The night I came to the apartment to tell you about your brother, I noticed a resemblance. Kind of gave me a start, but I blew it off as coincidence. I've seen an awful lot of young men that looked a little like Charlie. Usually they don't really, not if I get close. Then you said your dad was a cop and I started wondering again. But Lee never had any kids. At least none I knew about. But now...with the short haircut, in his uniform, the resemblance...you had to be related."

"What are you talking about, Stryker?"

"Lee Westin was my cousin. Charlie always did look more like Lee than he did me."

I placed the photo on his desk and thought back to all the times I'd caught an odd look in his eyes when he glanced my way. Now I knew it was because I resembled his dead son. I walked back to the window. Dean talked while I stared through the glass.

"Lee's mother left her husband when Lee was maybe eight years old. They didn't have any money so they moved in with us in Springfield. Lee and I were like brothers. They moved to Stantonville when he was thirteen and I was sixteen. That's when we started drifting apart. Then I left for college and he went into the service. There was a long stretch where we didn't hear much from each other, mostly just traded Christmas cards. I knew Lee was living here in Stantonville when he was killed. I'd talked to him just a few weeks before that when he called to invite me to the wedding. I never met Marilee, but I could tell when he talked about her that he loved her very much. I never knew about you, Brocs."

It was an apology of sorts, I guess, for the childhood I'd ended up with. I rested my forehead against the glass and thought how different my life could have been. Too late now to change things.

I sighed and sat down in front of Dean's desk. I wanted to know all about my father. I wanted to ask how Dean ended up living in Stantonville, but I didn't. Instead I asked what we were going to do next. Dean wanted me to come home with him. I argued against the idea, but in the end that's what I did. I let Dean Stryker take me home. At nine o'clock that morning, after Dean made his statement to the press, we strolled down the front steps of the police station and got into his car. No one gave us a second glance.

We entered the front of his house as his wife Judy came into the living room. She was short, with curly brown hair shot through with grey. She took one look at me and sank onto a chair.

"Charlie," she whispered.

I glared at Dean. "You didn't tell her."

He ignored me and wrapped his arms around her. She laid her head on his shoulder and they just held each other. I felt out of place. Dean spoke softly to her for a minute. Then she ducked out of his arms and walked across the room to me. She paused for a minute, then pulled me into a hug. Her eyes were bright with tears as she stared into mine.

"You are welcome to stay as long as you like, Brocs."

"Thank you." I paused. "You know I'm not Charlie?"

"I know that, dear." Her tears threatened to spill over and she blinked them away. "He would like the whole idea. He was always playing practical jokes. If I didn't know better, I'd say he set this up himself."

She let me go and hurried into the kitchen talking about breakfast. At the thought of food, my stomach growled.

Dean smiled. "Come on, she's a great cook."

"I'd like to change clothes. I...this..." I sighed and flapped a hand toward the uniform.

Dean motioned for me to follow him.

I entered a bedroom. A single bed with a blue bedspread and a walnut frame was scooted under the window. A matching dresser sat against the wall. Blue curtains fluttered in the breeze. A photo of an aircraft carrier hung above the bed, the only decoration on the walls. This was Charlie's room. There were no childhood toys or books on the shelves above the desk in the corner. No trophies or rock star posters on the walls, just the photo of the carrier. Probably the last one he'd served aboard. I had the sudden urge to go home, to get away from their pain. Dean and Judy had packed their memories away, only the photo of the aircraft carrier still hung in tribute. And now, here I stood in Charlie's dress whites. Dean motioned toward the dresser and spoke in a husky voice.

"There's some of your stuff in there. If you need anything else from your apartment, let me know."

He paused in the doorway and stared at me, lost in a memory of his son.

"Thanks, Dean."

He shook himself into the present and waved away my thanks as he stepped out of the room.

crashed after breakfast. When I awoke, it was late afternoon. I made my way down the hallway into the dining room. The sun shone through a big bay window and painted blocks of light across the hardwood floor. Judy Stryker was sitting at a harvest table with a photo album open in front of her. One end of the table held scraps of fabric, a sewing machine, and a half finished rag doll. I picked it up when I came into the room. Judy's face crinkled into a smile when she saw me.

"I make dolls and take them to the hospital. The nurses give them to the little kids." She shrugged her shoulders in a dismissive gesture. "It keeps me busy."

I laid the doll next to the sewing machine and sat down across from her.

"You feeling better?" she asked.

"Yes, ma'am. Thank you."

"Can I get you something to eat or drink?"

"No thank you, I'm fine."

I lounged in my chair and tried to ease the tension in my shoulders.

"I got this photo album out," she said. "I thought maybe you'd like to see some pictures of your dad. You look an awful lot like him, you know."

I caught my breath and sat up. "Very much. I used to have one of him and mom. It disappeared when I was a kid. I always figured Halston found it and threw it away."

My voice came out husky. I cleared my throat as she turned the album toward me. I let my eyes roll down a page of photos that showed Dean and Lee together as kids. I slowly flipped through and there was Lee alone. A couple were taken at the beach, one was of Lee sitting on a motorcycle, and old Harley that looked a bit like the Heritage Softail I'd last seen crumpled in the valley outside of town. I turned the page and saw him in an army uniform and next to it a formal portrait taken in his highway patrol uniform. My hand brushed over the photo as if I could get closer to him by touching it.

"That one was taken just before he died," she said. "His mother gave it to Dean after the funeral."

I looked up at Judy. I'd forgotten she was there.

"I wish I'd known him," I said.

"I think he would have been very proud of you."

I closed the photo album and tried to clear the lump from my throat. Judy picked up the album and put it away in the bottom of the china cabinet.

"What can we do to help, Brocs?" she asked.

"You're already doing it. I needed a safe place to stay and you gave it to me."

"There's got to be something else. What are you searching for?"

"I don't know. I thought I did, but now I don't have any idea. Drew was murdered because he found out something he shouldn't have. I don't know what that was. I don't even know where to start."

"You'll find it, you and Dean."

I smiled. "I hope so."

She left the room and went the kitchen. "You sure I can't get you something to eat, Char...Uh, I'm sorry... Brocs?"

"Sure, that'd be great."

"Well come on in the kitchen. Eating alone at that big table will make you feel silly."

I moved into the kitchen and watched as she put together a sandwich. It was bright and cheery in there—the heart of the house. Copper-bottom pots were lined up on hooks above the stove. The walls were a muted burgundy, which made the copper seem to glitter. A painting hung above the entry—a still life of vegetables and canning jars. Judy saw me staring.

"Dean painted that."

She grinned at my surprise. "He used to paint a lot, before...he used to paint."

I knew what she was going to say, "Before Charlie died." She put the sandwich on a plate and scooted it in front of me. I was still eating when Dean strolled in a few minutes later. He snagged a couple of beers out of the fridge, pushed one to me and straddled a chair on the other side of the table. I asked him about my dad.

"Lee was a daredevil. You didn't want to dare him to do anything. He'd do it. Jump off the roof, climb the highest tree. He was always pushing just a little harder than the rest of us. He used to scare me sometimes."

He took a long pull from his beer and spun the bottle around on the table.

"He took Dad's old farm truck and tried to jump a gully in the back pasture once. He didn't make it, the truck went off one side and nosed into the gully and that was that. Lee hit the steering wheel and busted his nose, but he came out laughing. Nothing ever got him down." Dean paused, remembering. "That old truck, the only thing holding it together was baling wire and rust. After that, it wasn't much more than a chassis and a seat. If I'd tried that, Dad would have skinned me alive, but he just laughed at Lee and got the tractor to drag it out of the ditch."

I told Dean about doing something similar with Halston's Buick. Lee probably did it thinking he'd make it across. I'd done it just to piss Halston off.

Judy came in and fixed Dean a sandwich, then left. The sound of her sewing machine in the background made the kitchen seem even more like home.

I asked Dean about Charlie. His voice got rough when he started talking, then became animated as he started a story. Judy came in and he asked if she remembered the time Charlie decided to ride his bike to Riker. They told the story in tandem, finishing each other's sentences. Judy got a fresh beer out of the fridge and gave Dean's shoulder a squeeze before she left the room to go back to her sewing. I relaxed in the comfort of the kitchen. I felt happy and connected in a way I'd never felt before. A couple of hours later, Judy came in and said goodnight, then Dean and I traded war stories. He told me about a guy that robbed a convenience store. They busted him when he came back later the same night to buy tampons for his girlfriend. That led to my story about the PMS repo and my recent adventure with the twin Crown Vics. Finally, Dean checked the clock and stood. "Time for this old cop to head for bed," he said.

"What made you change your mind?" I asked.

"What do you mean?"

"About me. What made you change your mind?"

He stared at me from the doorway, his eyes hidden in the shadows. When he spoke, his voice was husky with unshed tears, "You said when I busted you, back when you were just a kid that I was the kind of cop that you always hoped your dad was. That hit home. Lee was a good cop. I used to be, before Charlie died. You made me see how far away from that I'd gotten."

He turned and disappeared down the hall. I heard the bedroom door latch behind him. I sat in the kitchen thinking about the father I'd never known, the mother I'd lost, the brother that had been taken from me and the family I never realized I had. With a shake of my head, I shut off the lights and went to bed.

◼ ◼ ◼

Drew was screaming at me, but I couldn't understand him. I kept asking him what he was talking about. He kept yelling. I could see my mom in the background. Tears were running down her face. Halston was standing beside her shouting and shaking his finger in her face. She was repeating over and over, 'But I loved him, how could you'?

"Pay attention," Drew yelled. "You're not paying attention."

"I don't understand, Drew. What?"

"Pay attention to Mom."

I watched Mom. Halston had faded to the background. Mom was staring skyward. I looked up to see what was there. Mom was mumbling something. I stepped away from Drew to try and hear her words.

"I love you, Lee," she repeated over and over.

"Mom?"

Startled, she turned toward me.

"You look just like him."

"Who, Mom?"

"Don't let them get you too."

"Who? Who's going to get me?"

Mom started fading away. I turned to ask Drew what was going on. He was staring at me.

"Drew?"

"Start at the beginning and pay attention."

"At the beginning of what?"

"The beginning."

. . .

I woke with a start. The sky outside was dark. The dream was still running through my head. I got up, found a pen and paper and wrote, "Start at the beginning." I felt stupid writing down a dream. I put the pen and paper on the bedside table, turned off the light and relaxed against the headboard. What beginning I wondered? I mulled the question over and fell asleep before I had an answer. I woke again to sunlight streaming through the window. The answer was clear in my mind, the work of my subconscious. Judy's eyes crinkled at the corners when I walked into the kitchen. I had a sudden urge to give her a big hug and kiss. I didn't, I just sat down and she put breakfast on the table in front of me.

"You're going to make me fat," I said.

"Nonsense, eat."

I didn't argue. Dean was right; she was a great cook. She poured a cup of coffee and joined me at the table.

"Is Dean already gone?" I asked.

"He left about an hour ago."

I scooped up scrambled eggs on my toast, chewed, swallowed and picked up my coffee cup.

"Did you know my mom?"

"Marilee and I went to high school together. I grew up here. I met Dean at college in Springfield. We moved up here after Charlie was born.

"What about Halston Harley?"

"Oh, what a pain he was. He pestered your mother constantly. She was so glad to get away from him. He finally backed off when she started going out with Lee. I think Lee had a little discussion with him one night, if you know what I mean." She smiled. "After that he stayed away. I couldn't believe it when I heard she went back to him after Lee died. Of course, we didn't know she was... well we didn't know about you. We weren't living here then." She paused and stared into her coffee cup. "I wish she'd come to us. She didn't have to marry that ass."

I was glad these people had cared about my mom. I finished eating and pushed my plate away.

"How did Lee die?" I asked.

"I thought you knew."

"I'd like to hear it from you."

"His mom said he stopped to help an old man out on Highway Ten. The poor man was trying to change a tire. It was raining and dark and there's hardly any traffic out on that road. I guess the old guy didn't have a clue what he was doing. Anyway, Lee was changing the left front tire and a car came speeding down the highway and ran into him. I guess the driver didn't see him because of the rain."

"Did the old man say anything about it afterward?"

"He said the car came right at them. He jumped out of the way just before the car hit. I guess Lee never even knew it was coming. The old man didn't see the license plate number, and I don't think they ever found the car. They assumed it was a drunk driver."

"Do you know who the man was?"

"I don't remember his name. Dean might. If he doesn't, I'm sure he could find out."

"Is he still around, the old man? Do you think I could talk to him?"

"Oh, no. He'd be dead by now I imagine."

I sighed. Drew, I thought. I started at the beginning and got another dead end...or another dead witness. I stopped with the coffee cup halfway to my mouth.

"How did he die?"

"The old man?"

"Yeah."

"I don't know. Is it very important?"

"It might be."

"Go in the study and call Dean. Maybe he knows."

"Thanks."

Coffee forgotten, I went into the study, dialed the police department and asked for Dean.

"Brocs, what do you need?"

"Can you get the accident report on my dad?" I asked.

"I guess, what for?"

"I don't know yet. I'm just sniffing out a hunch."

I paced around the desk in his study as we talked. I couldn't stand still.

"Anything else you need?" he asked.

"Do you remember the old man that Dad stopped to help the night he died?"

"No. I wasn't on the force here then. We were still in Springfield."

"Could you find out what ever happened to him? Judy thinks he died. Do you think you could find out how and when?"

I could hear the scratch of a pencil as Dean took notes.

"Where you going with this, Brocs?"

"I don't know, Dean. It's just a hunch. I'm going with my gut on this."

"I'll see what I can find out."

I hung up the phone, then wrote notes about all the deaths in my family and all the others that seemed connected. I was searching for a pattern. I thought I had one, but I wouldn't be sure until Dean got home with the information I'd asked for. I paced the living room, waiting for Dean to arrive. I finally felt like I was on to something.

At lunchtime, Dean came in with the police files. I sat at the dining room table, files and papers spread out in front of me. I read through every piece of paper and made notes on a legal pad while Dean asked questions. If I was right, five murders had been committed. We knew who was behind it, but didn't know why. I was comfortable at Dean's house. It felt like home, but this wasn't the time for hiding. I needed to rattle the tree branches one more time.

I thanked Dean and Judy for taking me in, packed my things, and Dean gave me a ride home. He didn't want to and spent the drive trying to talk me out of it.

"You sure this is the right thing to do, son?" He asked.

"I'm sure."

Chapter 26

I wandered through the unfamiliar streets of Riker until I finally found Carmichael's building. It didn't look like the base of operations of a multi-faceted crime endeavor. It looked like it should be condemned. The once red exterior had turned a dusty brown. Deep fissures wended their way toward the roof, following the mortar between the bricks. The outside wall was losing the battle to gravity as it bulged outward and sagged. One day soon, the side face of the building was going to topple onto the sidewalk. I hoped no one was strolling by when it happened.

I circled the block searching for a parking place and finally edged in between a delivery truck and a bright orange Plymouth Valiant. I scooted down in the seat and waited to see what kind of visitors came and went. It was a wasted effort. No one was going in or out of the building. I glanced up and down the street. It was the middle of the day, but there was no foot traffic here and very few vehicles. If I didn't know better, I'd think there were 'keep out' signs posted at the corners.

As boredom set in, my mind wandered over my dreams. No longer cloaked in shadows, they wove through my head one after another. All but the last one, it was still hidden. I tried to concentrate on it, but nothing came. I scooted up for a better view as a large man scuffed down the street toward me. He turned onto the walk and pushed inside, the bulge of his gun visible beneath his light summer jacket. He looked like the guard that was working the gate the day I made my visit to Carmichael's house. I filed that information away and settled in to watch some more.

Memories that I'd forgotten or blocked joined the dreams and I tried to pick out the relevant pieces. A picture was slowly coming together and Rayburn had been right. He'd said I might not like what I found. I didn't.

I checked the time and wondered if the news had had time to filter down to Carmichael. Dean had issued a statement to the press that I'd been cleared of all charges. He told the newshounds that new evidence had come to light and the investigation was ongoing. He didn't want to do it, but Carmichael needed to know the police were still looking. I wanted him to be on his guard. I hoped to force his hand and push him into making a mistake.

I eased out of the truck and stretched cramped muscles before I crunched down the cracked and broken walk. A filthy pebbled glass door led inside. I pushed through and took in the sights. To my left, what was once a reception counter sagged against the wall. It was still a counter, but no one manned it anymore. I stalked across the lobby. The dust was shuffled away from the tile in a direct path to the elevator. It was so thick on the rest of the floor that it looked like carpet.

I punched the button for the elevator and waited while it clanked its way down. It finally settled and wheezed open. I stepped inside and pressed the broken button for four and wondered if it even worked. I took it on faith I was on the fourth floor when the elevator creaked open again. I stepped out of the decrepit box and walked down the grungy hallway. I had no trouble picking out which office belonged to Carmichael. The glass doors sparkled in the dim light seeping through the dirty hall windows. I pushed through and accosted Carmichael's secretary. She was mid-forties probably, slender and dressed in a sexless gray business suit that did little to hide her curves. She didn't look like she would intimidate easily. Not like Rayburn's little blonde plaything.

"I need to see Carmichael," I said.

"Do you have an appointment, sir?"

"I don't need an appointment. Just tell him Brocs Harley is here and he knows what's going on."

"He has a very full schedule this morning. You'll have to make an appointment."

I placed my hands flat on her desk, pressed into her personal space and stared deep into her eyes. I held her captive until she swallowed once.

"He will see me, now," I said.

I had pegged her right. She stood her ground. She didn't move until I stepped away from the desk, then she gave me a haughty glare and disappeared through the door behind her. When she reappeared, she motioned me inside. I barged into the office and parked in the chair across from Carmichael's desk. He didn't stand when I entered or offer to shake hands.

"Mr. Harley. I hope you've recovered from your accident. Those hill roads can be murder."

His lips turned up in a parody of a smile.

"I'm not here about the crash."

I slouched into his visitors chair and forced myself to relax. I wanted to pace and yell. I wanted to shoot him. My fingers itched for the feel of my gun. I placed my hands flat on my thighs and looked him in the eyes.

"What can I do for you, Mr. Harley?" he asked.

"Why did you go into business with Halston Harley?"

"Who told you we were in business together?"

My hands clenched into fists. I took a deep breath, slowly opened my fingers and relaxed my muscles. "Carmichael, I'm not here to spar with you about whether or not you and Halston are in business together. That's a fact I've already ascertained. What I'm asking is why you went into business with him."

"Mr. Harley. What kind of business could I possibly have with your father?"

I scooted to the edge of my chair and enunciated very clearly. "Halston Harley is not my father."

Carmichael smiled. I took a deep breath and slouched down into my pose of relaxation. I swore at myself for letting him get to me. Round one to the bad guys.

"What does it matter to you what I purchase through Harley Real Estate? You're not part of the business."

"I'm not interested in your real estate deals. Those are fairly straightforward. I want to know about the rest."

Carmichael paused before he answered, weighing his words before he spoke. "I'm afraid I can't help you, Mr. Harley. That's all the business I've ever had with your... with Harley Real Estate."

"Don't lie to me." I hunched forward in the chair and gave up all pretense of being relaxed. "I've seen the books, Carmichael. I know what kind of business you do with Halston, you sell with one company, buy with another, and Halston takes a nice big cut out of the middle. I don't really give a shit what kind of circle jerk you guys have going. All I want to know is why you're involved with him and when it started."

Carmichael's smile disappeared. His eyes narrowed as he glared at me across the desk. He pressed a button on the phone and the door behind me opened. The goon that guarded the gate at the lake house strode in and stood behind my chair.

"What are you insinuating, Mr. Harley?"

"I'm not insinuating anything, Marcus. I just want to know how you got Halston Harley to start laundering money for you."

Carmichael motioned with his eyes. The bodyguard moved away from my chair and stood behind the desk. The muscles in my shoulders relaxed. I hadn't realized they'd tensed up.

"Let me get this straight. You think I approached your...Halston and set up a money laundering scheme through his business?"

"I don't think he's laundering money for you, Carmichael. I know he is."

Marcus relaxed in his chair. His thug moved away from the desk and took up a slouch against the wall. Tension leaked out of the room. Shit. I didn't like the way this was shaping up. Carmichael, smile still in place, rolled his chair forward and leaned his forearms on the desk.

"You are operating without all the facts, Mr. Harley."

"Then why don't you fill me in? That is why I'm here. I want to know what the hell's going on."

"To find that out, you need to go to the source."

"Who's that, Billy Rayburn?"

Carmichael laughed. "Billy was just a fortunate acquisition. He's been very helpful."

"I'll just bet he has."

"Hmm, quite helpful, but I think he's just about fulfilled his usefulness to the organization. In any event, he doesn't have the information you're searching for."

He cut his eyes toward his guard and received a slight nod in answer. I caught the look and the answering nod, but the significance didn't hit me until later, I was too intent on getting Carmichael to part with some information.

"Quit yanking me around, Carmichael. Just tell me what's going on."

Carmichael shook his head. "You are talking to the head of Austin-Kline Investments. You are not talking to the person responsible for the business dealings between Austin-Kline and Harley Real Estate."

"Then tell me who else is involved."

Carmichael leaned back and stared at me with something close to sadness in his eyes. "Mr. Harley, I won't give you that information. You're better off without it."

I leapt from my chair and slapped my palms down on the desk. It sounded like a pistol shot in the silent building. The bodyguard jumped forward with his gun out. Carmichael waved him away.

"I'll decide what I'm better off not knowing."

He shook his head. "You are too stubborn for your own good, Mr. Harley. If you're not careful, it's going to get you killed."

"By you?"

"Maybe, maybe not. Trust me, you don't know all of what's going on here. Just leave it alone. You're not going to like what you find."

"I can't leave it alone." The words came out before I'd thought, but as soon as I said them I knew it was true. I couldn't turn my back on this. I had to know what was going on and why. It was important in a way I didn't yet understand. I stepped away from the desk and stared at Marcus Carmichael. He knew I wasn't going to let it go. He could read it in my face.

"See Mr. Harley out."

He motioned his muscle and I was grabbed by the arm and escorted to the exit. I jerked away from Carmichael's thug and he backed off from the look on my face. Carmichael spoke again, softly this time. "You'd do well to heed my advice, Mr. Harley."

My fists were clenched at my sides, my anger was barely under control. "Carmichael, if I find out for sure that you killed my brother, you'd better hope the cops get to you before I do."

The thug made a move toward me and I caught him with an uppercut. His eyes rolled back as he stumbled into the wall behind him and slithered to the floor. I stalked through the receptionist's office and onto the elevator.

Chapter 27

Dean was waiting in my parking lot when I arrived. I motioned with my head for him to follow and went up to my floor. The light was out in the stairwell and I made a mental note to call the landlord. He'd probably tell me to change it myself and send him the bill. I stepped out onto my floor and turned to say something to Dean. Before I could speak, something connected with the side of my head. Lights exploded behind my eyes, then went dark as I crumpled to the floor.

Dean shoved me aside and took off down the hall toward the rear stairs. I raised myself to my hands and knees and tried to shake out the cobwebs. Nausea washed over me. Two sets of footsteps thundered down the rear stairs. A shot thumped into the wall and Dean yelled, "Police! Drop your weapon." Another shot sounded and a set of footsteps faded into the distance.

I managed to get into a sitting position with my back against the wall, and hung my head between my raised knees.

My eyes wouldn't focus and my head felt like it was going to explode. I sat up as footsteps thumped across the floor behind me. I hoped it was Dean. I was a sitting duck. I tried to stand and my vision went dark. I sank to my knees and gagged.

Dean kneeled by my side, still breathing hard from his run. "Brocs, you okay?"

"Help me up."

He pulled me to my feet and kept an arm around my waist. I reached up to feel the lump on the side of my head and my fingers came away bloody.

"What the hell did I get hit with?"

"Looked like a baseball bat. Come on, let's get you inside."

He let go of me and I sagged toward the floor. He grabbed me under the arms and we wobbled in tandem toward my apartment. I fumbled the keys from my pocket and tried to find the doorknob. Dean lifted them from my fingers and fitted the key into the lock. My knees started to buckle. He snagged a handful of shirt collar and dragged me inside. I sank onto the chair beside the door and dropped my head to keep from passing out. I gagged and closed my eyes against the pain.

"Don't move, okay. Just stay put for a minute," Dean said.

I wasn't going anywhere.

He left me and walked into the kitchen. I heard him on the phone. The words were indistinct except for "God dammit, you were supposed to be here." The receiver clattered onto the base. I slowly sat up and squinted around the room. It didn't appear to be messed up. Whoever hit me hadn't made it inside.

Dean came back with ice wrapped in a kitchen towel. I held it to my head and tried to get my brain functioning again. It was a slow process. My head had taken too many knocks in the last few days. I finally swayed to my feet and stumbled to the recliner. Dean sank onto the couch. I lifted the ice pack away and looked at him.

"Did you see who it was?" I asked.

He shook his head. "This shouldn't have happened. Morris was supposed to be here. God dammit."

I leaned back, pressed the ice against my throbbing head and closed my eyes. Dean got up and paced around the room. His adrenaline was still kicking and he couldn't sit still.

"Any idea why that guy tried to knock your head off?" he asked.

I started to shake my head, thought better of it and mumbled no.

"Bullshit, Brocs."

"I don't have any idea."

"Where did you go today?"

"I went to see Carmichael."

Dean stopped his pacing and glared across the room. I didn't have to open my eyes to know it. I could feel his gaze boring into me like a laser.

"Dammit, Brocs. I thought you were going to wait for him to come to you. You gotta quit doing this shit without telling anybody. Jesus."

He resumed his pacing, but he was starting to slow down. A few more laps around the room, then he sighed and sagged onto the couch.

"Dean, he knows something. I'm sure of it. I didn't want to wait to find out what it was."

"Did you learn anything?"

"He admitted Billy was feeding him information."

As soon as I said Billy's name the look and nod between Carmichael and his thug popped into my head. "Carmichael said Billy had just about fulfilled his usefulness."

I jerked forward in the chair and the dizziness came back full force. I groaned and pressed the ice to my head to keep my brains from erupting.

"They're going to get rid of him, Dean." I said as soon as I could form words. "You've got to find him before they kill him."

Dean went to kitchen to use the phone. I kicked the footrest up on the recliner and leaned gently back. The towel was damp from the melting ice and turning red from the blood on my head. Dean brought back a plastic bag filled with ice, wrapped it in a dry towel and traded them out. I squinted and willed the headache away. It didn't help much.

"I called Morris, he's going to try and locate Rayburn."

He nudged two Tylenol into my hand. I popped them in my mouth and washed them down with the glass of water he handed me. He sat back down. I waited for the Tylenol to kick in. When I opened my eyes again, Dean was standing over me.

"I was getting ready to try and wake you."

I dropped the icepack on the floor and tilted the chair upright. Pain thundered behind my eyes and settled into a steady ache around the knot on my head.

"What else can you tell me about your meeting with Carmichael?"

"I asked him when and why he got involved with Harley Real Estate."

"He tell you?"

"Not really, he said I was asking the wrong person."

"What'd he mean by that?"

"I don't know yet."

I shook my head. Bad move. I gritted my teeth and waited for the jackhammers to stop. I took a deep breath and let it out. The hammers subsided a little.

"That's the second time this week someone's gone after me with a baseball bat."

"You life's just one adventure after another, isn't it?"

"I'm glad you were here."

A knock sounded and Dean got up to answer it. Wil was standing outside. He came in, glanced from me to Dean and asked what the hell was going on.

"Someone took a homerun swing at my head."

"Why?"

"Not sure."

"Who was it?"

"Don't know."

"Who sent them?"

"Not sure about that either, Wil."

He folded himself to the floor.

"You sure got a lot of people trying to kill you these days," he said.

"You may make detective yet, Wil."

"Wise-ass."

I smiled and eased the recliner back while Dean told Wil about Billy.

"You want me to go with Morris and locate, Billy?" Will asked.

"No, you stay here with Brocs. I'll help Morris."

Dean left to catch up with Morris and file a report on the attack. Wil took his place on the couch. I nursed my headache and tried to figure out what I knew that had

Carmichael worried enough to take a swing at my head. Wil gave voice to my question.

"You have any idea what the hell's going on yet?" he asked.

"I've got bits and pieces, nothing's really clear yet."

"Want to share what you've got?"

"Not yet."

"Okay."

Wil was silent. I picked up the ice pack and put it against my head.

"Brocs."

"What?"

"I'm sorry about the fight at The End Zone."

I turned my head and grinned.

"You really think I'd do anything to hurt Annie?"

"I just saw those pictures and went nuts. Besides, she's had a crush on you since college. I don't know why she didn't marry you instead of that dickhead she ended up with."

"Oh I don't know, Wil, maybe 'cause I never asked her."

"I always wondered why you didn't"

Until I met Melinda, I'd never felt deeply enough about anyone to consider a permanent relationship. I wasn't going to try and explain that to Wil.

"She's better off without me. Ronnie may be a dick, but he's not carrying around a bunch of emotional baggage."

"Ronnie doesn't have enough brain cells to carry emotional baggage."

I laughed and it turned into a groan as the pain inside my head exploded.

"Brocs, what the hell's going on with Billy?"

"I don't know, man. He always did like to live on the edge. Maybe he's been hooked up with Carmichael all along."

"He's gonna go to jail over this."

"If Carmichael doesn't kill him first."

We were both silent for a while after that. When something or someone you think you know well turns out to be completely different than you always thought, it's hard to wrap your mind around the change. My mind wasn't in shape to wrap around anything at the moment.

"Hit the rack, Brocs. I'll stick around and make sure they don't get another shot at you tonight."

I hated to be so weak. It seemed like Wil had been playing nursemaid to me for a month, but it was all I could do to remember to breathe in and out. I needed to rest. I eased out of the recliner and managed to make it to the bedroom before my knees buckled again. I sprawled across the bed with my feet still on the floor. I gave some thought to dragging myself all the way up, but passed out before I could do it. I woke a couple of hours later when Baldwin swatted at my pants leg.

I sat up slowly, swallowed a groan, undressed and got the rest of the way into bed. The next time I woke there was dim light coming through the windows from the streetlamp. I eased up and squinted at the clock on the nightstand. It was after midnight. Next to the clock was a glass of water and two Tylenol. I swallowed them and settled onto the pillows. My headache was down to a dull throb. As long as I didn't move my head too much, I was okay.

I lay in the semi darkness and tried to puzzle out what Carmichael meant when he said, "If you want to find out, you need to go to the source." If Carmichael wasn't the source, who was?

The answer didn't come right away and I slipped into a light doze. All the dreams I'd had over the past days flickered through my mind. Drew kept saying, "Pay attention to Mom," and "Start at the beginning." Mom said, "I loved him, Halston. How could you?"

I woke up then, knowing I'd just figured out something important, but unable to pin it down. The harder I thought about it, the further away it slipped and the worse my head throbbed. While I lay waiting for sleep to overcome the headache again, I thought through everything that had happened, both in the present and the memories I'd relived through my dreams. There had to be a common thread. On the edge of sleep, that thread appeared.

I jerked upright. My head started pounding, my stomach rolled, bile climbed into the back of my throat. I crawled off the bed and made it to the bathroom just in time. I rinsed out my mouth, slumped to the floor and pressed my cheek against the cold surface of the tub. I wasn't sure if I was sick because of the concussion or what I'd just figured out.

"That can't be right," I mumbled. "That can't be it. Come on, Drew, please tell me I'm wrong."

I sat on the floor of the bathroom a long time waiting for an answer that never came. Wil found me there an hour later. He helped me off the floor and poured me into bed.

"Brocs, maybe you need to go to the hospital. Your color's real bad. You might have a skull fracture."

I waved him off and closed my eyes.

"Can I get you anything?"

I didn't answer and he went away. When I woke again, my head was better. The throb was down to a dull ache. I got out of bed, stepped into my jeans and didn't get dizzy. That was a definite improvement. I laced up my tennis shoes, brushed my teeth, and walked into the living room. Dean and Wil were watching a ball game. I sat down and told them what I'd figured out.

Wil shook his head. "That can't be right," he said.

"Tell me what else makes sense."

"That's crazy, Brocs."

"What do you want to do, Brocs?" Dean asked.

"I haven't decided yet. Go home. I'm going back to bed. I'll talk to you guys tomorrow."

"Promise me you won't do this alone," Dean said.

I looked up at Dean's face. "I can't do that."

"Please, Brocs. Let us back you up. There've been too many deaths already."

His face filled with fear and maybe love. It scared me.

"I'm not Charlie, Dean."

He stared at the floor for a minute before he looked up into my eyes.

"I know that, but you're Lee's son. I don't want to lose you."

My eyes prickled with unmanly tears. I stared at the floor to hide them. When I raised my head, Wil was shifting his eyes between Dean and me in confusion.

"Don't do this alone, Brocs," Dean said.

I nodded. He smiled and headed out. Wil watched me in silence after Dean left, waiting for me to fill him in. I just sat there. He finally couldn't take it any more.

"What was that all about, Brocs. Who's Charlie? Who's Lee? What the hell is going on? Christ, I feel like I walked into the middle of a movie."

"I'll tell you later," I promised as I got out of my chair.

I felt Wil's eyes boring into my back as I made my way down the hall to the bedroom. A few minutes later I heard the door close softly behind him as he left.

Chapter 28

I showered the next morning and washed the blood from my hair. The lump on my head was egg-sized and tender to touch, but my headache was down to a manageable throb as long as I didn't move too quickly. I only did that once. Baldwin sat on the kitchen table and watched while I washed Tylenol down with my orange juice. I filled his dish, gave him fresh water and rubbed his head. He ignored the food, jerked away from my hand and stared at me. His tail swished back and forth in agitation. He could feel the tension gathering inside me and he didn't like it.

I shuffled together all my notes and left for the office. It was windy and damp. Dust rocketed around the parking lot. I cupped a hand over my eyes as I made my way to the truck. Inside I felt shaky, but my fingers were steady as I stabbed the key into the ignition. A few minutes later, I parked in my lot downtown. The wind died and thunder rumbled in the distance.

I made my way into the building and unlocked my office. The light coming through the windows was dim, but I didn't turn on a lamp. I opened the blinds and the murky dimness brightened a little. I retrieved the files from my safe and sat down with them one more time. I wanted to find something that told me I was wrong, but it wasn't there. There was only one common denominator linking everything together.

I turned my chair toward the window and propped my feet on the sill. Black clouds were rolling in the western sky. The trees bent over as the wind picked up again. I sat and watched the storm move closer. There was one more piece of the puzzle we needed before I could move forward. Before the confrontation, I wanted absolute proof.

I called Dean.

"We found Billy," he said.

"Alive?"

"Barely, he's in intensive care. Doc won't say what his chances are yet, it doesn't look good."

I thought about Billy and didn't speak for a minute.

"You there, Brocs?"

"Yeah, I'm here."

"Even if he does recover, life's not going to all that great for a while. He's staring at a pretty long sentence."

"He's still my friend, or I thought he was. He still feels like a friend."

It was Dean's turn to go quiet.

"Is he conscious? Is there any chance he can help us out here?"

"Sorry."

"There's one person that I know of that could verify most of it," I said, then told him what I needed and where I thought he could get it.

"I'll get back to you."

I hung up and went to the window to stare out. The wall of black cloud was getting taller. The wind died out again and the room was filled with a dusky twilight. It felt like evening. I picked up the phone and dialed Melinda's number. She answered on the first ring.

"Mel, it's Brocs."

The silence on the other end of the line spoke more than words ever could.

"Mel, please don't hang up. You don't have to say anything, just listen for a sec, okay? I understand, about Danny. I'm sorry..." I sighed. "I'm sorry you had to go through this. I...I'm sorry."

"It's not your fault, Brocs. I know that, but I...I just need some time, okay?"

She hung up before I could answer. I dropped the receiver back into the cradle on the desk. Gravel and grit rattled against the window behind me as the wind gusted outside. I checked my watch, glanced at the phone, then out at the approaching storm. Tension curled up my insides. I slumped into my desk chair and reached into the bottom drawer where I kept the bottle. My hand stopped before I picked it up. Time for that later. I tipped back, propped my feet up on the open drawer and waited. When the phone rang, I jumped and let my feet slide to the floor. It rang again and I just stared at it. I didn't want the information that Dean had. I needed to know it was true and not my imagination, but I didn't really want it. On the third ring, I picked up the phone.

"Brocs, Lester talked. I'm afraid you're right. You want the details?"

I didn't need them. I was going to get those from the source. I told Dean what I was going to do and when, then opened the drawer of my desk and lifted out the bottle. It was less than half-full and the outside was coated with a thin film of dust. I wiped it on the tail of my shirt. I got a glass out of the bathroom and poured. The liquor was golden in the bottom of the glass. I swirled it around, but didn't drink.

Lightning flashed in the distance. I counted off the seconds until I heard the thunder. It was still a long way off. I put the glass on the desk and turned my chair around to face the window again. I knew what I had to do, but I didn't want to leave the office. I didn't want proof that what I thought I knew was really true. I just wanted to forget about it, but it was too late for that.

I watched as the storm crept closer. I thought about Drew. How close we were. How much I missed him now. The things in our childhood that had drawn us together could have just as easily torn us apart. If our roles had been reversed, I'm sure that's what would have happened.

Drew seemed like the weak one, but he was stronger than I, he always had been. I thought about my mom, spending all those years with Halston, still in love with Lee. Anger curled in my stomach.

I picked up the glass. Before I could drink I walked back into the bathroom and poured it out. The picture of Lee Weston in his Highway Patrol uniform flashed across my mind. My muscles clenched. The glass in my hand shattered. The pieces clattered into the sink. Blood oozed from my palm. I didn't feel a thing. I picked the slivers of glass out of my hand, rinsed it under the faucet and wrapped it in gauze.

I came out of the bathroom as my office door opened. Dean and Wil strode in. I picked up my jacket and shrugged into it, then I took the .22 out of my pocket and dropped it into my desk drawer, unholstered my nine and placed it next to the .22.

"You're not taking a gun?" Wil asked.

"No. I might use it."

"You don't have to do this." Dean said. "With Lester's statement, I have enough to pick him up."

"Just let me talk to him first. I need to hear it from him."

Dean nodded and they followed me out of the office. I drove through town and parked in the drive outside of Halston Harley's house. Dean braked to a stop behind me. He and Wil stepped out and we mounted the stairs together. I slapped the brass knocker hard against the door. A man I didn't recognize opened it.

"I'm here to see Halston," I said.

"He's not to be disturbed right now, sir. Would you like to leave a message?"

I pushed past him into the house. Dean and Wil edged in behind me.

"You guys stay here," I said.

Dean and Wil drew their guns and encouraged Halston's help to stay in the front hall. I went in search of the man who had raised me. I found him in the study, desk chair tipped back, feet propped up, hands behind his head. When I stepped into his office, his feet hit the floor with a thud.

"What the hell do you think you're doing here?"

"I'm here to talk."

"Get out. I have nothing to say to you."

Lightning creased the sky and thunder crashed overhead. The windows shook. Halston jerked and swallowed hard. Rain came down in sheets against the windows. He glared at me.

"I want to know what happened to my mother, Halston."

"Don't be ridiculous," he said. "You know what happened to her. She died in a car accident."

"She was run off the bridge by another car."

Halston's golf tan paled, he swallowed hard and hunched forward, hands braced on his desk. "That's nonsense. Who told you that?"

"Lester Crawford."

I took a step forward and caught his eyes with mine. Our gaze held for a moment before he turned to stare at the opaque windows.

"The police have it on file," I said.

"Well they got it wrong."

I noticed he didn't ask who Lester Crawford was. I sat down across from him. He didn't turn around.

"What happened to Lee Weston?" I asked.

He jerked away from the window and stared at me. If anything, his skin lightened another shade. He picked up the glass at his elbow and took a long swallow.

"How the hell should I know?"

"I think you do."

"Well I don't."

His answer sounded weak. He heard it and set his face into a scowl, daring me to dispute him. I sat silent. He started to take another drink. Ice clinked against the sides of the glass, loud in the quiet of the room. He put the tumbler down on his blotter and stared over my left shoulder.

"Why was Drew murdered?" I asked.

"Andrew killed himself."

"With my gun?"

"Serves you right, you little bastard." He voice rose and his eyes widened. "That makes you responsible for his death."

His gaze flickered around the room, never lighting on anything for more than a second. His hands were clenched on the desk in front of him. He faced me, but his eyes never took me in. His skin was the color of milk. He took a deep breath and relaxed his hands. They trembled and he pressed them flat against the desktop. Bright spots of color dotted his cheeks. His chest rose and fell as he took quick panting breaths.

I stood and strode slowly around the room. Pictures of Drew covered the walls. The only family pictures were of the three of them. If you hadn't known there'd been two children, the pictures wouldn't have told you. All the years I'd lived in that house, I'd never noticed that before. I walked across the room and sank into the chair in front of Halston. He was breathing easier now, no longer panting, but his color was still off.

A thunderclap sounded before the lightning flash was gone. Halston jumped and stared around the room, his eyes finally stopped on my face.

"You were the cause of all my problems." He pointed the finger of one hand at me. "Everything that happened was your fault."

He was almost shouting. I leaned back and said nothing. Rain covered the windows like a curtain. We were locked together in a silence shattered only by the thunder. I broke the spell.

"When did you go into business with Austin-Kline?"

His eyes opened wide as he stared across the desk at me and his breath huffed out. "How did you find out about that?"

He shrank into his chair when he realized what he'd said. I pressed my advantage. "When, Halston? When did you get into bed with Marcus Carmichael?"

He pinched his mouth into a thin line of displeasure. An expression I was intimately familiar with from my childhood. "I don't know what you're talking about," he said.

My anger, tightly controlled until now, leapt out. "That's bullshit and you know it!"

Halston scooted back in his chair. My fingernails dug into my palms as I reined in my fury, and exhaled. Slowly I relaxed and slouched back in my chair. When I spoke again, my voice was soft and controlled.

"I'm not leaving here until you tell me everything."

Halston had to strain to hear me over the pounding rain.

"It's all your fault, you and your mother. That Bitch!" He spat out the last two words.

My anger was so hot I was sweating in the cool room. My hands were locked on the arms of the chair, my knuckles white as I forced myself to speak softly. "Explain, Halston. I'm not going away."

"You wouldn't understand. You were her son."

It sounded like a curse.

"Try me," I said.

Halston swallowed and searched around the room for a way out. I was between him and the only escape route. He hunched over and stared at his hands on the blotter. He looked old, older than he had at the funeral, his face lined and pale. His hair lay lank and unwashed upon his head. His suit was rumpled and slept in. When he glanced up at my face, I saw the dark rings under his eyes. His pupils were tiny pinpoints. The whites surrounding them were lined with red. He looked pitiful. I swallowed my disgust and waited in silence.

"She wouldn't marry me," he whispered.

"Speak up."

"She wouldn't marry me, dammit. She went chasing off after that damn cop. You don't understand. I couldn't live without her. She was my life."

I narrowed my eyes.

He met my gaze and shouted. "You could never understand. She was my whole life. Without her I was nothing."

A tear slid down his cheek. He didn't notice.

"Tell me what you did."

"I had to get rid of the cop," he whispered.

I edged toward him to hear above the rain and thunder outside. The storm was on top of us and the noise was almost continuous.

"She would come back to me if he was gone. I knew she would, but I was running out of time. The wedding was almost here. I tried to see her. She just laughed at me. She was so beautiful."

Another tear joined the first. He sniffed and went on. "I went to Marcus Carmichael, I heard he had contact with people that could do stuff like that." He caught my eye. "I couldn't let her marry him. She was mine."

I swallowed my reply. I was seething inside, but I didn't want to interrupt.

"Marcus said he thought we could work out a deal. I agreed, the cop died, Marilee was mine. That should have been the end of it, and it would have been except for you."

The expression on his face was madness fueled by hate. I met his glare and he ducked his head. "She didn't have to die," he whispered. "She just wouldn't leave well enough alone. She found out about Lee. She overheard me talking to Marcus and figured it out. I told her how much I loved her, but she just looked at me with contempt."

My lip curled. I swallowed the bile that rose in my throat.

"She didn't have to die. I would have given her anything. I loved her." His voice trailed off and was swallowed by the storm. He sniffed again and more tears ran unheeded down his face. "She was going to go to the police. I couldn't let that happen."

I sat like a stone, not moving a muscle. Hearing the story from his lips was a waking nightmare.

"What about Drew?" I asked softly.

"He was worse than your mother," he snapped. "He was clearing out some old files and found a letter from Carmichael that I thought I'd thrown out. I gave him a story, but he didn't buy it. He threatened to go to Carmichael for the truth. I put a stop to that by telling him about the Austin-Kline business, but he just kept picking at it—asking questions about Lee and your mother. He wouldn't let it go. I knew it was just a matter of time before he went to you. He was my son, I loved him, but he never came to me, he always went to you. I hate you!" he screamed.

I jerked away from the loathing that radiated from him. It was as forceful as a blow.

"I had to kill him and it was your fault. It was supposed to look like you did it. You should be in jail. Why aren't you in jail?"

I slumped in the chair, stunned by his last words. I thought Lester Crawford had killed Drew.

"You killed him? You killed Drew?"

"I couldn't go to Carmichael again. I had to take care of it myself. I just wanted to talk to him, to scare him into staying quiet. But he wouldn't listen."

"My God, Halston, you killed your own son."

Halston reached over and fumbled around in his desk drawer. I closed my eyes and tried to gather my scattered thoughts. I pushed up from the chair and started out of the office. I couldn't stand to hear any more. It was time to get Dean.

"Turn around, Brocs."

I stopped. Halston's voice was level and hard. Not the same voice he'd just used to tell me his story. This one wasn't filled with pain; it was filled with hate. I slowly turned to face him. He was standing braced against the desk, a .45 leveled at my chest. His arms were extended in front of him. The gun never wavered. I cursed myself for leaving my gun at the office.

"Now it's your turn to die," he whispered. "I should have killed you when you were a child."

I stared at the man who had hated me since birth—the man who was responsible for the deaths of my father, my mother, and my brother.

"What good will it do to kill me now?" I asked. "They're already dead. It won't bring them back."

"SHUT UP!"

I swallowed and took a step away from Halston and his .45.

"DON'T MOVE."

I stopped. A shot winged over my head and thudded into the bookcase behind me. A book tumbled off the shelf and onto the carpet.

"Halston, don't do this."

"SHUT UP. I HATE YOU."

His eyes were glazed and tears ran down his face. The gun wavered in his hands. The study door crashed open behind me. When he turned toward the noise, I dove for the gun. Halston leapt away.

"Don't move, Halston. You're under arrest," shouted Dean.

"I won't go to jail."

I lunged for Halston.

Before I could reach him, he put the barrel of the .45 in his mouth and squeezed the trigger. Blood and brain matter splattered the walls and window behind him. The gun slid from his slack fingers as he slumped to the floor. I sank to my knees and covered my face with my hands, but the picture of Halston Harley's last second was seared into my mind.

"God dammit!" Dean swore.

He picked up the phone and dialed the department. I turned my back on the carnage. The room was filled with the smell of cordite and the copper tang of blood. I sat, bent my knees up and rested my forehead on them. I thought I'd be free of Halston Harley when this was over, but he'd left me with an image that would stay for the rest of my life. Dean knelt beside me.

"Come on, son. Let's get you out of here."

I stumbled to my feet and let him lead me out of Halston's study. The thunder crashed overhead; the whole house shook. A shiver crawled up my spine. Dean guided me away from the horror.

"He was crazy," I whispered.

"Leave it be for now, son."

Outside, rain fell in sheets and soaked us as we trudged across the drive to Dean's car. I collapsed onto the passenger seat. Dean closed me inside and walked slowly to the house. I rubbed my temples and waited for a reaction. Tears, rage, something. Nothing came. I was empty.

I closed my eyes. Memories of Drew and Mom played across my eyelids like a movie. A flash of Halston's last moment intruded and I shuddered. I felt a hand grasp my shoulder and snapped around to look in the rear seat. It was empty, but I wasn't alone. Drew was still with me. The knot of emptiness around my heart started to loosen.

I got out of the car. The storm had passed leaving only a shower. I turned my face to the sky as a shaft of sunlight broke through the clouds. My tears mixed with the rain and my emptiness washed away. Drew was okay now. My dreams would go back to being my own.

kd easley

Author kd easley is a union carpenter who spends her downtime in Missouri trying to keep two psycho cats from tap dancing on her keyboard while she's trying to write.

Get to know kd at www.kdwrites.com where she shares information about upcoming books, writer's conferences and resources, and blogs about writing, life, and living with crazy felines.

www.ingramcontent.com/pod-product-compliance
Lightning Source LLC
Chambersburg PA
CBHW050923120626
46552CB00001B/16